BEATRICE
AND CROC HARRY

BEATRICE
AND CROC HARRY

A NOVEL

LAWRENCE HILL

HarperCollins*Publishers*Ltd

Published by HarperCollins Publishers Ltd

First edition

HarperCollins Publishers Ltd
Bay Adelaide Centre, East Tower
22 Adelaide Street West, 41st Floor
Toronto, Ontario, Canada
M5H 4E3

www.harpercollins.ca

Library and Archives Canada Cataloguing in Publication

Title: Beatrice and Croc Harry : a novel / Lawrence Hill.
Names: Hill, Lawrence, 1957- author.
Identifiers: Canadiana (print) 20210313692 | Canadiana (ebook) 20210313722
ISBN 9781443463362 (hardcover) | ISBN 9781443463379 (ebook)
Classification: LCC PS8565.I444 B43 2022 | DDC jC813/.54—dc23

Printed and bound in the United States of America

LSC/H 9 8 7 6 5 4 3 2 1

For my beloved daughter
Beatrice Lucinda Freedman

CHAPTER 1

An Awful Lot of Places for Something to Go Wrong

Beatrice was not entirely sure if she was dead. She raised two fingers to her lips and felt her own warm breath. She appeared to be awakening from a deep, dark dream in which she had either died or come close to it. As she opened her eyes and studied her circumstances, the facts confirmed that she was alive. She didn't know much, but she knew this: her name was indeed Beatrice. It had a certain flow. Three syllables and never just two, thank you very much.

Beatrice was lying in a single bed in a one-room, wooden cabin. She had never slept in that bed before or seen the cabin. She had no idea what awaited her outside, except an incessant woodpecker. Eight pecks in a row. Pause. Another eight pecks. And again. And again. There was nothing like a woodpecker to get her attention. It sounded like an electric hammer in the hands of a toddler. The message, being banged right into the grey matter of her brain, seemed to say, *I am here and you are there and if you don't get up this very second I am going to tap tap tap tap tap tap tap tap until you go completely mad.*

Beatrice swung her legs off the bed. Straight ahead: three rows of shelves, stacked with books. To her left: a bedside table, and on it, two more books. On top was a manual with meticulous purple handwriting on the cover. It said: *Survival Tips, Argilia Forest, 2090.* Beatrice turned to the first page, which consisted of a simple message in purple ink: *Outhouse is outside. Climb down the ladder and head to the river.* Ladder? River? Outhouse? Was this some sort of joke?

The second book on the bedside table was filled with the same handwriting. Each letter was tiny and printed and looked like it had been smacked into place by a typewriter key. Typewriters? How did she even know about typewriters? Beatrice remembered nothing about herself or her past, except for her first name. But she knew about typewriters. Once, she had seen several of them in a museum and was quite sure that she had laughed as she pounded the keys and slammed the carriage return and rolled out a sheet of paper. For a girl who did not even know her own age or the name of her mother, if she had a mother, Beatrice found it unsettling that she could recall typewriters and the museum sign that said people had used them as recently as a century ago.

Perhaps the second book would explain who she was, or where she was, or where she had come from.

Nope.

No such luck.

It was a dictionary as thick as two bricks. So heavy she needed both hands to pick it up. It was entitled *The St. Lawrence Dictionary of Only the Best Words, Real and Concocted.*

Beatrice sighed. She was hungry and in no mood to be trifled with. Still, she was curious. She flipped open the dictionary and landed on the B page. *Beatrice. That is your name.* Well, thanks for the information. She read on. *Bumfuzzled: To be utterly confused and somewhat dazzled.*

That pretty well summed things up. She was bumfuzzled. Absolutely, totally, completely bumfuzzled.

What kind of dictionary knew her name and spoke to her? She flipped through the huge book and located a few more words, each one strange and faintly ridiculous. The dictionary seemed like a wound-up friend, talking at her between every breath. One could only take so much of that. Beatrice shut the book. She looked all around her.

Pots and pans hung from hooks above a table. There was a hatchet. There was a sign: *No cooking in the tree house.* Beatrice stood up and examined herself in the mirror. She saw a girl. Not a toddler nor a teenager. Maybe eleven or twelve? In her opinion, she looked short for her age. She studied her own face. Brown skin. A litany of freckles. Tight black curls, which were in a state of complete bedhead. She'd have to comb out the kinks and do something with them.

How could a person see herself in the mirror and not even know her own last name?

Beatrice was wearing a set of onesie pyjamas decorated with zebras. Really? She was too old for that. Had someone selected the zebra pyjamas for her? If so, they had underestimated her. Beatrice did not care to be underestimated. She found a stack of clothing on a dresser. Socks. Underwear. Pants. Shirt. Sweater. Sturdy runners.

She dressed quickly. The whole cabin swayed. Was she on a ship? Was it an earthquake? Beatrice ran to a window opposite the door. She looked out and saw huge leaves as big as soccer balls and branches thicker than her own body.

A shiver ran down her spine. She was alone in the tree house, high above the ground. She had no clue where she came from or how she got there, but she had caught a memory, as if it were an autumn leaf twirling through the air. The memory was connected to the dream from which she had just awakened. There had been screaming. But it was not her screaming. She was too badly hurt to speak. The screaming came from other people: men, women and children. She heard the terror in their voices, rising and falling. The wailing went on and on. But that was all she remembered. No images. Just sound.

Enough of that.

Beatrice shook her head. She had to pee, and she was hungry. On a solid wooden table that looked just the right size for eating alone, reading and writing, Beatrice found an open knapsack. On the top was stitched the word *Beasack*. All right then. Beasack it was. It contained two small cooking pots, a bowl, a wooden stirring spoon, an eating spoon, cloth bags of dried oats, cinnamon, brown sugar, raisins, slices of dried apple, salt and a packet of butter. She poked around to see what else was in the Beasack: matches and a slingshot and a bag of perfectly round stones—presumably to be used with the slingshot. Beatrice grabbed the hatchet and stuffed it into the Beasack. She slung the pack over her shoulder. She opened the door and stepped out onto a giant branch that was wider than the span of her arms. She was fifteen feet off the ground. She was in the middle of a massive forest. No sign of people. Just birds. A veritable cacophony of birdsong. The birds sang out in a concert of tiny voices. She heard them. She could actually make out their tiny, individual voices: "Worms here. Airstream coming. Updraft. Downdraft. Mind my nest. Look out. Human approaching."

Beatrice climbed down a rope ladder. It swung as she descended. She let the ladder rock her back and forth like a swing and hopped down onto a spongey forest floor. She stepped back. The tree that held the house looked like an elephant, seen from the side. The base of the tree spread out like a giant foot. She stood beside the tree and walked from one side of the trunk to the other: it took fifteen steps. The branch on which the tree house rested shot out in a straight line and looked like an endless trunk.

Near the base of the tree, Beatrice found three signs staked in the ground. One said *biggest fig tree in Argilia*. The second said *outhouse* and pointed to the left. The third said *cookfire* and pointed to the right. She tallied what she knew so far. She was in a massive forest named Argilia. She lived in a cabin perched on a huge branch of a giant fig tree. Apparently, there was a place to cook nearby.

Beatrice picked up a stick and scratched at the rich forest floor. She dug under some moss and saw tiny bugs running away. When she listened carefully, she could hear one of them complaining: "Hey. That hurts. Easy with that stick. I have feelings, too, you know."

"Sorry," Beatrice said. She dropped the stick and stood up. She left the tree and took a narrow, winding forest path. Paw prints marked the path, but there were no signs of humans. The trail wound past trees and bushes, and after a few minutes, led her to a big river. It was fast flowing and wider than a house. Wider than three streets, back-to-back. The current seemed to say, *Try me. Just try me. See what happens.* Beatrice tried to throw a stone across the river, but it landed with a plop in the middle of the water.

A handwritten sign near the riverbank said *Potable water*, which, according to *The St. Lawrence Dictionary of Only the Best Words, Real and Concocted*, meant drinkable. If the water was fit to drink, why not just write *Drink here*? Or *Drinkable*? Or *Knock yourself out*?

She scooped water into her oatmeal pot. She found the firepit, which was covered by an iron grate and had been dug into a clearing close to the river. It was a good place for a fire—no trees or bushes nearby, so she would see if anything or anyone was approaching her.

It was a clear, sunny day. Was she safe? Might there be lions or grizzly bears? She pulled out her slingshot, loaded a stone into it, pulled it back, aimed at a tree and let the stone fly. It travelled only a few feet and dropped onto the earth. She couldn't harm a flea with that thing. Not unless she practised. That would have to come later.

With her hatchet, Beatrice chopped some dead branches into kindling and started a fire. She set the pot down on the grate. Beatrice had no idea if she had a mother, father, sister or brother, or why someone had left her in a tree house with instructions, but she knew how to make oatmeal. To the water, she added oats and all the additional ingredients.

As the pot heated up, Beatrice stirred in some butter. In the dictionary, she had seen a definition for the word *ingrease-ments: The finest oatmeal additions mixed with two pats of melted butter*. Beatrice stirred the oats and the ingreasements until they thickened and bubbled. Cooking comforted her. It gave her something to do. Beatrice prepared to pour her breakfast into the bowl. But the pot had no handle, so she had to return to the tree house for oven mitts.

She stuffed the slingshot in her pocket and left the Beasack and hatchet by the fire. She filled the spare pot with river water and carried it back toward the tree house. As she walked, she felt a mounting irritation about not knowing where she had come from. But whatever the country, city or village, Beatrice felt in her bones that something had gone wrong. She kept checking her arms and legs. No scratches. No broken bones. There were any number of vital organs in her body—for instance, heart, lungs, stomach, kidneys, liver and pancreas—so there were an awful lot of places for something to go wrong. The dream had suggested that some part of her body was broken or damaged. But everything seemed to be working. She was in no pain.

Still, it was frustrating not to be able to walk up to a person and ask for explanations. This put her in such an irritable mood that she put down her pot of water, retrieved the slingshot from her pocket, placed a marble-sized stone in the sling, pulled back hard and let it fly. The stone shot through the air and thwacked against something. From behind some bushes, she heard a low, angry voice.

"Watch it." The bushes thrashed.

Beatrice clenched her slingshot.

The voice came at her again. "Some people have no clue. No broughtupcy. No manners at all. Throwing stones here, there and everywhere. Really!"

It was a deep-throated, irritated, expressive voice. Beatrice understood every word, but the voice did not seem human. She took a step back as the thrashing continued and the bushes parted.

There, before her, appeared an immense crocodile. She guessed that it was at least three times the length of her own body. Its scales were soaking wet. In the sunlight, they shimmered a deep, rich turquoise. Although the blue-green colour looked like it came from a beautiful jewel, the reptile terrified her. Its thick, powerful tail swished. It unhinged its jaws to reveal two rows of sharp teeth. Its breath smelled like rotting meat. It looked her up and down as she froze in her tracks.

The crocodile straightened its legs to lift the front of its body off the ground. It looked like it was doing a push-up. "Who in tarnation are you?" the crocodile asked. It thumped its tail twice. Beatrice felt the vibrations under her feet.

Beatrice stared at the beast. How many teeth did it have? She could only see the sharp ones perched outside of its mouth. Sharp teeth waiting and ready made her nervous.

"I am Beatrice," she said.

"How astonishingly unhelpful," it said. "Can you do any better?"

The crocodile stopped moving. Beatrice wondered if it was getting ready to lunge. Would a crouching crocodile be getting ready to lunge, like, say, a cat or a tiger?

"I am under no obligation to reveal my personal autobiography," she said, holding one hand with the other, to keep them from shaking. "And just who are you?"

"I am a King Crocodile. Biggest kind going. You may call me Croc Harry. And I happen to have just emerged from my burrow. It was a perfect estivation, until you struck me, entirely unprovoked I must say, with that stone."

"Estivation?" Beatrice muttered.

"Hot weather hibernation for crocodiles and certain other species, but never mind that. I'm annoyed. Frankly, I am quite piqued." Croc Harry opened his mouth and bellowed.

Beatrice took one step back. The crocodile had teeth like knives. He was loud and unpleasant to behold, but he did not look like he was king of anything. She gripped her slingshot. She pulled another stone from her pocket and loaded it into the sling.

"Don't even think about it," Croc Harry said.

"You have teeth, so I have a slingshot," Beatrice said. "Even-steven."

Croc Harry bent his front legs and lowered the top half of his body back down on the ground.

"So you are a talking crocodile?" Beatrice asked. "And what are you doing here, anyways?"

"The word you intended to use is *anyway*, which has no need for the *s*. You said it entirely wrong."

Beatrice felt her face grow hot. "Pardon me?"

"It's any*way*," Croc Harry said, "not any*ways*. Were you educated in a barn?"

Beatrice said nothing. She could find no words to match her anger.

The crocodile nodded his head. Up and down. Like a human. "You are clearly a willy lump lump," he said.

"Willy lump lump," Beatrice repeated. "Is that an insult?"

"In the same ballpark as fool. Ignoramus."

"I don't appreciate being called a willy lump lump," Beatrice said.

This monstrous turquoise reptile sure had a knack for getting under her skin. He knew how to get her blood boiling.

Beatrice took another step back. The slingshot shook in her hand. If he were to attack, how should she defend herself? His eyeballs were his only vulnerability: they sat curiously atop his head. It did not seem wise to get into a fight with a crocodile. What she had to do was stand up to him. Maybe all he needed was a verbal slap down.

"We are not in school," Beatrice said, "and I have no need of grammar lessons from a beast whose centre of gravity is pitifully low."

"What is that supposed to mean?"

"Your centre of gravity. It's how low you sit to the ground. The lower your centre of gravity, the less likely you are to have a viable brain. As a matter of fact, your centre of gravity is lower than that of a pig. Infinitely lower!"

The crocodile snorted. Water shot from his mouth. "Pigs. I've eaten pigs."

"I doubt that," Beatrice said.

"Little ones. Piglets are most succulent!"

"You shouldn't go killing animals. Why don't you pick on someone your own size?"

Croc Harry snorted again. "You clearly know nothing about the laws of nature. Let me spell it out for you: if I don't kill, I don't eat. Also, in this world, if you're big, you chase. If you're small, you run. Picking on someone your own size won't get you far. Not in this forest."

At that moment, an armadillo and two of her pups raced across the forest path and disappeared into the woods.

"If I were you," Croc Harry said, "I wouldn't take on anything bigger than an armadillo."

Beatrice knew a thing or two about armadillos. She must have read about them, before she wound up in this mysterious forest. "You shouldn't go near armadillos. They can give you leprosy."

The crocodile took two steps back. "Let's de-escalate. You may go on your way, without fear of becoming my breakfast, if you apologize."

Beatrice put her hand on her hip. "Breakfast? Apologize?"

The crocodile rolled his eyes. They looked like billiard balls spinning in the sun. "An apology is a statement that you're sincerely sorry," he said.

Beatrice let out an angry shout. She was overcome by a desire to throw something. Hard. She stuffed the slingshot in her pocket, picked up the pot and tossed the water on Croc Harry's head.

He stared at her without blinking, as if nothing had happened. This made Beatrice even angrier.

"Why should I apologize?" Beatrice said.

"I'm choosing to ignore that you threw water on me," Croc Harry said. "You do realize that I am a crocodilian. You throwing water on me is like me breathing on you. No effect! Let's focus on your original sin: you shot that stone right into my scutes." The crocodile swished his tail and, with the end of it, pointed to the hard scales on his back.

"And you came up on me by surprise in the forest," she said, "which is equally rude, so we're even. And by the way, your name is quite ludicrous. What kind of crocodile is named Harry?"

He opened his cavernous jaws and bellowed. His teeth glinted in the sun. Beatrice jumped back. She was sure she saw the leg of something—a rabbit or a groundhog?—stuck in his back teeth.

"From you," Croc Harry said, "I require a modicum of respect."

Beatrice did not know how much a modicum was, but it was more than she was willing to give.

"Don't sneak up on me again," Beatrice said.

Croc Harry exhaled loudly. "Attitudinous brat!"

"How dare you call me attitudinous," Beatrice said.

"Well, you are!"

"Is that even a word?"

"It's a word in my books. It means too mouthy for your own good."

"Well, if I'm attitudinuous, it so happens that you smell like an unwashed bear. And you are positively assitudinous."

"I bathe daily," Croc Harry said. "And *assitudinous* is not a word."

"It is in my books," Beatrice said.

"So what's it mean, then?" Croc Harry asked.

"Stubborn like a donkey."

"I don't recognize that word or accept the definition," Croc Harry said.

"Well," Beatrice said, "this is goodbye."

Keeping her posture perfect so her fear wouldn't show, she walked as quickly as she could to the far side of the path. She hurried to the fig tree, climbed up the rope ladder and pulled it up behind her.

Fifteen feet below, Croc Harry watched her.

She stomped her foot. Curds. Smut balls. Pokey mud! Her stomach was rumbling. Her oatmeal was probably burning. But Croc Harry was out there, wallowing around between her tree house and cookfire.

Only when she stomped her foot and cursed again did

she realize that she had just had a long argument with a crocodile. Not only did they understand each other, but he appeared to have a superior vocabulary. This would not do.

Tarnation, attitudinous, scutes . . . she could barely keep up with him. She would have to study *The St. Lawrence Dictionary of Only the Best Words, Real and Concocted*. She would spend twenty minutes a day on vocabulary, to learn how to insult a crocodile. She would learn one zinger of an insult right now, just to have it on hand.

She flipped open the dictionary and landed in the O pages. She put her finger down randomly. There. *Odoriferous*. It meant stinky. It was a good insult. Five syllables, with the accent on the third. It occurred to Beatrice that when you were trading insults, the more syllables, the better.

Beatrice waited five minutes and marched right back to her cookfire with her oven mitts. She saw no sign of the odoriferous reptile. She stirred the oatmeal. It was burnt on the bottom of the pot, but the rest was salvageable.

Beatrice poured the oatmeal into her bowl, sat on the riverbank, slingshot at the ready, and watched a heron dive headfirst into the water and surface with a wriggling fish. She squinted as the sun climbed above the river and was astonished to see the images of two more suns—one to each side. Sundogs. She'd seen that word, too, in the dictionary. *Sundogs: Bright spots on each side of the sun, formed by the way the sunlight passes through ice crystals high up in the air.*

Beatrice made a decision. She would not be afraid. Even in a terrible situation, how would fear help? Beatrice sat by the river, admired the sundogs and tucked into her first meal in the vast and magical Argilia Forest.

CHAPTER 2

Self-Control

This much was clear: Beatrice would not starve. Food, books and supplies kept arriving in her tree house, just as miraculously as she had. Beatrice tried to stay awake one night to see if she could discover the delivery system, but nothing came until she slept.

She looked in *The St. Lawrence Dictionary of Only the Best Words, Real and Concocted* but could not find an answer under B for books, F for food or S for supplies. She looked in *Survival Tips, Argilia Forest, 2090*, but found no answers there. She did, however, find a warning about crocodiles: *Don't bathe in the river at night, because you might fail to spot a crocodile lying in wait. Crocodiles are patient predators. They may not look smart, but it's an act. They wait for you to saunter up to their mouths. Don't be fooled. And don't be a fool.*

Survival Tips, the dictionary and a thick volume about crocodile biology were the only books that appeared to speak to her directly. Beatrice picked up every other book off her shelves. There were 120 books—mostly novels for children. One by one, she flipped through the pages of each book, but found no messages scrawled into the margins. She held each book by the spine and shook it, but no loose papers with clues fell into her hands. The novels were of no practical use to her, but on rainy days and in the early evenings, they kept her good company. Indeed, they were the best of friends. She calculated how long the books would last. She usually read about one-third of a book each day. So, three days per book times 120 books equalled 360 days—almost a full year. If she ended up being stuck any longer in Argilia Forest, she'd double back and reread them.

The books were the most exciting part of her tree house. For a tree house, the room was utter luxury, but for a place she lived in day after day, all alone, it was pretty spartan. There were two small windows—no curtains. Her door could be locked from the inside with a sliding bolt. She had a single bed with two pillows, which was perfect, because when she lay down to read, she liked to have one under her head and the other under her knees. She had a mahogany table for eating, reading and writing. There was one wooden chair, with thick, solid wooden legs. She would have appreciated a cushion to sit on, but at least the chair was well made and did not creak or squeak. As for the pots, pans, dishes and cutlery—just enough for one person. One broom and dustbin. The hatchet, the slingshot and the Beasack. No candles, but there was a solar-powered flashlight. She also found a comb, a washing pot, and a large, open cylindrical container with the words *honey bucket* written on it. She had to look that up in her dictionary. *Honey bucket: Use it if you are stuck in your cabin at night, don't want to go out in the dark, and really need to go. Carry it down with you the next morning, empty and wash it out, and set it back by your bed. Not too fancy, but you'll be grateful for it.* Honey bucket, Beatrice mumbled. Of all the strange definitions in her rambling dictionary, this one seemed to be the most useful.

* * *

For four days in a row, Beatrice walked the entire morning in one direction, and then she turned around and spent the whole afternoon walking back. This, according to her dictionary, was the act of reconnoitering, or checking out her surroundings. She found no end to the forest, so she kept on reconnoitering.

To the east, Beatrice passed under fig trees so tall that if she threw a stone as high as she could, it only hit the bottom quarter of the trunk. To the west, she found raspberry bushes teeming with fruit.

She came upon a huge tree with a shocking variety of colours—entire sections of magenta, pink and lavender— that offered peaches, nectarines and plums. The three different fruits all hung from the same branches. It looked like a splendid picnic tree. She stopped to pick a peach. She bit into it. The skin was good and firm, but not fuzzy. The flesh, juicy and sweet. The picnic tree peach was truly succulent. In Beatrice's humble opinion, a peach at its very best had no rival in the world of fruit. With the back of her hand, she wiped away the juice running down her chin. Beatrice decided that no matter what happened to her in Argilia Forest and no matter what bad things might befall her, she could always look back and remember the day when she had stood in the morning sunlight under the three-fruit picnic tree and devoured a perfect peach.

She continued walking. A flock of geese flew overhead, and Beatrice could hear them chattering. "Two-legged hairy newcomer looks lost," the leader squawked.

"I heard that!" she shouted. She wanted to inform them that she was not the least bit lost, but they were already gone.

To the south, she crossed endless meadows of every shade of green—emerald, forest green, jade and lime. The lime-green meadow was covered in poppies, which waved like a human hand under the breeze. She did not enjoy walking through that meadow because the waving poppies reminded her of a recurring dream: she was hurt and people were screaming. The distressed sounds of her dreams kept flooding her mind. She tried walking faster to avoid thinking about the dreams.

To the north, she encountered more rivers and lakes. In the distance, she could see a mountain whose snowy peaks glinted in the sun. On the far side of a field, she saw a grizzly bear in a river, browsing for food. It swiped through the water with its paw, brought up a big fish and ate it in two bites. She shuddered to think how powerful its jaws must be to turn a fish the size of her arm into a two-bite meal. Thanks to *Survival Tips* in her tree house, Beatrice could identify poop dropped by moose, kangaroos, rabbits, antelopes and other animals. She paid special attention to bear scat: large, sweet-smelling, tube-shaped, tapering deposits of black, brown or green, often containing bits of berries, moss, hair or bones. *Note to self*, she thought, *walk far away from fresh bear poop.*

No matter how far she walked, Beatrice could not find any end to the forest. No gate. No fence. No road. No sign of people. Somebody must have brought her to the tree house in Argilia. Where were they, and why had they abandoned her? Would they come for her or know how to find her? Hello! Had anybody noticed that she was missing?

She did not feel homesick because she had no idea whom to miss. Still, she felt a certain dissatisfaction. She didn't feel lonely. Not a single solitary bit. Beatrice was an independent thinker, and loneliness was a waste of time. But something irked her.

Even though her tree house kept out the rain and her bed was firm and fresh food appeared every morning, Beatrice knew that she had to find her way home. Wherever that was.

* * *

Early one morning, the rain hammered so hard on the roof that Beatrice wondered if her tree house would split. But it held fast, and Beatrice comforted herself by reading in her dictionary about the names of groupings of animals. Geese in a bunch were called a flock, the dictionary said. Buffalo, all together, were called an obstinacy. *You may not believe this,* the dictionary said, *but it happens to be true that a group of ravens is called an unkindness.* Camels, a caravan. Toads were a knot. Turkeys, a gang. Pandas, an embarrassment. *Get this,* the dictionary said, *sharks in a bunch are called a shiver. It would be understandable to wonder who came up with such ridiculous names.* Beatrice wondered if it was the same silly person who had invented her dictionary.

The rain finally stopped. Before going out, Beatrice had to do something about her hair. She tried sprinkling some water on it, but that didn't help. She could barely run the comb through her tight curls. She combed and combed. All the tugging stung her scalp. She kept combing through the pain until her hair acquired a consistently frizzy look. She examined herself in the mirror. Not bad. Not bad at all. She saw a girl who looked smart. Full of personality. Her hair was unfinished, but jazzy. She liked what she saw. It would do for now.

Quickly, Beatrice put her clothes on, including a red sock on one foot and blue on the other, because she believed that same-coloured socks were deadly boring. She stuffed her slingshot, hatchet and two apples into her Beasack and climbed down the rope ladder.

She tacked a sign to the base of the tree. The sign, which she had written the night before, said, *A person lives here.*

Answers to the name of Beatrice. (For clarity: this person is a Human Being. She is a child of Uncertain Age.) She was not sure that she had identified herself clearly, so at the bottom of the sign she added in small print: *Awfully short, but with plans to grow. Brown eyes. Black curls. Brown skin. Abundant freckles. Always carries her Beasack. P.S., A Beasack is a purple knapsack with many pockets. It contains survival gear and supplies to repel crocodiles.*

Since she had awoken from her nightmare and found herself in Argilia, Beatrice had the impression that someone, or something, was following her. Monitoring her movements. This spooked Beatrice. She did not appreciate being tailed. She was not sure if she was imagining it. She wondered if somebody or something was trying to peek into her mind. She spun in a circle to see if she could spot an intruder. But none of the animals of Argilia seemed to be of the spying kind.

Survival Tips had said nothing about what to do if you felt that someone was watching you. Beatrice could only think of two strategies. The first strategy was offensive: throwing and slinging rocks. Accuracy would be necessary if she ever needed to protect herself.

The second strategy was defensive: Beatrice smeared the trunk of her tree house with bear fat she had found in a large metal tin in her cupboard. Bear fat made the trunk pretty well impossible to climb. Each night, before she settled into bed, Beatrice pulled up the rope ladder that dropped from her tree house to the ground. However, she had to lower it in the morning. What about when she was out and about in the day?

Beatrice began writing another sign to attach to the tree. Her first effort said: *This ladder is for the sole use of Beatrice.* But she didn't like it. Too long. She tried another approach. It said: *Keep out.* But that didn't work, either. Too short and somewhat inconsiderate. Finally, she settled on a sign that said: *Private residence and ladder (both).*

* * *

Beatrice decided it was high time for a constitutional: a fine, five-syllable word that she had also discovered in the dictionary. A constitutional was simply a long walk that you took for good health. She could call her outing a walk, but constitutional sounded so much better!

The mist began to lift off the forest floor as the sun came out from behind the clouds. As Beatrice headed through a row of trees, she walked straight into a spider's web. There, before her, a bug was stuck in the fine threads of the web. She listened carefully and could hear its tiny voice.

"Got to . . . got to . . . got to get out," it said.

Beatrice broke the web with her hand.

"Thanks," the bug said. It ran free and disappeared.

A spider dropped down on a thread and faced her, eye to eye. "Hey! That was my lunch!"

"Sorry," Beatrice said. She dodged the spider and kept going.

She tiptoed over a massive log that had fallen across the

fast-flowing water which, according to *Survival Tips*, was known as the Argilia River. She headed into an endless meadow covered in brilliant yellow dandelions. They were beautiful. Dandelions were thought of as weeds, she knew, but as they covered the massive field, they looked like flowers to her. How many were there? Thousands? More. Millions? Maybe.

At the edge of the meadow, she picked a bunch and placed them on the low-lying branch of a tree. She took ten steps back, put a rock in her homemade slingshot, drew back the band and let the rock fly. It smashed through the dandelions. She repeated the sequence at a distance of fifteen and then twenty steps, and hit her target again. On the fourth attempt, when she drew back her slingshot, the wooden handle cracked. Curds! It would not do to have a broken slingshot.

Beatrice looked up. Opposite the sun, she saw a rainbow in the sky. It was the biggest rainbow she had ever seen. Its seven colours expanded until they covered a whole section of the sky. They vibrated as she stared.

"Holy comoly," she mumbled. "That's some rainbow."

"I'm glad you noticed," the rainbow said back. It had a low, calm voice. It sounded like a woman—like a woman who knew how to take charge and never raised her voice because people behaved when she said so.

"Your colours are exceedingly pretty," Beatrice said. "Especially the purple. It's my favourite."

"Mine too," the rainbow said. "Next time, I'll put on a bit more violet."

"Well, I hate to admit it, but it is a bit lonely being the only person in this forest," Beatrice said.

"I know," the rainbow said.

"Not a person to be found," Beatrice said.

"I know," the rainbow said.

"I can take care of myself," Beatrice said. "But it's a bit weird, with nobody around."

No answer came back, so Beatrice asked, "Who are you?"

"Ms. Rainbow."

"You sound like a person," Beatrice said. "I mean, a real person. A human. So where are all the people?" Beatrice asked.

The sun disappeared behind a darkening cloud. The rainbow shrank and shrank. At the moment it disappeared, the rainbow made the very bang you hear when you take a paper bag full of air and pop it with your hands. Paper bags. Lunch bags. What was that memory? The memory fled like a rabbit down a hole. Beatrice looked up again. The rainbow had entirely vanished.

For a moment, Beatrice was unsure if she had been dreaming. Had she really just been conversing with a rainbow? She knew two things: more rain was coming and her slingshot had broken.

* * *

Hot chocolate would have been good. It would have been delicious. But there was no hot chocolate in the tree house, so Beatrice heated some water over the cookfire and made tea. She returned to the tree and set her cup and saucer on the ground. She began underlining the word *private* on her sign when she heard a familiar rustling.

A voice called out. "Beatrice, oh Beatrice. Could we speak during your elevenses?"

Curds. Double curds. Croc Harry was there again, emerging from the woods and approaching her tree.

Beatrice retrieved her teacup and saucer. She quickly sipped the tea. Not hot anymore. Since it would be hard to climb the ladder with the tea in her hand, Beatrice placed the cup and saucer on top of her head and climbed the ladder smoothly. She made sure not to spill a drop. She had no memory of learning how to do it, but she sensed that she knew exactly how to walk with objects balanced on her head. Back straight, chin up, and moving always with perfect dignity.

As Beatrice climbed, Croc Harry called out, "Please, don't go. The other day, we got off on the wrong foot."

Beatrice kept going till she reached the top of the ladder. She removed the saucer and cup from her head, sat down on her branch, checked to make sure that her feet were dangling a safe distance above the crocodile's head, and then sipped her tea.

"I'll say," she said.

"I smelled your tea," Croc Harry said. "Couldn't you just sit there and drink it? Couldn't we converse for a wee bit while you enjoy your elevenses?"

Beatrice wondered how a crocodile could possibly know that word. But he seemed to know every word, including many that she did not. Beatrice remembered reading about elevenses. It was the snack between breakfast and lunch that the hobbits took in *The Lord of the Rings*.

She looked down at the King Crocodile. She found his teeth both intimidating and unsightly. What self-respecting animal would show his teeth, even with his mouth shut?

He talked on and on and on. He talked so much that it seemed the word *loquacious* had been invented just to describe him. It was pronounced "low-KWAY-shus" and it meant "big mouth, won't shut." He talked so much that Beatrice ached to smack his mouth. But even when he was silent and hanging onto her every word, Beatrice could still see his bottom teeth sticking up over his upper lip and his top teeth snaking down outside his lower lip.

Perched outside his mouth, Croc Harry's teeth seemed to say, "Go on and keep talking while I contemplate having you for lunch."

Rude!

Earlier, in her tree house, Beatrice had consulted the textbook *Basics of Croc Biology*, so she knew that at any given time, Croc Harry stored a few dozen stones called gastroliths in his stomach. He used them to crush his food. This aided with digestion. Crocs did not eat frequently but took an eternity to digest their food.

Whenever he was not acting like a hopeless carnivore, Croc Harry seemed friendly enough.

"Oh Beatrice, oh Beatrice," he called out from the base of the fig tree, "this is a dreadfully slow and uneventful morning, so would you puh-leeze just stay there and sip your tea and palaver? Could you give this King Crocodile some idle conversation to aid in the passing of time?"

Beatrice checked again to see how far her own feet hung below the branch. No crocodile could jump that high. She curled and straightened her toes.

"What shall we discuss?" she said.

"Could we just palaver?" he said.

Beatrice did not have a personal relationship with any other crocodile, but she was convinced that no other reptile trotted out fancy words.

"Wait a sec."

Beatrice ran inside, knelt by her bookshelves and consulted her dictionary. *Palaver*, she discovered, meant *to blather, yackety-yak*, or, put plainly, *to talk on and on*.

She returned to the branch and sighed.

"I so do enjoy watching you take your elevenses," Croc Harry said. "But today, I am worried about you."

Beatrice had difficulty believing that the crocodile had her best interests at heart. He could talk her head off. But he could also rip her head off. She could well imagine what it looked like when Croc Harry got ravenous. At that point, he would gladly capitulate to his basest instincts and eat a dozen bunnies, or a goat or an antelope, or even Beatrice, for breakfast. Or lunch. Or dinner.

However, Beatrice had problems to solve and a family to locate. She had no desire to become somebody's main course.

"The only thing you worry about is how long you have to wait before gobbling me up."

"You underestimate me," Croc Harry said. "Can't we be friends?"

"What if you get hungry?"

"I will exercise self-control," he said.

"Hardly reassuring," Beatrice said.

"Then stay perched on that lofty branch. But I need to say this: someone, or something, is following you."

How could he know that? Was he the one? Was he trying to trick her? What, exactly, was Beatrice to make of the one creature who sought her out like this, slapping his tail emphatically on the ground, dying to converse with her about the nature of the stars and the moon, or about the strange sounds emanating at night from the high plains above the forest, or about whatever happened to be on Beatrice's or his mind.

Croc Harry was an energetic conversationalist. He did not tire of talking. What was Beatrice to make of him? Was he friend or foe? Would he help her figure out where she came from? Would he help Beatrice leave Argilia? Or would her life end one day if she fell asleep while reading on the branch of her fig tree and dropped straight into his yawning jaws? On the branch of her tree, she could simply not allow herself to read boring books. She could not risk *Basics of Croc Biology*, or *Survival Tips*, or *The St. Lawrence Dictionary*. While sitting out on her branch, it would only do to read a story that was Rooftop Good.

In her private list of Great Books as Deemed by Beatrice, Rooftop Good meant the book had to be so great that she would be willing to stand on the roof of her tree house and shout out about it. *The Hobbit* qualified as Rooftop Good. *The Miraculous Journey of Edward Tulane* also qualified as Rooftop Good. Which brought Beatrice to a question she could not find an answer for: How come she had amnesia but still remembered which books were Rooftop Good? How could a book be more stuck in her brain than, say, the memory of a dress, a home, a sibling or even a mother? The only thing Beatrice knew was that she was better at asking questions than answering them.

CHAPTER 3

Good for Any Constitution

Someone was trying to sneak into her brain. Waking up was the best way to keep them out. As she did every morning in Argilia, Beatrice lay on her back, raised her knees, kneaded her fingers and reviewed what she knew.

She knew her first name, but as for the middle or last names, no clue. Parents? If they existed, they had been wiped from her memory. Her book, *Survival Tips, Argilia Forest* was dated 2090, so she had to be living in that year or later. She had cracked open *A Brief History of Argilia* a few times, but she always fell asleep. She had retained one fact from the book: the gated forest was so massive that it would require "days of hard traversing" to walk from one end to the other.

Gates! Where were those gates? And what was outside them?

Beatrice wondered if she might find answers in her own dreams. It was uncomfortable digging into her dreams, because they seemed to be filled with two horrible scenes. In the first, there was singing. The choral voices—altos, sopranos, tenors and basses—were achingly beautiful and made her think of family, home and community. But in a flash, the singing became screaming and she was covered in her own blood. She felt a hot pain in her belly. In the second scene, she was no longer near the singing or the screaming. She was in Argilia, and someone was whispering to her in a low, urgent voice. *Let me in. Let me in. I'm not going away until you let me in.*

In her dream, Beatrice sensed that it was a man speaking to her. A tall man. A man who would not hesitate to use his size and height against her. Because Beatrice was small and still a child, he assumed that she was weak, so he decided to pick on her. He was the sort of person who would not give up easily. What did this tall man want? He was trying in some strange way to take control of her, to use her to enter the forest. But Beatrice was strong—far stronger than he could possibly imagine. As she woke up breathing hard and lay still in her bed to calm down and sort out her dreams, all she could tell was that he was tailing her. Following her. Lurking like an evil shadow.

With the aid of her steel ruler that could expand to three feet, Beatrice decided to measure herself. She notched a tall, straight tree in the forest at one foot, two feet, three feet, four feet and five feet. Above four feet, to monitor her growth, she notched every inch into the tree—up to five and a half feet. She measured herself and determined that she was merely four feet, ten and a half inches. This was inadequate. Thoroughly unacceptable. A girl in Argilia had to defend herself. The only way to compensate for being so diminutive was to become a dangerous slingshotter with unfailing accuracy.

Beatrice had not seen the person or being or thing that was tailing her in the forest. But she could already pitch a stone three-quarters of the way across the Argilia River. Using her slingshot, she could hit a target on a tree twenty paces away. But the slingshot had cracked during her last practice sessions, and she was determined to fix it. So, after making breakfast, Beatrice searched in *Survival Tips* for the letter G, for glue.

The writing, in perfect purple calligraphy, indicated exactly what to do. It even instructed her to find, hanging from a nail in the pantry, a giant spoon with a three-foot-long handle. Beatrice lowered her rope ladder, carried the glue fixings and the spoon to the pit near the river, set a fire, hung a pot over the burning embers and followed the instructions. Easy as pie. She did not know why people said easy as pie, because good pie was surely hard to make. Making glue would be easier.

Beatrice boiled one cup of steel-cut oats. When they were cooked, she stirred in a cup of crunchy peanut butter. Then she added three tablespoons of flour and three tablespoons of beeswax.

The trick, said the purple handwriting in *Survival Tips*, was to bring all ingredients to a temperature that was warm to the touch, stirring as it thickened. *This is no time to look away, and no time to lose focus,* the book said. *Put a lid on the pot. You now have one minute to assemble whatever parts are broken and to bring them near. Remove the lid. For heaven's sake, use the bearskin pot holders and do not burn yourself.*

With the back of a spoon, Beatrice shoved some glue into the cracks of her slingshot. The glue wasn't strong enough yet. It needed more cooking. She was utterly focused, with nothing else on her mind, when Croc Harry slid out of the river and dropped onto the patch of ground beside her. His tail thumped. She felt the vibrations in the ground. She had never been this close to Croc Harry. She could barely move. Or breathe. She sat cross-legged by the fire, holding the glue pot with her bearskin pot holders.

"What's up this morning, Big Bea?" Croc Harry said, which Beatrice detested. He only called her big because she was tiny. She did not appreciate his mockery. However, at this moment, Beatrice had other concerns. The best policy was to appear unflappable.

"Making something to eat," she said.

"Meat?" he asked.

"You know I'm a vegetarian," she said.

"Some vegetarian. You are using bearskin pot holders."

"I'm kind of busy right now."

"No 'good morning' to me?" he said. "No warm salutation? No special indication of the fact that you and I are kindred spirits?"

"Good morning, Croc Harry." She tried to sound as disinterested as possible. It would not do to appear frightened. Maybe he would forget that she was made of meat and bones. Or perhaps he would have considered that she would be mostly bone, and would thus be unappetizing. Maybe he would lose interest and slither right back into the Argilia River. Perhaps he was still busy digesting his last antelope.

"Oh, come on, Beatrice, work with me. Let's palaver. I am in the mood for conversation."

"Okay," Beatrice said.

"Did you see the fog hanging so thick over the water this morning, and then watch it disappear as the sun rose? Wasn't that a thing of beauty?"

She removed the lid and stirred the pot. "Yep," she said. The glue was nearly perfect now. But soon it would harden. *If you let the glue harden in the pot,* the manual said, *you might as well throw out the whole thing. You'll never get it out with a spoon. You will not get it out with a spatula, either.*

Beatrice hoped that Croc Harry had no clue what she was doing. She imagined the conversation. It could not go well:

So what exactly are you doing, Beatrice?

I'm fixing my slingshot. Why?

And then what would she say?

Thankfully, Croc Harry did not seem to know what she was up to. His mouth hung halfway open. He looked innocent. When the instinct to kill was dormant, a predator looked rather foolish. Was he truly not hungry? Or was he playing with her, enticing her to get closer? Crocodiles did that. *Survival Tips* had warned her about that! Beatrice took a good look at him.

Croc Harry stared right back at her. His black pupils hung like vertical daggers. He stared and waited.

"Earth to Beatrice," he said. "Trying to get a little conversation going. Your thoughts on the beauty of the morning fog?"

Beatrice added more beeswax and resumed stirring. She needed her glue to have maximum stick factor. MSF, she reasoned, might be the only thing that could save her life. He continued to stare at her.

Finally, Beatrice spoke. "Why should I care about the beauty of fog when this might be my last breath?"

"Oh, so is it that?"

"Yeah," Beatrice said. "It's that."

"If I wanted to eat you, I would open up my jaws wide and toss you down the hatch before you could say your name."

Survival Tips had said to *practice nonchalance in the face of danger. A predator can smell fear, which exacerbates their hunger.* Beatrice had needed to consult her dictionary. *Exacerbate.* Just a fancy word for making a problem worse. *Nonchalant.* Appearing to not have a care in the world.

"Aren't you so very funny," she said, trying her best to appear nonchalant. Beatrice stirred the pot. It was reaching maximum stick factor. She glued her slingshot back together. It held fast. Powerful glue, indeed.

Beatrice considered her options. There was no point in

running. There was no point in fighting. Croc Harry would thwack her with his monster tail and knock her out and eat her at his leisure. She abhorred the idea of passing over reptilian teeth smelling of swamp water and half-digested rabbits. If Beatrice was going to perish, she did not want her last thought to be about Croc Harry's swampy breath. He outweighed her, and ten-to-one was not fair. But it had not been fair, either, when David had fought Goliath. Beatrice had read all about that fight. The lesson was perfectly clear. The only way for her to do battle with a crocodile was to outsmart him.

"Are you brown from being in the sun all day, or were you born like that?" Croc Harry asked.

Beatrice didn't appreciate the question. Croc Harry barely knew her. His question was too personal, so she refused to answer it. She would never admit this to him, but the question forced her to think about herself in a new way. She liked the kinks in her hair, and she liked her own skin and its colour. But was there something wrong with brown? Was brown unusual? How would she know what she'd looked like at birth, and at any rate, it was none of his business. She didn't even know where she was born, or to whom, or if she still had a family. If she did, she was sure that nobody who loved her would be looking at her all weird because her skin was brown. Her skin was her skin, and that was all there was to it.

It was most unnerving to have those two hungry eyes

staring at her. He had to be the only forest creature who had eyes atop his head, like periscopes above a submarine.

Beatrice kept stirring and chose to ignore his question.

"Does it get lonely in that tree house?" he asked.

"I get on perfectly well." This wasn't entirely true. Beatrice always read until she fell asleep and had a bump on her nose from having dropped one too many books. She had been wondering what it might feel like to be tucked in, or to have a lullaby sung for her, or to fall asleep during a back rub.

"Aren't you the independent one!" he said.

"You don't exactly spend your afternoons swimming with otters," Beatrice said.

"Mammals tend to think I will eat them."

"Can you blame them?" she asked.

"Things would look smackifyingly bleak if I ate all my friends," Croc Harry said. "But they don't know that. They refuse to fraternize. It's the price I pay for being a King Croc."

Beatrice felt her own legs trembling, but she hoped he didn't notice.

"You aren't anybody's king," she said. "You just happen to have big teeth, expandable jaws and a stretchy tummy."

Beatrice looked over at Croc Harry, to see how he would reply. In that instant, his eyes transformed into mean, hungry bulbs. The reptile beside her was no longer friendly. He was now a carnivorous crocodile with an empty stomach.

Croc Harry swivelled. He faced her. He opened his massive jaws. Crocodile spit flew from his mouth. Gross.

Beatrice grabbed the pot, removed the lid and poured the maximum stick factor glue into his mouth. With the giant spoon, she spread the glue all over his teeth and his flat tongue.

He closed his mouth, saying "yummy" as he did, but then he could say no more because his mouth was glued shut.

She stood up and gathered her things. "Enjoy your breakfast, Crockers," she said. "There's molten beeswax in that glue. Good for any constitution. Even that of a crocodile."

"Mmmm," was all Croc Harry could say.

Beatrice climbed up into her tree house, pulled up the ladder and looked out the window. Croc Harry was gone. Surely, he was back in the river, hoping that the water would unstick his mouth. Fat chance of that.

Beatrice felt no pity for him. He had come awfully close to eating her. Although she was still a child of uncertain age, she did accept that one day she would die. All creatures died. It was in the natural order of things. You lived, you died and someone else came along to take over. All that was fine. But she had no intention of kicking the bucket any time soon, or of perishing in the stinking, stone-filled second stomach chamber of the biggest, baddest crocodile in Argilia. Beatrice stomped her foot. How dare Croc Harry get all friendly, and in the very next moment, attempt to have her for breakfast? Some friend!

CHAPTER 4

Horace Harrison Junior the Third

Of all times of day, Beatrice most loved the evenings because she didn't have anything to do. She did like to keep a busy daytime schedule: oatmeal prep, cooking, gardening, cleaning, combing her hair, consulting the dictionary in her tree house and trying to figure out why she was in Argilia. However, she shoved her to-do list into her desk drawer and gave herself a break in the dying light of day.

Beatrice lay on the purple rug in the middle of her tree house floor. She got into her favourite reading position: flat on her back, little pillow under her curly hair, one leg bent up with the foot close to her behind and the other ankle resting on the bent knee, and the book held up over her face. Light from the western-facing window spilled in behind her and illuminated the pages of her book. This was the life.

She had opened *A Brief History of Argilia*, which she had been confused to find lying on her floor. Beatrice always put away her books. She wondered how the book had gotten there. How could it slip off the bookshelf and land in the middle of her rug? Had she removed the book earlier, left it on the floor and forgotten about it? She doubted herself. She read another line from the book. It was slow going. *Argilia was created in the Year 2060 as a living bio-experiment*, the book began, *in which most species of animals on earth would live in a boundless forest . . .*

Bump. She had fallen asleep. The book had hit her nose, again. This same book had hit her nose and awakened her three times that week. It was a sure sign that a book deserved to be abandoned when it put you to sleep and bopped you on the nose.

She picked up the book and yawned. There was no glossary. She had no clue what *bio-experiment* meant. All she knew was that the writer tended to bloviate. That word, she knew. It meant to write, or say, too much. Beatrice yawned. She put down the book. She had endured enough bloviation for one evening. The light was fading and all she wanted to do was close the windows, climb onto her bed and go to sleep.

However, she had to go to the bathroom. She hated that. Why was it that every single time she yawned and was ready to sleep, she'd get a little *ding ding ding* from her bladder? Her bladder seemed to call out to her like a bird pecking at the door: *Time to pee, time to pee, it's really time to pee right now.*

"Curds," she said. "That's it, I'm getting up now." She stood, shelved the book and wondered if it would be better to use it as a fire starter.

She took a long, careful look out the window. Nothing. No activity out past the fig tree, except for birds, squirrels and other creatures no bigger than her foot. Beatrice had theories about the four sizes of animals: smaller than her foot—she had little reason to worry; the size of her leg—exercise caution; the size of all of her—avoid when possible; twice the size of her—run like stink. But right now there was nothing out there bigger than her foot. And no trace of that thing that still seemed to be monitoring her. Could that thing have come up into her tree house and moved her boring book?

She walked out her door, climbed down her rope ladder and began the six-minute walk to the outhouse that faced Argilia Mountain.

Beatrice sat down in the outhouse, appreciating the thick, pink Styrofoam toilet seat that kept her bum well removed from the scratchy pine. She closed the door. She felt grateful that she had repaired her slingshot and had it with her, just in case the tall man from her dreams appeared.

Suddenly, the door creaked open an inch.

"Keep out, and who's there?" she shouted. "Croc Harry, is that you? If so, cease and desist right now. This is not one bit funny." The door closed. Then it opened again. She drew her sling back and shot a stone out the door. Had she hit a living creature, she would have heard a sharp cry, because stones flew from her slingshot at a mighty speed. But as the door closed, she heard the stone crash into the bushes.

"Who's there?" Beatrice found it tiresome to shout in an outhouse. Was this someone's idea of a game, or was her life in danger?

Before she could reload her slingshot, the door creaked again. A large, speckled rabbit opened the door, hopped inside, stole the single roll of toilet paper that was sitting on a shelf beside Beatrice and hopped back outside. The door clattered shut.

"Double curds," Beatrice muttered. She felt relieved that she wasn't being attacked, but now she was angry.

"Hey," she shouted, "that's my toilet paper! Bring it right back!"

A small, annoying voice called out with a trace of a whine. "Don't 'hey' me. I have a name, and it's Horace Harrison Junior the Third."

However, sometimes the rabbit could not pronounce the consonant R and turned it into a W, sounding like this: "Ho-wiss Ha-wison June-ee-oo the Thewed."

Beatrice could not stop herself from giggling. "So, who are Horace Harrison Junior the First and the Second?"

"No idea," Horace said. "But I'm here. Focus on me!"

"Never barge in on someone in the bathroom," Beatrice said. She could hear him hopping up and down. She hoped he was not hopping on her roll of toilet paper.

"I will give back the toilet paper under one condition," Horace said.

"Not negotiating," she called out.

"Come on! Work with me."

"I do not negotiate with thieves of toilet paper."

"You have books, wight? Your own libwawy?"

"How did you know that?" Beatrice asked.

"Everyone is talking about the two-legger who weads under the three-fruit tree. You're Beatwice. Famous in the fowest!"

"Flattery will get you nowhere. The toilet paper, now!"

"One condition," he said. "Lesson me. I want lessoning wight now. I can alweady wead and wight."

"Would you say that again?" Beatrice asked.

When he repeated himself, Beatrice understood that he meant to say "already read and write."

"They say I hop too much but I can wead and hop at the same time. The Argilia Wabbit Academy won't let me in. Lesson me, Beatwice. Lesson me now so I can wead better than any of those other bunnies in the Academy."

"The toilet paper," Beatrice said. "Open the door and roll it in."

The door cracked open. Beatrice saw a rabbit paw set the roll on its side and push it toward her. The door closed. Beatrice finished in the outhouse and stepped back outside. She washed her hands in the creek, brushed a strand of hair from her forehead and turned to face the creature. He was a most unusual-looking rabbit. Except for his pink paws, every inch of his fur was polka-dotted beige and brown. He was chewing on the outhouse's wooden door.

"Stop that," she said. "You're not a beaver."

"Twue," he said. "But I'm like a beaver. Gotta chew, gotta chew, just gotta chew. I go out of my mind if I don't have something to chew."

"Why?"

"I chew to grind my teeth down. Otherwise, I'd be a wabbit with a mouth like a beaver."

Beatrice handed him a broken branch from a willow tree. "Here. Chew on this. It will last longer than an outhouse door."

"Why, thank you. You are a lady and a scholar, whose wisdom is only exceeded by her good looks."

"Knock it off, furball," she said.

"Okay," he said. "No more formalities."

Beatrice studied the rabbit's face. Like her, he had a litany of freckles.

He hopped up and down on the spot, moving so incessantly that Beatrice found it exhausting to watch him. She tried to look peeved, but could not help grinning.

"Tell me about yourself," Beatrice said.

"How vewy diplomatic of you," Horace said. Between hops, he added, "I'm a wabbit. Of the speckled variety. I used to live with the other speckled wabbits on the far side of Argilia Mountain. But a flood washed out our warrens. So here we are."

Beatrice bent down and extended her hand. "Nice to meet you."

Horace lifted a paw and shook her hand. "Are you leaving me alweady?"

"I must get on with my evening."

"While you are getting on with it, may I hop along?"

Beatrice smiled. "Hop along, then," she said as she walked toward her tree house.

"Do you have a nickname?" she asked.

"I prefer Horace Harrison Junior the Third," he said, "but you can call me HHJ the T if you wish. If you must economize your syllables, Horace will suffice."

"All right then, Horace it is."

"Gonna teach me, gonna teach me, gonna teach me to wead even better," he said. Horace gave a giant hop. He sailed high over a bush that was taller than Beatrice. Then he sailed back over the bush and landed at her feet.

"How did you do that?" Beatrice asked.

"I defy gwavity."

Beatrice bent over and slapped her thighs as she laughed.

"You say you defy gravity?"

"Pay it no heed. I have no wespect for gwavity. A wabbit's gotta hop. I can hop halfway to the moon."

"I'll say! You're the best hopping rabbit I've ever met."

"I want you to learn me. So I can wecite pams."

"You want to recite poems?"

"Yes. To the best of my limited ability."

Beatrice stroked his soft ears. He stood still for that.

"You know, Horace, I could give you some speech therapy, so you could get your teeth and tongue around those Rs and those blended vowels."

"Don't need speech therapy. Don't need blended bowels, either. Pewfectly good the way I am."

Horace had a point. He was a perfectly good speckled rabbit, in equal measures charming and annoying.

CHAPTER 5

Complete and Total Calamoflation

Beatrice was stuck in that awful nightmare again. She could not escape. In the dream, something bad was going on where she lived. As a result, Beatrice had been banished from her homeland and had to start life all over again in Argilia.

In Beatrice's nightmare, no animals would speak to her in the forest. She had nothing to do. Her punishment was to remain stuck without hope of returning home unless she could say the name of the place she had come from. And since she had forgotten everyone and everything, how could she do that?

In the nightmare, a voice kept coming at her. It was insistent. Incessant. Like a fist at a punching bag. The voice belonged to the tall man who knew her name. *Open the door, Beatrice*, he whispered. *I require just the tiniest crack. Let me into your brain, and all will be well again.* His voice was sickly sweet, but Beatrice did not trust it. It sounded like that of a Grade 5 teacher who was faking kindness, but who might at any time explode into a fit of anger. Nothing scared Beatrice more than pretend niceness.

Beatrice kept ignoring the voice. Soon it turned nasty. *I say open that door, child. Were you not taught to respect your elders?* As a matter of fact, Beatrice didn't remember any elders, or being taught anything, ever. *All will be just fine if you just go along*, the voice said. *But you will suffer grave consequences if you do not obey. I'm sliding a key under the door.*

In the nightmare, a silver key slid under the door and stopped at her feet. *It won't hurt a bit. Put the key in the lock and all will be solved. You will be happy. I will be happy. Don't you want us both to be happy? Beatrice! Insolent child!*

Beatrice would not do it. The door thumped. The door banged. The tall man was indeed a giant, pounding at the door. But now Beatrice was waking to the sound of real pounding on a real door. She finally woke up. She was drenched in sweat. Who could be knocking in the middle of the night?

"Beatwice Beatwice, please please pwetty please open up."

It was Horace Harrison Junior the Third. Thank goodness he had eased Beatrice out of her nightmare. She got up and unlocked the door.

Horace hopped in. "It's a disaster. Complete and total calamoflation." Beatrice knew that word. She had seen it in the dictionary. It meant escalation to the point of calamity. She stroked his long ears and got him to calm down and take a breath, and then invited him to speak again. It was worrisome to see the rabbit hyperventilate. Every time Horace drew in a panicky breath, his front paws and ears flew up again. Then he would settle down on all fours, only to inhale so deeply that his ears and front paws flew up again.

He thumped a hind paw on the floor and told Beatrice he had just learned that an unusual number of speckled rabbits had been disappearing after they showed up at the Argilia Rabbit Academy.

Beatrice sat beside Horace. She listened to his worries. She whispered in his ear that, together, they would find a solution. She stroked his ears and rubbed the furry spot between his eyes. The rabbit's breathing settled down. They both fell asleep.

In the morning, Beatrice could not awaken Horace. For a moment, she stood with her feet apart and hands on her hips and admired the slumbering rabbit. When he inhaled, he sounded like ten purring cats. Beatrice found it comforting. He sounded like family. Then Horace held his breath. When he exhaled, he sounded first like a goose honking and then a piglet snorting. His whole body shook, and then he inhaled all over again. How adorable. Horace was a rabbit with sleep apnea.

Each time he exhaled, Horace mumbled a few words under his breath. Beatrice leaned closer and put her ear near his mouth. In the moments between snores, this is what she thought she heard him mumble, like quiet instructions to himself about how to live: "Jump high, wead pams, find out about Beatwice. Sister is huwt. Badly huwt. Save Beatwice."

What was that silly rabbit dreaming of? Read poems? Find out *what* about Beatrice? Sister is hurt? Badly hurt? There had been no talk of Horace Harrison Junior the Third having a sister. And what did he think he had to save Beatrice from?

Horace kept snoring and mumbling. He was even cuter when he snored than when he was awake. When he wasn't snoring or mumbling, he seemed to breathe fast. Beatrice counted his breaths. Horace seemed to take about sixty breaths in just one minute.

She looked out her window at the sky, which was dark and cloudy. The wind was picking up. Perhaps rain was on the way. She hadn't seen rain for weeks. The clouds reminded her of her nightmare.

The giant had been trying to walk into her brain, the same way you could turn the key in a lock and walk through a door. In the dream, her mind was protected by a solid oak door, but the person kept pounding. The door barely held. The person was not used to taking no for an answer, but Beatrice refused to give in. The voice got louder, and the fist pounded harder. Finally, Beatrice had awoken, trembling and cold.

Beatrice looked outside again. Dawn had broken. She saw some pink in the clouds above the trees, but dark clouds were also clustering in the western sky.

Rain or no rain, it was time to investigate Horace's problems at the Argilia Rabbit Academy.

Horace hopped up the minute Beatrice opened the door.

"Where are you going?" Horace asked.

"To the Rabbit Academy. You coming?"

"No sir. Matilda scares me."

"Who's that?"

"The boss of the Academy."

"How do I find the Academy?"

"Easy. Head to the hill in the distance, and then follow the wabbits carrying books to school."

The Argilia Rabbit Academy turned out to be located in the Grand Warren Underground Castle. Its door sat at the base of a steep hill, beside an unoccupied grass throne that rose as high as Beatrice. A rope was attached to a doorknob. On the rope, a handwritten sign said *No chewing on this!* Beatrice saw that a notice had been posted to the tree nearest the Academy: *Attention speckled rabbits. If you can read this, get out and go home. If you cannot read this, get out anyway. Trespassers will not be tolerated.*

While a stream of book-carrying grey rabbits arrived, pulled open the door and slipped inside, Beatrice noticed two large rabbits with extra big teeth leading away a small group of speckled rabbits.

"You can't stay here," the tallest soldier rabbit said. "Tell your friends. The Academy is full. So sorry about that."

But the soldier rabbits did not look sorry, and the speckled rabbits limped, as if they had been kicked or pelted with stones.

The soldier rabbit suddenly opened the door and bowed down low.

The biggest rabbit Beatrice had ever seen emerged from the

door and hopped up on the throne. She was a Flemish giant—the size of a small dog. She had fat, furry jowls and feet the width of a big tomato. She called out in a high-pitched, confident voice, the voice of someone accustomed to standing in classrooms and telling others what to do.

"You must be the famous Beatrice," she said.

"Nice to meet you, Matilda."

"You may call me Your Excellency, the Highest of the Head Rabbits."

Beatrice could not bring herself to say such a thing, so she decided not to call the head rabbit anything at all, and only to think of her as Matilda.

Matilda stared at her for a minute, and then, not receiving the answer she had been expecting, said, "Well, you've clearly been socializing with the wrong sorts. I hear a high-jumping speckled rabbit has been pestering you. Don't put up with that. Send him back. You can't show those speckled ones any latitude. Give them an inch, and they'll take a . . ."

Beatrice raised her hand to interrupt Matilda as politely as possible. "May I explain the purpose of my visit?"

"For such a little girl, you have elevated diction," Matilda said.

Beatrice took that as an invitation. She had not planned what, exactly, to say to Matilda, but she knew that she needed an opportunity to see for herself how the Academy worked.

"The purpose of my visit is to see if you have any vacancies for teachers."

"In fact, we do need a new teacher. Someone who can teach our rabbits to be aware of predators and to take pride in their elevated place in the world."

"Are you teaching all rabbits? Grey rabbits and speckled?"

"Heavens no, child. Haven't you been listening? Speckled rabbits need no training in crocodile avoidance. If a few of them run in the wrong direction and end up in some croc's stomach, well that's a few less that we have to send back to the other side of the mountain. And we can't have them reading. The next thing you know, they would claim to be our equals."

"Can you deny that speckled rabbits have hearts and bones and blood, just the same as you?" Beatrice asked.

"Are you arguing with me?"

"I simply wish to inquire why you won't educate them," Beatrice said.

"They are not of us. They are not from here. They are an inferior species. They are invading our lands." Matilda suddenly put her paw to her head, as if she had felt an electrical shock. She looked unbalanced. She nearly keeled over. "My head," she said.

"Are you quite all right?" Beatrice asked.

Then, as if nothing had happened, Matilda was able to sit straight and tall again.

"How impudent. Of course I am all right. What were we discussing?"

"The speckled rabbits."

"You are not from here, and you do not know our ways. We only have so much room to house, feed and educate rabbits, and the speckleds do not belong here. When you are as old and experienced as I am, you will understand."

Beatrice stared at Matilda. She did not see what this had to do with age and experience. "I don't think they would appreciate being called speckleds," she said.

Matilda said, "I don't care what they are called. Let's focus on my rabbits. Flemish rabbits. You can tell us from the others. We have an attractive grey colouring. And no speckles. Not a single one. So. Can you come back to teach one class? As a tryout?"

Beatrice paused. Was this really a good idea? Would she be able to help Horace by entering the Academy to teach a class?

"From your diction alone," Matilda said, "I believe you must at least be Level 10 in English. You clearly have the intellect to teach a basic course in crocodile biology."

"I don't know your levels, Matilda, as I am not familiar with everything in Argilia. But my English is close to flawless. It will be unparalleled once I have memorized all the entries in the *St. Lawrence Dictionary*."

"Confidence is a good thing, child. But you should know your limits."

"I have no limits," Beatrice said.

Matilda's ears shot up in amazement. "All right then, spell *dysfunctional*."

Beatrice stood straight and puffed out her chest, as if she

were at a spelling bee, and said, "Dysfunctional: not functioning properly." And then she spelled the word. Letter for letter. Correctly.

"And you," Beatrice said. "Are you a master speller? Can you spell *gastificated*?"—which she knew from the dictionary meant a person who was accumulating much gas and unable to expel it.

Matilda huffed. "I do not accept spelling challenges from my inferior," she said.

"I am not your, or anyone's, inferior."

Matilda sniffed. Beatrice sniffed right back at her. Matilda sniffed again, broke a bunch of carrots away from their green tops, tossed the carrots away as if they were garbage and munched on the greens. When she saw Beatrice staring, she said, "We can't eat carrots. Too sweet for rabbits. It's one of the first things rabbits learn in my academy. If it's green, go for it. If it's orange, toss it out. Our resources are limited. We can only offer you ten carrots an hour. Let's start with one class, one hour exactly, next Tuesday evening."

Matilda appeared ready to launch into a lecture, so Beatrice raised a hand timidly.

"Yes, what is it now?" Matilda said.

"Are all rabbits unable to eat carrots? Speckled rabbits too?"

"All rabbits, yes. But speckled rabbits are not my concern."

"As for payment, I require ten sets of carrot greens. No carrots for me."

"Are you attempting to negotiate with me?" Matilda hopped

right over to Beatrice and opened her mouth to show her teeth. They were big, for a rabbit, but Beatrice had now seen crocodile teeth up close, so she found little reason to worry.

"No," Beatrice said. "I'm just explaining that I won't teach unless you promise to let me have . . . to give me . . . ten bunches of carrot tops for the test lesson."

"Fine," Matilda said.

"Tuesday it is, then," Beatrice said.

"I expect you to run a disciplined shop. No shenanigans permitted. If you fail to teach my rabbits well, they will start to disappear with a hungry crocodile on the prowl."

"I'll do my best," Beatrice said.

"I expect nothing short of excellence," Matilda said. "And Beatrice?"

"Yes."

"Next time, wear socks of the same colour. We have standards to uphold."

Beatrice was not prepared to consider dropping her habit of wearing different-coloured socks, but she decided to say nothing about it. She would wear what she wanted, and when she did, it would be too late for Matilda to object.

As they spoke at the entrance to the Argilia Rabbit Academy, a speckled rabbit who looked like he hadn't eaten in a week limped toward the door.

"I don't mean to bother you, ma'am," the speckled rabbit croaked in a hoarse voice, "but could you spare a bite to eat?"

Beatrice watched as Matilda's back hairs suddenly stood

up. She thumped her hind paw down hard on the ground. It was strong enough to sound like a drumbeat. *Thump thump thump.*

"Get out," Matilda screamed.

The speckled rabbit backed off.

"Did you not see the signs? No speckleds here. Do you want me to hurt you? Do you? Do you?"

The speckled rabbit turned and hopped away. It leaned to one side as it hopped with a limp. One of its legs seemed to be broken.

Beatrice's mouth fell open. "Matilda! That rabbit was in pain. And hungry."

"And speckled," Matilda said.

Beatrice turned to run after the rabbit. She meant to tell it to meet her at the fig tree, where she'd give it something to eat. But it had disappeared into a thicket of bushes, and Beatrice could find no trace of it. She returned to speak to Matilda, but the head rabbit was holding her head in her front paws.

"My head is killing me. Something is pounding on my brain. Goodbye, Beatrice," she said. "Servant! Take me to my napping chamber."

One rabbit soldier opened the door to the Academy and escorted Matilda inside. Another soldier rabbit led Beatrice away. "Can I come live in your tree house?" he asked.

"Sorry, I live alone," she said. "But why? Isn't it comfortable in the Academy?"

"You saw her, didn't you? Reign of terror, here."

"Has it always been like that?"

"No, she used to be fine. She started up this rabbit training academy. She used to be kind to everybody. But lately, she has been acting funny. It's as if her brain changed."

To Beatrice, Matilda seemed so extreme that she was a bit clownish. Teachers, Beatrice suspected, could sometimes be like that. But why was Matilda so mean? It didn't seem natural, or believable. But whatever the reason, Matilda was more worrisome than a clown, because clowns didn't hurt people. Or rabbits.

CHAPTER 6

So Can We Be Friends Now?

Beatrice wondered what it would be like to be part of a family. Perhaps if you belonged to people and they belonged to you, and if you slept under the same roof and woke up together, they would not ask your name or why you had freckles. They would not ask why your skin was brown because they would know it was normal to have brown skin. They would play chess with you in the afternoon and Scrabble at night, and not throw a fit if you beat them every time.

Even if they had a bone to pick with you for some silly reason (had you read their book before they cracked it open, or nibbled at their blueberry scone, or used their toothbrush to clean a boot?), their anger would only go so far. This struck Beatrice as the true meaning of trust. Trust, according to her dictionary, was a kind of belief. It meant you felt a person was reliable. Trusting them meant believing that they would not try to eat you, no matter how angry or hungry they were.

Here he came now, slinking out of the Argilia River, high-walking up on his short, stubby forearms and powerful but undersized legs, and stopping under Beatrice's tree house for his morning conversation. He could only converse so much because the oatmeal glue prevented him from opening his mouth more than halfway. His mouth was not a pretty sight. Strands of oatmeal, elastic and sticky like lines of a spider's web, held his lower and upper teeth just a foot apart.

Even though his mouth was still half-sealed with oatmeal glue, he jumped up in the air to see how close he could come to Beatrice's feet as she sat on her favourite reading branch, which jutted out horizontally from the tree trunk and then curved smoothly upwards until it pointed directly toward the sky. Not even close.

"I don't know why you bother," Beatrice said, yawning.

"I don't really want to eat you," Croc Harry said.

"You can't fix your instincts," Beatrice said. "What if I fall from the tree and land in your mouth?" Beatrice asked.

"We can be friends," Croc Harry said.

"No offence," Beatrice replied, "but the answer is no. Why would I be friends with a carnivore who looks at me and sees breakfast?"

"Lunch, actually," Croc Harry said. "I don't do breakfast."

"You are not good material for friendship." Beatrice looked away and opened her book.

"While you are amusing yourself with your little story, I'm having trouble eating. I have not eaten since you glued my mouth shut. This is the moment to solve that problem. I want you to watch."

Beatrice yawned. She read another page of her book. But she put down the book and stared when Croc Harry opened his mouth halfway and called out weakly, "Toothbirds. Toothbirds. Come now, my sweet hygienists."

Beatrice liked to read with her dictionary on her lap, so she looked up the word *hygienist*. It meant someone who worked in a dentist's office and cleaned people's teeth. Yuck. The job sounded like a hole in a road. Best avoided.

Four birds with purple heads and yellow bellies drifted down from neighbouring trees and landed on Croc Harry's head.

"I wouldn't do that if I were you," Beatrice called out to the birds.

"My friends won't listen to a word you say," Croc Harry said.

Beatrice flipped through the thesaurus at the back of the dictionary for words that meant the same thing as dangerous. *Pernicious. Insidious. Vicious.* The best ones all ended with "ious."

"Careful," she called out to the birds. "He can be noxious." The birds paid her no mind. They kept pecking way at the teeth.

"You're in a foul mood today," Croc Harry said. "It must be hard to deal with all those digits. Utterly superfluous. Did you wake up with your toes in your mouth and your fingers in your ears?"

Beatrice flipped open her dictionary again. She'd never admit it, but she did like it when Croc Harry expanded her vocabulary. *Superfluous* was just a fancy word for more than enough. Digits could be single numbers, but they could also be fingers and toes.

The four birds settled into position in the crocodile's wide-open mouth.

"I'll take the right side, at the back," the first bird said.

"I've got the right side, at the front," the second bird said.

"Left side, back," said the third bird.

"That leaves me the left side, front," the fourth said.

Each bird started pecking around the edges of Croc Harry's four-inch-long teeth, cleaning out the oatmeal and gobbling up bits of decaying meat stuck to his gums.

"Got a taste of zebra, back here," said the first bird. "Crockers, when did you pull down a zebra?"

"A month ago," Croc Harry said.

"Very good, very nice, very smooth," said the first bird, pecking and eating away. "A good red meat. It has aged well. Robust. A hint of blueberry on my beak."

"That feels good," Croc Harry said. "I can feel my breath freshening."

"Is this baby rabbit over here, Crockers?" asked the second bird.

"I got ten of them not too long ago," he said.

"Scrumptious," said the second bird, who hammered like a woodpecker at Croc Harry's lower teeth.

"You birdies ought to watch it," Beatrice called out. "He could swallow you in the time it takes to blink."

"He wouldn't dare," the third bird called out, who was snacking on remains of wildebeest. "If he did that, he'd never get another plover to clean his teeth. All his teeth would fall out. He'd never eat again. Don't worry about us, Beatrice. We like this payday."

"Croc Harry, you won't eat us, will you?" said the fourth bird.

"My darling Flossie," he said, "I need you for dental hygiene. My arms are so short that I can't reach inside my own mouth with a toothbrush. My gums hurt when you birdies don't come by."

"Crockers," Beatrice called out.

"Yes, dear?"

"How about a meat-free diet?"

"Hey!" called out the first bird. "I can eat leaves and grass by myself, thank you very much. But can I taste wildebeest, zebra or rabbit without Croc Harry's help? If he becomes a vegetarian, there goes my protein."

"You've still got worms and bugs," Beatrice said.

"Croc Harry, can you open an inch wider?" Flossie said. "I need to get at that tooth at the back."

Croc Harry stretched his mouth open another inch, and the fourth bird finished pecking away at a bit of rotting meat.

"All done," the four birds sang out together. They hopped out of his mouth, flew to the closest raspberry bush, transported a few berries back to Croc Harry and dropped them into his mouth.

"Thank you, Croc Harry," they called out.

"And thank you for the raspberries," Croc Harry replied.

"Sweet, aren't they?" Beatrice said when she found herself alone with the crocodile.

"I'm very fond of those birds," he said.

"I meant the raspberries."

"A bit tart, today. But still good."

"You could live off raspberries, avocadoes, blueberries and grasses," she said. "You would have more energy. Feel better. Have less gas."

"I have no issues with gas. All that matters is that I am the biggest, baddest croc in Argilia," he said.

"After you've eaten, a moth could beat you up with its wings," she said. "After you've eaten, you're like an over-fed puppy. All you can do is lie there and moan and drop gas bombs. But your indigestion would vanish if you became a vegetarian. You would have more friends. You would be more fulfilled."

"Zebra fulfills me."

"You could change," she said.

"How would you like it if I absconded with your oatmeal and fed you zebra meat?"

"I don't eat zebra," Beatrice said, "but if you go without meat today, I'll bring you some tasty food."

"I'll try your fruits and vegetables and other such nonsense for a day. But no oatmeal."

Beatrice climbed down her rope ladder and walked beside Croc Harry to the riverbank, where she mixed up a huge calabash of raspberries, blueberries, boiled grasses, avocadoes, onions and mangoes. Beatrice also made him a thick stew of chickpeas, onions and sweet potatoes, which he ate hungrily, thinking at first that she had promised him chickens, not chickpeas.

While Croc Harry ate, a group of rabbits studied him. They hopped up to the edge of the beach, getting close enough to see if he was truly taking the food into his mouth and swallowing it, hoping this change in his eating habits might mean they would be safer in the future. Zebras, wildebeests, squirrels and raccoons all came closer to speak with Croc Harry, comment on his food sources and ask him about life in the swamp.

As Croc Harry kept eating, he began to cry. Tears formed in his eyes.

"Are they real?" Beatrice asked. "Do crocs truly cry?"

"I do," he said.

"Why?"

"My eyes get dry when I spend too much time out of the water, so I cry a little to moisten them. I use my lacrimal glands for that. Come take a closer look."

Beatrice stepped up close to examine Croc Harry's tears. "I'm only doing this because your mouth is still partially sealed," Beatrice said.

"At some point you have to trust me," Croc Harry said.

"Why would I trust a predator?" Beatrice asked. "You can't help yourself. You're a natural born killer."

Croc Harry shrank back several feet. His eyes drooped. He looked ashamed. He looked away.

"What?" Beatrice said. "The truth hurts?"

Croc Harry's voice wavered. He grew very still. He spoke so quietly that Beatrice had to lean forward to hear him.

"Look at you. Little afro. Freckles. All that light in your eyes."

Beatrice did not know what to say. She wrapped her arms around her belly.

"I can tell," Croc Harry said. "Beatrice, you're incapable of evil."

Beatrice felt a wave of gratitude but didn't know how to show it to the crocodile.

Croc Harry swished his tail from side to side.

"Why are you swishing?" Beatrice asked. "Is that the prelude to an attack?"

"Heavens to Betsy, no!" Croc Harry said. "I have something serious to tell you."

"And that is?"

"I will never eat you," Croc Harry said.

Beatrice swallowed. She nodded her head at him and smiled. "Thank you. But what will you do the next time you get hungry?"

Croc Harry sighed again. "Permission to approach?"

"Yes."

He crawled slowly forward. He flipped onto his back. Then he did a backward Croc dance, swishing his tail and pumping his forelegs, and thereby advancing inch by inch on his back.

"Come over here and place your hand on my heart."

Beatrice put her hand on his smooth, cool chest. She felt his heart beating slowly. About once every three seconds.

"I promise you that I shall never eat you. Or hurt you. Do you understand?"

"Yes."

"Do you believe me?"

"Yes."

"So can we be friends now?"

"Yes, if you agree to help me find my way out of here."

"So do we have a truce?" Croc Harry asked.

"Truce," Beatrice said, as she felt his heart thump against her palm.

CHAPTER 7

The Weight of 333 Broad-Billed Hummingbirds

Beatrice was relieved that she no longer had to worry about becoming Croc Harry's breakfast, lunch or dinner. However, she could not shake a certain feeling of melancholy. Her dictionary had described that word perfectly: *a gloomy mood*. She sat by the river with her head in her hands. She hated the idea of sadness. It got in the way of things. She was one hundred percent opposed to sadness, but she felt it anyway, like a weight in her chest. She felt like having a lazy day. Doing nothing at all. Leaving the river and going straight back to bed and spending all day despising her sadness. What could she possibly do all by herself to change the way Matilda was treating the speckled rabbits? If she were home, someone would surely advise her. Now that she had discovered a problem in Argilia, being alone made her even sadder.

Beatrice looked over one shoulder and saw a giant weeping willow. She looked across the river, where a deer ran into the woods. No one was watching. No one would see her. Good.

She bent over, put her hands on her knees and bawled her eyes out. She cried so loud that her nose ran. She removed some tissues from her Beasack. She wiped her eyes and her nose. There. She felt better. Now, instead of feeling sad, she was angry. How dare nobody come for her! How dare that nasty voice pursue her in her dreams! How dare something or someone be following her in the forest! In *Survival Tips*, Beatrice had read a chapter called "Managing Emotions." It said: "From time to time, it's perfectly normal to get angry." Perfectly normal. Was she perfectly normal? It was hard to tell, because there were no other humans in the forest. She thought some more about it and decided that she did not agree with *Survival Tips*. Just because it was written in a book did not make it true. Beatrice did not want to be perfectly normal. She wanted to be herself. Unique! She was Beatrice, and that was good enough. She kept on reading and thinking. "If your anger gets the better of you," *Survival Tips* said, "get a grip. Get on top of the situation. You're the boss of your own behaviour."

Survival Tips got that right. She knew what to do.

She slipped the heavy Beasack off her back, sat on a log resting over the damp grasses and exhaled.

In her kind, soprano voice, Ms. Rainbow called out from the skies above. "That sounds like a troubled exhalation," she said.

"My days in Argilia have been mostly lovely, but my nights are wretched," Beatrice said.

"What seems to be the matter?"

Beatrice told Ms. Rainbow about her nightmares. Ms. Rainbow listened attentively. She mixed a little extra violet into her palette.

"That sounds awful," Ms. Rainbow said.

"I have no idea why I am here, or who the giant is," Beatrice said. "I don't even know what a rainbow is, or why it can talk."

"I come out when the sun chases away the rain and light strikes the water droplets hanging in the air," Ms. Rainbow said.

"Not especially helpful," Beatrice muttered.

"You will only find one talking rainbow," Ms. Rainbow said.

"Still not helpful," Beatrice said.

"Sunlight is made of colours," Ms. Rainbow said. "Some bend more than others when light passes through a water droplet. Violet offers a gracious refraction. By that, I mean it bends the most. So it's my favourite. Red bends the least. It's a stubborn colour. Violet and red do not get along, so I keep them far apart when I come out to show my colours."

The explanation failed to tell Beatrice what she wanted to know. She had hoped for more from Ms. Rainbow.

"A rainbow can also be a portal," Ms. Rainbow said.

Beatrice was in no mood for a lecture. "What is that supposed to mean?"

There was a pause. Beatrice thought she heard a trace of

an irritated sigh, followed by the words "a door through which we communicate." But she was not sure, because the words made no sense at all. Beatrice did not like this manner of speaking. When she had a conversation, she liked it to be clear and concise. This conversation was pointless. Now she was angry and hungry. She reached into her Beasack for the snack she had made that morning: three blueberry flapjacks. She took a bite.

"How are the flapjacks?" Ms. Rainbow asked.

Beatrice took a second bite. And a third. They were so thick and moist and delicious that they did not even need syrup. "Mighty good," she said.

"The best thing about a flapjack is its name," Ms. Rainbow said. "It sounds so much better than pancake!"

Beatrice perked up. Now that she was eating, she started to feel better.

"Flapjack sounds better in my ear too," Beatrice said. "Pancake sounds boring. Dead. But flapjack sounds alive. Energetic. This flapjack is mighty good. The blueberries make all the difference. Downright superlative. Twelve out of ten."

There was another long pause. Beatrice was not entirely sure if Ms. Rainbow had heard her. Suddenly, her little monologue about flapjacks sounded silly. Perhaps all unique thoughts sounded silly if nobody was listening.

Ms. Rainbow's colours grew more vibrant. The violet morphed into a deeper shade of purple.

"Superlative flapjacks are good for the gouzelum," Ms. Rainbow said.

"What's a gouzelum?" Beatrice asked.

"One of your vital organs," Ms. Rainbow said.

"What's it do?" Beatrice asked.

"Cleanses your soul."

"What does that mean?" she asked.

"When you eat something fantabulous, it warms your gouzelum."

"This thing you call a gouzelum," Beatrice said. "Where is it?"

"Near your centre of gravity."

"Exactly where?" Beatrice asked.

"If you must know, it's next to your hippoflump."

"And where's that?"

"Well, as everybody knows, the hippoflump is located above your sybberly."

"Does everybody have a gouzelum?"

"Absolutely not. Only the best kind of people have a gouzelum."

"Do I have one?"

"People who make their own blueberry flapjacks are guaranteed to have a gouzelum."

After the snack, Beatrice was so full that she got off the log and lay down on the grass on her back, with her hands behind her head. She watched the sun climb the sky. Ms. Rainbow began to fade.

"In a moment," Ms. Rainbow said, "I will be on my way."

"Wait," Beatrice said. "You haven't even explained why I am here or why crocodiles eat children."

"You have not reported anything about crocodiles eating children."

"I came close to being a crocodile meal."

"As for your presence in Argilia, there is one more thing to say."

Beatrice jumped up. She wanted to be as close as possible to the rainbow, whose voice had faded to a secretive whisper.

"You passed the first test," Ms. Rainbow said.

"What?"

"You are in Argilia and you want to get out, correct?"

"Yes, I want to go home."

"That is not a sure thing. But to have any chance at all, you first had to pass a test. Which you did."

"What test?"

"You befriended a potential enemy," she said.

"Croc Harry?"

"He could have ended your life, but you made him an ally. You formed a friendship."

"We're not exactly close. He merely agreed not to eat me."

"Good enough. You passed."

Beatrice picked up her Beasack and slung it over her shoulder. "How do you know all these things?"

"You only see half of a rainbow," Ms. Rainbow said.

Beatrice shook her head. She was tired of non-answers.

Ms. Rainbow continued. "A rainbow forms a complete circle, but from where you stand, you only see half. There is more to me than you know."

"So about that test?"

"Because you passed it, you will have the opportunity to try to find your way out. To find your way home. The only way to do so is to collect eight clues. Once you collect the first clue, you will have seven more days to find the remaining ones. But you must begin by finding four clues. One a day, four days in a row. If you succeed, you must pass another test. Only then will you have a chance to find the final four clues."

"What exactly do you mean by clues?"

"Little messages," Ms. Rainbow said.

"Messages from whom?"

"All will be revealed, if you are clever enough."

"Will the clues help me figure out how to go home?"

"Not necessarily."

Beatrice stomped her foot. "Then what is the point?"

"You must prove yourself."

"Why? What's wrong with me as I am?"

"If you can't find all eight clues in eight days, you will never get out of Argilia."

"Never?"

"Never."

Beatrice gulped. She could barely see a trace of Ms. Rainbow anymore, and she could barely hear her speak.

"How do I find the first clue?" Beatrice asked.

The words came to her faintly. To hear better, Beatrice cocked her ear to the sky.

"Look for a message under a perfectly round and flat rock, thrice the size of your palm and the weight of 333 broad-billed hummingbirds."

"I'll find that clue," Beatrice said. "But I have something to say. Are you listening?" No reply came back, but Beatrice kept speaking anyway. "I don't appreciate all this testing. I see no need to prove myself."

Beatrice recalled a fabulous word she had discovered that very morning in her dictionary. A word that described the bothersome nonsense that she was about to be put through. "It's a whole lot of rigmarole," she shouted.

There was no reply. No movement in the sky. No more arching colours. Beatrice heard the popping sound that accompanied Ms. Rainbow's exit. But what about a two-way dialogue? Beatrice wasn't finished!

"Do you hear me?" Beatrice shouted. "Rigmarole!"

CHAPTER 8

The Noble Art of Decrockestation

One of the benefits of being the only human in Argilia was that nobody told Beatrice what to do. *The Late-Twenty-First-Century Book of Table Etiquette*, from her second shelf, had an entire chapter on how to eat oatmeal. A civilized person, the book said, should eat it with a mid-sized spoon from a bowl set on a plate. The book said one must never allow sticky oatmeal to fall from the table or onto one's lap. It was rude to lick your bowl or eat from the pot. But Beatrice saw no harm in eating oatmeal straight out of the pot. Did manners matter when you lived alone?

Another benefit of living alone was that she could read while she ate. This was one of Beatrice's favourite things to do. This very morning, while reading her dictionary, she had learned a new word.

Decrockestation, she read, was a survival skill developed in Argilia Forest. Sounded interesting. She read on. The noble art of decrockestation involved saving the lives of small mammals who had just been swallowed whole by a crocodile. If one acted swiftly, it was possible to help the victims hurl themselves back out of the stomach of a crocodile.

Beatrice jumped up to consult *Survival Tips*. The books were piling up beside her bowl and spoon. She found *decrockestation* in the book and flipped to the steps describing how to escape the gastroliths and stomach acid of a crocodile. She read with interest.

"Beware of the stomach juices of a crocodile," it said. "When it's time to digest a big meal, the heart reroutes its blood flow. Instead of sending blood to the lungs, it pushes croc blood straight to the belly. This helps the croc unleash a wave of gastric acid—powerful enough to incinerate the hind quarters of an antelope, a slew of rabbits, or a human being. If a croc swallows your loved one, you have one chance to save its life. It's called decrockestation. But it must be done before gastric acid fills the stomach."

The book gave a complicated explanation. Beatrice gulped. She let three spoons of oatmeal fall on her lap. But she had no time to keep reading. She had to start looking for her first clue.

* * *

Beatrice was walking beside the Argilia River and had already kicked fifteen stones. None of them were smooth, flat or close to the weight of 333 broad-billed hummingbirds.

Where was that blasted rock? How would she find a

perfect rock if it was underwater, sitting on a riverbed? *No,* she told herself. *Stop that foolish thinking. Use logic.* Someone had written a message to her. No reasonable person would hide a message on the bottom of a river. The stone had to be on dry land. One way or another, Beatrice would find it.

Beatrice had been looking for hours. She kicked another stone. It went flying. It was light, smooth and flat. Maybe that was hers. Underneath, she uncovered a bright blue tarantula. She had never seen a live tarantula before, but she had read about them and seen pictures. There could be no doubting her discovery: bright blue, eight hairy legs and lying on its back. It flipped over, waved its two front legs in the air and said, "Why, thank you. I have just moulted. Time for me to get moving again. And who are you, anyway?"

"I am Beatrice," Beatrice said.

"Nice to meet you, child. Do you know who I am?"

"I believe you are a tarantula. And I see that you can speak."

"Of course I can speak. If you can speak, why can't I? At any rate, for your future information, I am a Blue Sapphire Tarantula, but let's proceed on a first-name basis. Call me Fuzzy."

"Hello, Fuzzy."

"Hello, Beatrice. By the way, you should be careful about kicking stones. I happen to be in a good mood and can see that you could be my friend, but another tarantula might not be so happy to have you kicking off its roof. I've got some potent venom. Not enough to kill you, but I have enough stuff to mess with your mind and make you sick. Very sick."

"I'm glad you're not angry," Beatrice said. "For an arachnid," she added, "you are very pretty."

"For a human girl, child, you're not so bad yourself, although you could use a comb."

"I've got a comb," Beatrice said, "but I need to put something in my hair first. To loosen the kinks. Maybe bear fat would work, too, but—"

"But we can't have you smelling like a bear, because then you'd have no friends at all," Fuzzy said.

"Exactly," Beatrice said. "I'm looking for a smooth, flat rock the weight of 333 broad-billed hummingbirds. Have you seen it?"

"When it's time for me to moult, I usually hide under a stone just like that. Let's go look at the one you kicked off me."

"It's way over there," Beatrice said, pointing to a spot by the water.

"Mind if I hitch a ride?" Fuzzy asked.

Beatrice hesitated.

Fuzzy took a step closer. "I only bite animals that threaten me or that I desire to eat. Here. Put your hand down."

Fuzzy's soft, hairy legs scampered across Beatrice's hand and all the way up her arm until the tarantula perched on her left shoulder.

"Let's check out that stone," Fuzzy said.

Fuzzy seemed like a trustworthy friend, so Beatrice described her nightmares while she walked. Fuzzy listened carefully. Her leg hairs trembled, a sign that she was paying close attention. She said she was very sorry to hear of Beatrice's bad dreams.

As Beatrice walked along the riverside trail, Fuzzy said, "So why are you looking for a stone? Don't you have better things to do? Such as calisthenics?"

"Calisthenics?" Beatrice said.

Perched right on Beatrice's shoulder, Fuzzy lifted her body up and down, several times. Then she stretched out her front legs. Then her side and back legs. She rolled over twice. By then, she was panting.

"I'm out of shape from all that moulting," Fuzzy said, "but that's calisthenics. Exercises to stretch and limber up. I do them to stay fit, because when I'm fit, my poison is more toxic. I do need to keep a strong dose of poison handy. You'd be surprised how many creatures want to get up in my face. They see me and want to prove something. I don't get it. I never look for trouble. Unless I'm hungry."

"But you're so blue and beautiful," Beatrice said.

"If you don't mind me saying so, you are so brown and beautiful," Fuzzy said.

Beatrice blushed. Nobody had ever called her beautiful before. At least, not that she could remember. And certainly not since she had awoken in Argilia.

Beatrice reached down to the sand by the river and picked up the smooth, flat stone. It was light in her hands. It was very possibly the weight of 333 broad-billed hummingbirds.

It was so smooth that it felt polished. It felt like waves of water had splashed over it for thousands of years. It was as round as a clock and was three times the size of her palm. It was not too heavy to throw, but too heavy to throw a great distance. It felt close to what Beatrice imagined 333 hummingbirds might feel like if they were all perched on a platter on her hand. It was a beautiful rock.

Beatrice flipped the stone in her palm. There it was. Her first clue! On one side of the stone, in perfect lettering so tiny that Beatrice had to squint, appeared these words: *Arriving in Argilia causes complete memory loss, but individuals of exceptional intelligence have been known to recapture memory fragments.* It occurred to Beatrice that if she got smarter, she might figure out where she had come from. But how to make herself smarter? Were there calisthenics for the brain?

Beatrice turned the rock over and saw four additional tiny words: *Show me to Killjoy.*

"Who is Killjoy?" Beatrice asked.

"The forest dentist," Fuzzy said. "She is kind of wise, but a real grump."

"What does she look like?" Beatrice said.

"She is a blue-eyed, black-and-white lemur. Cute face. But don't be fooled. She does not have a cute personality. A bit anti-social. And she is missing a tail."

"Where can I find her?"

"Ask around. Everybody knows Killjoy."

Beatrice decided that she would go to see Killjoy as soon as she could. As they walked along the river, Beatrice spotted another smooth, flat, beautiful stone. She bent to pick it up.

"Don't!" Fuzzy said, but it was too late. Fuzzy fell off Beatrice's shoulder, somersaulted twice through the air and landed on her feet, just like a cat.

"Rude awakening," Fuzzy said.

"Sorry," Beatrice said. She picked up the rock.

A brown snake was coiled under the rock. It raised its fangs and drew itself closer to her. Beatrice heard it spit out the words, "Stand still. Just a little bite of poison to open the door to your brain."

Beatrice jumped back, and at that moment, Fuzzy sprang forward and bit into the back of the snake's head. It twirled a few times and fell to the ground, lifeless.

"You saved my life," Beatrice said.

"It wouldn't have killed you, but it would have hurt like the dickens," Fuzzy said.

Beatrice bent over to pick up Fuzzy, but the tarantula waved her off with a hairy front leg.

"Hang on a moment. Snack time."

"How can a tiny, beautiful thing like you eat a plug-ugly snake like that?" Beatrice asked.

"I can't chew, so I just suck up the juices."

From its mouth, the beautiful Blue Sapphire Tarantula placed a straw-like device right over the spot where it had bitten into the back of the snake's neck. Beatrice heard the tiniest slurping sound.

"Succulent!" Fuzzy said.

"What are you doing?"

"Snake juice is the tastiest. Tangy and spicy, just how I like it."

"What did you just do?" Beatrice asked.

"Girl's gotta eat. So I melted the flesh with a bit of my acid and sucked up the juices through my proboscis."

"Your what?"

"This little straw-like thing helps me drink my prey. All I need is a sip or two."

"I sure hope you never do that to me," Beatrice said.

"At a certain point, you have to trust your friends," Fuzzy said as she crawled back up Beatrice's arm. "You've got a fine shoulder, by the way. I'm sitting pretty up here."

As they walked, it struck Beatrice that trust was something to treasure, but that not every creature in the Argilia Forest had her best interests at heart. It wasn't a nice feeling, but Beatrice would have to prepare herself for that. That snake, for example, had tried to hurt her. It seemed to know about her bad dreams. Beatrice didn't trust Matilda, either, and told Fuzzy about their meeting.

Fuzzy said that some time ago, Matilda had been bullying her. Pestering her. Claiming that she was getting too close to the rabbit warren and kicking dirt at her. In a fit of anger, Fuzzy had bitten Matilda.

"I bit her hard. She was too big for me to kill, but I gave her enough venom to cause hallucinations."

"What are hallucinations?" Beatrice asked.

"When your mind is not working well and thinks all sorts of bizarre and unreal things, like it's raining oatmeal and elephants are stampeding upside down in the forest," Fuzzy said.

"So if she was bullying you and you gave her a little dose of venom, what's wrong with that, and what does it have to do with me?"

"Well," Fuzzy said, "maybe the hallucinations led to nightmares, and maybe the nighttime giant you have been telling me about got into her brain and is gaining strength and is trying to get into your brain too."

"That's a lot of maybes," Beatrice said.

"Anyway, time for you to let me down," Fuzzy said. "I've got to run."

Beatrice felt disappointed that her new friend was already leaving. "Can you just hop off?"

"If I jump, I could break a leg."

"If your leg snaps off, can you grow one back?"

"When I moult, I can grow another leg. But it won't be as good as the first leg. Not as big or as strong. I could make do, but I prefer to have all of my appendages in working order."

"See you later, Fuzzy," Beatrice said.

"See you later, friend."

"Thanks for saving my life," Beatrice said.

Fuzzy gave out a laugh. "Besties now." She scurried into the bushes and disappeared.

* * *

On her way to have lunch in the tree house, Beatrice saw some plovers fly past.

"Hurry," the first plover said to the second.

"Why?"

"Croc Harry is hunting rabbits," the first plover said. "So we may get some free food, if he wants us to clean his teeth. Symbiosis is one of the joys of life!"

"Where is he?" one plover asked.

"Just up ahead, on the riverbank."

Beatrice ran in pursuit. She spotted a bunch of speckled rabbits sliding down a trail of mud and landing in the river. The rabbits climbed back up to the top of the riverbank and then slid down the mud again. One of the rabbits hopped much higher than the others. His hop was distinct, and his voice sounded familiar.

Beatrice dashed down the bank to warn the rabbits. Croc Harry lunged out of the water. He trapped five speckled bunnies in one mouthful, lifted his mouth high and swallowed.

"Croc Harry, a moment of your time," Beatrice shouted.

"Occupied at this moment," he said.

"Can I offer you the sweetest delicacy known to human or Croc?" she asked. "Look. I have five apples. And more in my bag."

"Drop 'em right here," Croc Harry said, yawning wide with his jaws.

Beatrice peered inside. His teeth were clean. He had swallowed the rabbits whole. That meant they were still alive. Not for long, but she could get them. Inside, she could hear one of them howling. She could tell her friend was in there, because his wild hopping caused Croc Harry's back to bulge, then his stomach, then his back again. It looked like someone was swinging a huge grocery bag back and forth inside Croc Harry's belly.

"Let me out!" a voice screamed. "Please, pwetty please, we-lease me from this undignified and unsightly end. Pwetty please!"

That voice from inside the crocodile! She would have recognized it anywhere. Even though they had only met recently, it was like Beatrice had known Horace all of her life.

"That howling rabbit is giving me indigestion," Croc Harry said.

"You can't eat Horace Harrison Junior the Third."

"Already ate him," Croc Harry said.

"If you release them," Beatrice said, "I'll give you apples."

"Decrockestation is the only way out," Croc Harry said, "and they don't have much time. My gastroliths are rumbling and the blood is heading toward my belly and the gastric acid will soon rise like a tide."

"Do you agree to release them?"

"Only if you give me the apples."

"Deal."

Beatrice ordered Croc Harry to swing around so he was looking directly into the sun. Then, following the steps set out in *Survival Tips*, she placed the apples in front of Croc Harry's mouth. Decrockestation, the manual had said, requires the placement of tasty food just outside the Croc's mouth. It has to be tastier than what he has just eaten. Next, Beatrice hollered to the bunnies inside.

"Rabbits. Do you hear me?"

"YES," they hollered from within.

"How many are you?"

"We are five, but we fear we will soon pewish."

"Horace, are you all right?"

"Yes. Beatwice. Get me out! Pwetty please! I smell acid on the rise."

"Do you see any stones in there?"

"YES, a pile of stones."

"And do you see a thin wall, with light on the other side?"

"YES, that is where we came in here, but then the wall came up."

"That is his palatal valve," Beatrice said. "Take those stones and throw them hard against it, and it will open."

"Hey," Croc Harry shouted. "Stop. That hurts!"

"Keep throwing," Beatrice shouted. She could hear the rabbits grunting as they lifted and hurled the stones.

"All right, stop already," Croc Harry shouted. He stared directly into the sun, opened his mouth wide and gave a massive sneeze. The five rabbits flew over his tongue, leapt past his teeth, somersaulted in the air and landed onto the rocky banks of the Argilia River.

"Thank you thank you thank you," one rabbit shouted. "Beatrice, you are our hero."

Horace Harrison Junior the Third stood up on his hind legs, shook the crocodile spit off his fur and gave Beatrice a giant hug. "You are the bestest. The vewy bestest. You are my hewo."

"You won't need a hero if you keep away from the riverbank," she said.

Horace hopped straight over to Croc Harry. "Don't you ever, ever, ever twy that again. I am Horace Harrison Junior the Third, abbweviated if you must as HHJ the T, and I will not be twifled with."

Croc Harry yawned. "Whatever." He turned to Beatrice. "I'll have the rest of those apples now."

Beatrice emptied her bag. The apples tumbled into a pile by the croc's mouth.

"I hope this helps you become a vegetarian," she said.

Horace hopped up and down three times on top of Croc Harry's head.

"Stop," Croc Harry said.

"I will not be ignored, diswespected or eaten," Horace said.

"Go away."

"Do you know how I can bite? Vewy vewy hard. If you eat me again, I shall bite a hole in your stomach and chew my way out. The hole will gwow and gwow and all the stomach acid will leak out." Horace kept hopping higher and higher, landing over and over on Croc Harry's head. "All of the stones will fall out of your stomach. You will be nothing when I am done with you. Nothing more than a big fat empty sausage."

"Is the tiny fellow always this aggravating?" Croc Harry asked Beatrice.

"I am wight here. Speak to me. Speak to me. I am Horace Harrison Junior the Third, and I demand that you speak to me."

"What an odd one," Croc Harry said. "Someone gave him an overdose of personality."

"I may be odd," Horace howled, hopping up and down furiously on Croc Harry's head, "but you . . ."

He did not get to finish his sentence. While Horace was in mid-hop, Croc Harry swivelled, raised his tail and batted the rabbit away. Horace did three backflips as he flew through the air and landed on a pile of soft grasses growing by the river.

"Hey," Horace called out, "that was not funny. It was not polite. I demand . . ." He stood up and got ready to spring back into action, but then suddenly yawned and lay down and began to snore in the grasses.

Croc Harry said, "He is the strangest rabbit I never ate."

Beatrice smiled. "He's got to be the only animal who can go from shouting to snoring in ten seconds." She saw the rabbit's chest rise and fall. How could she not love this rabbit now that she had watched him sleeping?

Beatrice noticed Croc Harry looking at Horace, and saw, for the first time, that a crocodile smiles by making its nostrils quiver.

Croc Harry turned his attention back to the apples.

"Load me up, Beatrice."

She picked them up and dropped the big red apples one by one into his mouth. Croc Harry didn't chew. He gulped them down whole.

"Delicious," he said.

"How do you know what it tastes like if you don't chew?" Beatrice asked.

"I have olfactory skills," he said.

"What's that?"

"My sense of smell. I can smell the essence of everything that I eat. The taste, for me, is in the smell."

"If you behave," Beatrice said, "one day I'll make you apple pie."

"I am a King Crocodile. It is not in my nature to behave. And anyway, if you are making a snack for me, I would prefer rabbit pie."

Beatrice sat down on the riverbank, next to the crocodile. The afternoon had barely begun, and she was already exhausted.

Croc Harry flipped over on his back, so that his belly was in the air.

"What are you doing?" she asked.

"Suntanning."

"You want to get darker? You want to have brown skin, like me?"

"No. The sun is out and I want to warm up."

For a few minutes, they sat together with neither saying a word. Finally, Croc Harry flipped back onto his belly, with his tummy down and his back up and the hard, mobile scales on his back facing the sun again.

"What are all those scales on your back?"

"Scutes," he said. "I have thousands of them. They are interlocking but move independently of each other."

"What do you have them for?"

"They are my armour," he said. "They protect me."

"Why would you need protection?" Beatrice said. "You are a King Croc."

"That I may be, but even a King Croc is mortal."

Beatrice wondered what could endanger a King Croc. The only thing she could imagine was a person with a gun, or perhaps someone strong who wrestled the croc and managed to get behind his head and hold his mouth shut. She had read that certain big men wrestled crocs. Why a man would do that, she did not know. If she ever met a man, perhaps she would ask him.

CHAPTER 9

The Bee's Knees

As Beatrice dressed and got ready to climb down from her tree house, she pushed a bad dream from her mind. She had things to do. Today, she had to go see Killjoy. She had to find clue number 2. She had no time to waste on dreams about some giant trying to break into her brain. She thought about something Fuzzy had told her: "Be prepared at all times to defend yourself. You may not be big, but you are smart. So use what you've got: your brain and your tools."

Beatrice had asked Fuzzy all sorts of questions about Killjoy, who was said to be knowledgeable about Argilia and its history and who knew all the constellations in the night sky. Killjoy ran a thriving business as a beautician, hairdresser and dentist. Killjoy could work, leap and hop at great speed. She could talk a blue streak. Rumoured to be a fine dancer, Killjoy was perpetually angry becasue someone had cut off her tail while she was sleeping. She was still looking for the perpetrator.

Killjoy's office was a huge, extra-wide chair that she had built out of large, flat rocks. She had stacked one rock upon another, fastening each addition with mortar until it was wide enough for her biggest customers—bears and antelopes. The chair was located next to the river, about half a morning's walk from Beatrice's tree house.

When Beatrice arrived at the chair, Killjoy was nowhere to be seen. So, while she waited, Beatrice practised with her newly repaired slingshot, aiming at mud balls that she perched on the riverbank. Just as her perfect shot obliterated a mud ball, Killjoy walked by. The mud splashed all over her black-and-white face and covered her snout.

"Who did that?" she called out. She put her face in the river, pulled it out and wiped her eyes. "I say, who did that? Did you hear me asking for a mud bath?"

"Sorry," Beatrice answered. She ran up and helped her wipe her face.

"And the neck," Killjoy said, so she washed her neck.

"And the shoulders."

"That's quite enough," Beatrice said. "You're clean now, and I already apologized."

"You're a good shot, I'll give you that," Killjoy said. She was a tall lemur, about half the height of Beatrice, with long, lean, powerful legs. Beatrice wondered if her tail had been black or white before it got cut off.

"I know what you are thinking," she said. "I saw you looking. My tail had been black and white. Both. Like the rest of me."

Killjoy indicated for Beatrice to have a seat. Beatrice climbed up on the chair. Killjoy climbed up, too, and peered at her face.

"Are you the one who made off with my tail?" Killjoy said.

"No."

"Do you know who did?"

"No, but I'm sorry you lost it."

"You could use a hairstyling, but I don't have time for that today."

"Didn't come for a haircut," Beatrice said.

"You'll find an avocado tree near the bend in the river," Killjoy said. "Pick a ripe one. Mash a bit up and rub it into your hair when it is wet. It will help with the combing."

"Thanks," Beatrice said. She told herself to try that soon. Very soon.

"But today," Killjoy said, "do you need your nails sharpened?"

"I would like to have them filed and made smooth, but I didn't come for that either."

"Sore tooth?"

"No."

Killjoy let out an exaggerated sigh. "Then why are you taking up my time?"

Beatrice wondered if Killjoy would just keep getting madder.

She summoned her most polite voice. "Do you have a clue for me?"

"Are you buying my services today?"

Beatrice reached into her Beasack and pulled out five blueberry flapjacks.

"Now we're talking," Killjoy said. She folded the first flapjack in half and then in quarters. "I like my flapjacks good and thick," she said. "It feels more substantial. Like I am eating more." She wolfed down the flapjack. One by one, she folded the other flapjacks and ate them too. "That was good," she said. "Mighty good. I thank you for the flapjacks."

"You are welcome," Beatrice said. "Now. About the clue. Maybe something that will explain my provenance?"

"'Provenance. A fancy word for where you come from. You possess a respectable vocabulary. I'll give you that."

The compliment sounded like an insult. Perhaps silence might be the best way for her to break through Killjoy's foul mood. If Beatrice just let her vent, maybe she would become cooperative.

"Left hand first," Killjoy said.

Beatrice stretched out her left hand.

For a primate so old and grumpy, Killjoy held her hand gently as she filed her nails smooth. Beatrice closed her eyes and felt the sun on her face.

"I can't say much about your provenance," Killjoy said, "but from all appearances, you seem to be human."

Beatrice was done being so polite. No more bending over

backward to get answers. "I'm not in the mood for funny," she said.

"You are human, but I don't know your people."

"Do you know *any* people?"

"What makes you think you can walk into my place of business and launch into a thousand questions?"

"Why can't anybody answer my questions?" Beatrice said. "And why do you have to be in such a foul mood?"

"I stay up at night. But you came to me in daytime. So you are interfering with my sleep."

"I'm sorry about that," Beatrice said, "but I did pay you. And you were awake when I found you. Anyway, I have to find things out, and I don't have much time." From her Bea-sack, Beatrice extracted the small, flat stone that was the weight of 333 broad-billed hummingbirds. She showed the underside to Killjoy, who studied the words and gently placed the stone back into Beatrice's hands.

"You found your first clue. Well, good for you." Killjoy turned to put away the nail file. "And yes, I have observed people."

"What are they like?"

"You think I'm a grump? You should see humans. They never get along. Fight about trivial things."

"Like what?"

"Who ate somebody else's grapefruit. Who isn't loved enough at home. Whose horse should go first down a road."

"They use horses?" Beatrice felt a vague memory stirring. She knew what it felt like to ride a horse at full gallop across an open field. She knew to keep herself relaxed and almost elastic under the power of a speeding gelding, but she could not recall any other details.

"They used to have cars and trains and planes, but they went out of fashion in 2040, when fossil fuels dried up."

"Fossil fuels?"

"Girl, do you know absolutely nothing? Gas, oil. Basically, fossil fuel is energy drawn from decomposed plants and animals buried deep underground. Once you use it, it's gone. So after 2040, horses made a comeback. One decade later, they invented teleporting. Humans aren't all kind, and some of them are downright nasty, but once in a blue moon they can be smart."

"Like me?"

"You're a little bit smart," Killjoy said.

"I'm not sure if that's a compliment," Beatrice said, "but I'm choosing to take it as one. What's teleporting?"

"Instead of driving a car or taking a bus or flying on a plane, humans learned to send themselves from one place to another by means of teleporting. You're in one place in one moment, and then, with the right machines, in an instant you are one mile or ten miles or ten thousand miles away."

"They can do that?"

"Yes. If you want to go somewhere, you have to get a

permit. Then you step into a machine that looks like a high-tech cabin with lights, batteries and wires. It looks like the cockpit of a rocket ship."

"I've never seen a rocket ship."

"Nor have I. But we can use our imaginations." Killjoy gave a little smile. Beatrice considered that a big breakthrough, so she smiled back.

"Anyway, after the technician does their thing, you're gone. Bye-bye. You get teleported from A to B, and Bob's your uncle."

"Who's Bob?"

"It's a figure of speech. 'Bob's your uncle' means 'there you go, that's it, all done.' That's how teleporting works. Oh, and they also use teleporting to send essential items, such as food and medicine. And books. And messages. But it takes a lot of energy. Humans are said to store energy from the sun in batteries. It takes days of sunlight storage to teleport a book or a sack of food. Weeks to teleport an animal. Months to teleport a human. It's a lot of work to teleport people or goods, so people disagree a lot over who gets to be teleported. Let me tell you, it's very few people. It's a great privilege because it consumes so much energy."

"Does it ever fail?"

"Mistakes happen."

"What do you mean?"

"They can send people one way, but they can't bring them back."

"So how do they get back?"

"If they get back, they walk. Swim. Steal a horse. Whatever. Also, individuals are not allowed to teleport themselves privately. It takes so much energy that it can only be done with the involvement of the authorities."

"Have I been teleported?" Beatrice asked.

"How else would you have landed in Argilia? Humans aren't normally here. We do just fine without you."

"Have you ever seen humans who looked like me? People from my family?"

"Couldn't tell you. But look in your tree house. You might find some answers there."

"How would you know what's in my tree house?"

"That tree house existed long before you were born. I'm not even sure if you were properly born."

"What is that supposed to mean?"

"Some humans are born in the usual way," Killjoy said, "but they've been working on boosting human intelligence, and some people come out of tubes."

"I prefer to think that I was conceived and born in the traditional way," Beatrice said.

"Whatever you say," Killjoy said. "Time's up. You're not my only customer."

Beatrice showed the flat stone to Killjoy again. "Don't you have a clue for me?"

Killjoy let out a long sigh. "Silly girl! You came to see me. I am clue number 2. And here is a tip to find clue number 3: look high up in a tree."

"Is that it?"

"There is one more part to the clue," Killjoy said.

Beatrice stepped closer to Killjoy. She didn't want to miss a syllable. "What is that?"

"It's not just about the clue," Killjoy said. "It's about the quality of the chase."

"What's that supposed to mean?"

"Maybe you'll figure it out."

"This is truly a rigmarole."

"Time's up."

"Would you tell me more if I brought ten flapjacks instead of five?"

"You make awfully good flapjacks. The blueberries add the perfect touch. So I'll give that due consideration."

"Killjoy, were you teleported? Why do you know so much?" She looked straight at her eyes, but Killjoy turned away.

With her back to Beatrice, Killjoy said, "Didn't anyone ever teach you not to ask personal questions?"

Beatrice climbed down off the giant chair and stomped her foot. She could not prevent herself from raising her voice. "Why are you always so angry? It's not just about the tail, is it?"

Killjoy swung around. She shook with rage. She hissed through her front teeth. "Well, aren't you the bee's knees? So smart and skillful and perfect. You have a chance of getting out of here. You actually do. So stop your kvetching."

Beatrice took three steps back. It was no time to press

for more information. But the sound of Killjoy hissing had unlocked a tiny memory. Beatrice could recall the sound of air hissing out from a leak in a bicycle tire. And she could also remember riding a bicycle for the first time. She had felt weightless, free and fast. That was it. Just a tiny memory fragment. She picked up her Beasack and slung it over her shoulder. "Thank you for the help. Goodbye for now." She turned to walk away.

"Beatrice," Killjoy called out.

Beatrice spun around to face the lemur, whose eyes had become perfectly round, blue lakes. The lakes began to leak.

Killjoy wiped her eyes impatiently. "When you are searching for clue number 3," she said, "it's not just about what you find. It's about what you learn while you are looking."

CHAPTER 10

Weighs on My Conscience

Beatrice was so worried about finding clue number 3 in time that she could not think clearly or figure out where to find it. So, to clear her head, Beatrice walked down to the Argilia River. She listened to the water rushing over rocks. She picked up stones and skipped them over the water. After she had thrown about a dozen, she got one to skip eight times before it sank. She imagined that she would live a full decade for every skip. Eight decades would be a full life, she concluded, but nine would be even better and ten would be the absolute tops. Just imagine all that Beatrice could get done if she skipped a stone ten times and got to live to one hundred.

Beatrice bent to the side, cocked her arm and prepared to throw her best skipping stone when Croc Harry slid out of the water.

"You gave me a fright," she said.

"Serves you right for standing by the river." He shook the water off his back, which soaked Beatrice.

"Hey!" she said.

"Move back if you don't want to get wet," he said.

"Why are you so grumpy?" she asked.

"One minute. I'm busy." Croc Harry dove, came back with a big salmon in his mouth, tilted his head and swallowed the fish whole. He caught and swallowed five more fish.

"Is it necessary to kill so many?" Beatrice asked.

"As an eater of oatmeal and apples, that's easy for you to say," Croc Harry said. "I'm a King Croc. I eat fish, fowl and mammals. If you don't like it, don't watch."

Beatrice stared at the crocodile. He did not seem himself.

"Something is bothering you," she said. "Stop killing salmon and talk to me."

Croc Harry crawled over a long, dead branch on the riverbank and smashed his tail down on it. The crack of wood splitting sounded like a pistol going off. Beatrice remembered the sound of guns. It made her shudder.

"Stop," she said. "*Ça suffit.*"

"What's that mean?" he asked.

"It's French, for 'that's enough.'"

"You know French?"

"I guess I do. *Basta* means the same thing, in Spanish and Italian."

"How do you know all those languages?"

"I don't know how I know the things I know," Beatrice

said. "My mind is full of information, but I have no idea where it came from."

"Totally," Croc Harry said. "I hear you."

"How could a crocodile know what it means not to know where you come from?" Beatrice asked.

"How could you know what lies in a crocodile's heart?" Croc Harry answered.

Beatrice shuffled from one foot to the other. She stared at the strange turquoise, talking reptile. It was true. She had no idea what Croc Harry knew or felt.

"I was ripping through that school of salmon," Croc Harry said, "because something is bothering me. I don't know why, but I feel upset." He thrashed his tail and another branch snapped. "Upset!"

Beatrice vowed to never again underestimate a crocodile.

Horace Harrison Junior the Third hopped up to join them and landed on Croc Harry's back.

"Hello, Harry, old pal," Horace said. "Remember me?"

"Not in the mood," Croc Harry said.

"I'm the one you're never having for lunch." Horace hopped up and down on Croc Harry's head.

"Basta," Croc Harry barked. He swivelled, launched the rabbit into the air and batted him with his tail. Horace sailed ten feet and landed in a patch of thistles.

"Ouch," Horace said. "Double ouch. That hurt!"

"Enough," Beatrice shouted. "*Ça suffit. Basta.* Stop it, both of you!"

Beatrice had no idea that she could shout that loud. Horace and Croc Harry fell silent.

"We're all in a bad mood, and I'm not sure about my purpose," Beatrice said.

"Porpoise?" Horace said. "Is there a porpoise in the wiver?"

"Purpose, silly," Beatrice said. "I don't even know what I'm doing in Argilia. I don't even know what you're doing here, talking to me as if you're humans."

"Actually," Horace said, "you're talking to me as if you're a wabbit."

Beatrice stomped her foot and pointed her finger angrily at both of them. "J'en ai ras le bol."

"What's that mean?" Croc Harry asked.

"It means I'm fed up. I'm going to see Ms. Rainbow."

"Do you want company?" Horace asked.

"No," Beatrice said.

"Not even my company?" Croc Harry asked.

"No. I need time alone."

"Come on," Horace whined. "Please?"

"No!"

Croc Harry and Horace gave each other a long look. Croc Harry slinked off silently, with Horace sitting peacefully on his back.

* * *

Beatrice took a long walk alone in the direction of the meadowlands—a giant, flat meadow with low shrubs and tiny grasses where, occasionally, the animals of Argilia gathered to communicate. Every animal in Argilia knew the rules of the meadowlands. There was no eating allowed. You could not eat the grasses or leaves if you were an herbivore, and you could not eat other animals if you were a carnivore. You could not threaten another animal, reptile or bird. You were not allowed to attack any creature coming to or going from the meadowlands.

It had rained in the early morning. The grasses were wet, and now that the sun had come out, the bushes glistened with dripping spider webs.

Beatrice stood out in the middle of the meadow and looked all around the sky. She raised both her arms above her head, bowed down three times, stood tall again and said, "Ms. Rainbow, are you there?"

A rainbow appeared faintly. It seemed to shrink and grow.

"Ms. Rainbow, is that you?"

The rainbow expanded. Soon, it formed a giant arc over half the sky. Beatrice detected vibrations in the sky, the air, the trees and the ground. A pleasant soprano voice spoke to her.

"There is no need to shout, Beatrice. I was tending to an issue elsewhere. I have a little too much on my plate, running everything. But I am with you now, and I can hear you perfectly."

"What do you mean, 'running everything'?"

"We won't worry about that just now."

Beatrice watched as the rainbow grew brighter. Her shade of violet gleamed like a flowering iris in the sunlight. Her green took on the brilliant hue of spring grass on a sunny day.

"I have never seen colours so fine," Beatrice said.

"Thank you for the compliment, Beatrice. When I reveal all of my colours after a rainstorm, it is nice to be admired. I put on some extra violet just now, as well as a brighter shade of green. What a shame it would be to shine like this and be ignored."

Beatrice stretched her palms up toward Ms. Rainbow. Tears welled in her eyes.

"Why do I have to chase down all these clues? I just want to go home. If I have a home."

Ms. Rainbow shone even brighter. The multicoloured arc in the sky vibrated. Beatrice could feel the pulsating air. On her shoulder, she imagined—perhaps she really felt—the light, reassuring pressure of Ms. Rainbow's fingertips.

Ms. Rainbow spoke again. "The world needs you, Beatrice. To survive, and to escape Argilia, you must find the clues."

"Why can't I just leave now?"

"You are being tested. You must prove yourself."

"Why?"

Ms. Rainbow did not answer. Beatrice could tell that no answer was coming. After a moment, Beatrice spoke again.

"Do you know the people who live where I belong?"

"I can't say."

"Are you my mother?"

Ms. Rainbow paused again. Just when Beatrice was concluding that no answer would be offered, Ms. Rainbow spoke. "That's frankly ridiculous."

"A talking crocodile and a rabbit who can jump halfway to the moon is also ridiculous," Beatrice said.

Ms. Rainbow paused again. Beatrice noticed that she certainly knew how to use silence to control a conversation.

"Do I look like anyone's mother?" Ms. Rainbow asked.

"You have motherly diction."

"Well. Believe me. I am no person's mother."

Ms. Rainbow shone even more intensely. Beatrice felt the vibrations in her very bones, as if she were a harmonica and the rainbow were playing her. Just as Beatrice was ready to ask another question, the vibrations stopped.

Croc Harry and Horace appeared together at the edge of the meadows. Croc Harry noticed that Ms. Rainbow was in conversation with Beatrice. To interrupt them, he opened his mouth and bellowed.

Ms. Rainbow shrank a little, let her colours fade slightly and said in a calm voice, "Croc Harry, that bellow of yours sounds like a threat."

"So what if it is?"

"We are in the meadowlands. There are rules."

"I am a King Crocodile, and you are up in the sky. What are you going to do about it, Ms. Muckety-Muck?"

"You may call me Ms. Rainbow," she said.

Croc Harry pushed up on his front legs. "Ms. Muckety-Muck!"

Beatrice looked down and said, "Croc Harry, stop that right now."

"I'll handle him," Ms. Rainbow said.

"Nobody handles the King Croc," Croc Harry said.

Ms. Rainbow spoke firmly, but quietly. Beatrice had to strain to hear her voice. "You're becoming a fool, and I don't suffer fools gladly. In truth, I don't suffer fools at all."

"Whatever you say, Ms. Muckety-Muck."

Beatrice kneeled down. She put her hand on Croc Harry's scutes. "A little respect!" she whispered.

"Beatrice, take ten steps back," Ms. Rainbow said.

Beatrice was so concerned about getting Croc Harry to settle down that she did not move.

"How about *me* being respected?" Croc Harry said.

"Beatrice," Ms. Rainbow commanded. "Ten steps. Right now."

Beatrice scooped up Horace. To be safe, she took twenty steps back.

Ms. Rainbow began to vibrate. At first, it felt like a dryer whirring as it spun clothes. Beatrice was shocked to remember dryers. She still had no memories of people, just one or two objects like dryers and bicycles. Ms. Rainbow's vibrations grew more ominous. It felt like an earthquake.

In a flash, Ms. Rainbow triggered a gargantuan vibration that split the ground under Croc Harry. The crocodile tumbled into a deep hole. When he began to climb out, Ms. Rainbow split the earth again. Croc Harry fell even farther down.

"Okay," Croc Harry called out. "Uncle. I give up."

Croc Harry crawled slowly out of the deep hole. Beatrice put Horace back on the ground.

Croc Harry looked up at Ms. Rainbow. "All right. You win."

Horace gave a giant hop that seemed to carry him halfway to the rainbow and back. "Lady, that was some show. Shall I call you Your Woyal Highness?"

Ms. Rainbow did not reply.

"Thank you for not hurting him, Ms. Rainbow," Beatrice said.

Horace was so excited that he could not stop hopping. He hopped onto Beatrice's shoulder, and off. He peered into Croc Harry's eyes and said, "Good effort, mate, but what can you do against a wainbow?"

Croc Harry said nothing.

Horace hopped twice more. Then he hopped on Croc Harry's back and bounced up and down a dozen times.

Beatrice wagged her finger at Horace, but he could not control himself.

"You delivered a ferocious bellow," Horace said. "But nobody competes with a wainbow, do they? And that isn't any ordinary wainbow. That wainbow is some powerful. Twuly omnipotent."

Horace jumped again on Croc Harry's back.

"Horace Harrison Junior the Third, get off my back," Croc Harry said.

Horace could not stop. He kept hopping up and down. Each time he landed on Croc Harry's head, Horace bent over to shout in his ear. "The mighty Croc Harry goes down after a technical knockout by Ms. Wainbow!"

Beatrice scooped up Horace and held him in her arms. "Quiet," she said. "And Croc Harry is not a trampoline."

The rabbit wriggled out of her arms and did a little dance on Croc Harry's head. "Not a twampoline, that's a good one. I'll tell you what he is." Horace hopped higher. "Here's what. He's a cwocowampoline."

Beatrice tried to grab hold of Horace and lift him away from the crocodile, but she missed. It was not easy to catch a speckled rabbit mid-flight.

Horace gave a mighty hop. When he reached the apex of his flight and began to drop again, Croc Harry flipped onto his back, opened his mouth wide and caught the rabbit. He pinned him between his eighth and ninth rows of incisors and turned onto his legs again.

"Heyyyy," the rabbit screamed. "That's not funny, let me go!"

"You're a pain in the scutes," Croc Harry muttered.

"No eating in the meadowlands," the rabbit howled. "It's a wule. An important wule. It's a . . . Wait. What are scutes?"

Beatrice noticed that the crocodile was not clamping down

on the rabbit or spraying him with croc juice. He was just teasing him.

Ms. Rainbow glowed with colours more vibrant than ever.

"I need you to listen, Beatrice. How many clues have you found?"

"Two."

"You must not tarry."

Beatrice nodded. She understood. She would resume her search for the next clue immediately.

At that moment, the vibrations began again. They shook the sky and the earth. They shook every bone in the bodies of Beatrice, Croc Harry and Horace Harrison Junior the Third. Beatrice looked up and stared. Croc Harry looked up, opening his jaws wide to do so. Horace fell out of the croc's mouth, stood on his two hind paws, looked up and said: "Holy comoly."

The rainbow was vibrating so fast that it felt like the whole world was spinning in circles. Beatrice could not take her eyes off the sky. The rainbow began to grow. Each of the seven colours—red, orange, yellow, green, blue, indigo and violet— expanded to occupy a huge, curving slice of the sky. The rainbow grew bigger and bigger and flipped so it looked like a giant horseshoe magnet lying on its side. The arms of the magnet began to stretch all the way across the sky. The rainbow curved the distant ends of its arms around the sun. Suddenly, with a resounding pop that sounded like the world's biggest firecracker, the rainbow disappeared. The sun disappeared.

The sky filled with dark clouds and it began to rain.

"Oh boy," Horace said. "That was some show, but here comes the wain. Worse than cats and dogs. It's coming down pigs and cows."

The rain fell in torrents. Beatrice reached into her bag and pulled out an umbrella. When she pushed it open, it spread out to completely shelter her head and shoulders, with room to spare. Horace hopped up onto her shoulder.

"I hope you don't mind," Horace said, "but I hate getting wet. Ruins my fur. Gets all matted. Then all the matted fur starts gwowing into my skin. Don't you hate that? Don't you just hate that?"

"Quiet," Beatrice said. "No huddling under my umbrella unless you are silent."

"Quiet, that is me," the rabbit said. "Perfectly quiet. Not saying a sound. Not even a syllable."

"Shush," she said.

Horace fell asleep on her shoulder. He snored by her right ear.

It began to hail. The icy stones pelted down hard and bounced off the umbrella. Croc Harry pulled in close to Beatrice as they left the meadow, re-entered the forest and walked the long trail back down toward the river.

"I knew you weren't going to eat him," Beatrice said.

"Next time I just might," Croc Harry said. "He'd be a right tasty wabbit."

"Don't mock him," Beatrice said. "He's a rabbit, not a

wabbit. It's not his fault his teeth are so big that he can't pronounce his Rs. But it's a good thing he doesn't have to speak Spanish. All those Rs. The poor fellow would be totally lost."

Horace kept snoring like a purring cat. Croc Harry pushed up on his front legs and, keeping his entire body except for his tail off the ground, high-walked under the umbrella to keep the hailstones from hitting his eyes. Beatrice thought about the rainbow's words, and about her explosion in the sky.

As she walked beside Croc Harry, Beatrice felt calm and purposeful.

"You know," she said to Croc Harry, "you really can't be acting like that."

"What do you mean?"

"Mouthing off, giving Ms. Rainbow a hard time. You need to up your game, Croc Harry, if you want to move on."

"Move on to what?"

"To a better friendship with me. We could get to know each other better."

"I would like that more than anything in the world," Croc Harry said.

"Well," Beatrice said, "I will not be friends with someone who is rude to others. There was no need to disrespect Ms. Rainbow. You could have avoided that confrontation."

"You're right."

"So what happened?" Beatrice said. "You had a whole different personality out there."

"I was in a terrible mood," Croc Harry said. "I still am, but I was out of line and I see that now."

"I like you, Croc Harry. We could help each other."

"Ditto," Croc Harry said.

The rain ceased. As they came out of the forest and travelled through another meadow, Beatrice brought a butterfly net out of her Beasack. She caught, examined and released butterflies as she walked.

"Aren't you going to eat them?" he asked.

She laughed and kept letting them go. He knew perfectly well that she would not eat a butterfly.

"Then what's the point of catching them?"

She asked if he had ever caught something that he did not eat.

"Friendship," he said. He had caught friendship, and he did not want to eat that.

She gave him a puzzled glance.

"You are my friend, Beatrice. We converse very well. Some people need coffee. I need palavering, and not just with anybody."

Beatrice said that during a long walk, conversation helped pass the time.

"I am hoping for time to pass as soon as possible," he said.

"Why?"

"I do not belong here. It's lonely being a King Crocodile."

"I notice you do not congregate with other crocodiles. Is it because you are turquoise and don't look like the others?"

"I don't want to be around other crocodiles. It's hard to hunt alone, but I do have to eat."

"It's not your fault you were born a carnivore," Beatrice said.

"What about before?" Croc Harry asked.

"What do you mean?"

"There was a time when I had little to eat. I lashed out and did something wrong. I don't remember what I did, but it weighs on my conscience anyway."

Beatrice stopped walking and stared at her friend. "It must be awful to not know what you did, but to still feel bad about it," she said.

"It feels like I am trapped," Croc Harry said.

A light flicked on in Beatrice's brain. Now she understood that crocodiles also had deep, unexpressed feelings.

CHAPTER 11

Thanks for the Permission

Even in Argilia Forest, which was so big that she had never found the end of it, Beatrice needed time alone. Lately, it had been challenging to go to bed at night or to wake in the morning and eat her breakfast in peace. Horace had taken to leaping, entirely uninvited, up to her tree house and trying to open her door. She had to put a lock on it.

"Beatwice Beatwice Beatwice," he shouted on a particularly aggravating morning as she stirred her oatmeal, "I know you're in there." He gave a giant hop from his place on the branch outside her door. When he was high enough to look through the window, he saw her and waved. He kept rising, reached his maximum height, began to fall and waved at her on the way back down. He kept going up and down like a yo-yo, ears hanging low as he rose and standing straight up to salute the sun as he fell, until Beatrice gave up and unlocked the door.

"What took you so long?" he said. "I've been hopping and bopping for five minutes here. I like to hop, but I like all that effort to count for something. Don't make me waste my hops!"

"Horace," she said, "I have never seen a rabbit jump so high."

Horace gave another demonstration. Over and over he hopped, each time muttering, "You can do it, you can do it, you can do it," before inhaling deeply and pushing off with his legs. When he began to clear the top of the fig tree, Beatrice waved at him to stop. He stood before her, panting.

"Impressive," she said. "Now settle down and tell me why you have taken me from my oatmeal."

"Sorry," he said. "You eat now. And I will talk."

Beatrice sat. She poured some cream over her bowl of food because nothing was worse than burning the roof of your mouth with hot oatmeal. She did not stir her bowl, because that was against all rules. Oatmeal had to be served with a slight pool of cream at the very top. Under that, the blueberries and the raspberries. And under that, the sprinkling of brown sugar. And under all of that, the oatmeal. This, and only this, was how to eat a bowl of oatmeal. As Beatrice dipped her spoon into the breakfast, Horace came to the other side of the table, stopped hopping and stood on his hind legs on the chair facing Beatrice.

When he began to speak, he raised his front paws. Five sharp nails on each paw. He was small, but those nails could cause some serious damage. They could cut through clothes and skin or scratch out an eyeball. He waved them about as if they were batons. His paws appeared to make exclamation marks at the end of each sentence. He said that speckled rabbits were disappearing faster than before. Horace said that the Flemish giant rabbits—the ones who were covered by light grey fur and ruled by Matilda—were doing just fine.

"When I go to teach, I'll see what I can do," Beatrice said.

Horace hopped onto her lap. "I heard that Fuzzy helped you find the first clue, and that Killjoy gave you the second."

Beatrice thought for a moment about Killjoy's advice: it wasn't just about finding the clue, but also about what she learned. Perhaps she would learn more with Horace by her side. "Would you like to help me now?" Beatrice said.

"Yes!" Horace began hopping wildly. "I am your best fwiend. Your one and only."

"We talked about this," Beatrice said. "You are not my only friend."

"Okay," Horace said. "As long as I'm the one you love the most."

"Friends can't be telling friends how to be with other friends," Beatrice said.

Horace sat still. He rubbed his brow with his paw. "If you say so."

Beatrice explained that she had been looking for clue number 3 in her tree house but had not been able to find it.

Horace tapped his head with his paw. "Looking in your twee house is too easy."

"Where, then?" Beatrice asked.

Horace suggested they go outside. Beatrice climbed down the rope ladder. Horace joined her, and they both looked up.

"I'm too low here to see anything up in the tree," Beatrice said.

"You do the talking, and I'll do the hopping," Horace said. "Teamwork!"

Horace began to hyperventilate as he hopped higher and higher and higher. He hopped six feet. He hopped ten feet. He hopped clear above the top of the tree house. He sailed up, up, up beyond the top of the tree house, and on his seventh hop up, he caught a little bag hanging from a branch, untangled it and hopped back down with it. He kept a distance from Beatrice and showed her the bag.

"Say 'I'm your bestie.'"

"No. I'm not saying that. Let me see the bag."

"Say 'Horace is my bestie.' Come on. Four words won't hurt you."

"In this moment, Horace is my bestie. Now give me that bag!"

Horace hopped closer and handed it over. It was a cloth bag, drawn together at the top with a string. Beatrice untied the bag, reached inside and removed a folded sheet of paper. She unfolded it and studied it.

"Wead it to me," Horace said.

Beatrice read the message aloud. "Clue number 3. Crocodiles are social reptiles, so why does Croc Harry fail to fraternize? Why does he never swim, hunt or eat with other crocodiles? Is Croc Harry who he says he is? Is he worthy of your friendship? Find clue number 4 on Croc Harry's belly."

Beatrice sighed. What a strange message. It appeared to cast doubt on Croc Harry. Beatrice had read in her dictionary about casting doubt. It meant painting someone in a bad light. Making them look bad. Beatrice did not appreciate anyone casting doubt on her friend. As for failing to fraternize, who cared if Croc Harry did not make friends with other crocodiles?

"You and I are mammals, wight?" Horace said.

"Yes."

"And Croc Harry is a crocodile. A crocodilian. A reptile. In the animal kingdom, he is one step down from mammals."

"That is no way to talk," Beatrice said. "Are you so perfect?"

"He is not the friend to you that I can be," Horace said.

"You are jealous."

"I am not."

"Yes, you are."

Horace thumped his hind paw on the ground. "I am your noble fwiend, and I am not jealous!"

"You can't be noble if you are jealous."

"Okay, maybe I am. Just a little. Why do you have to spend so much time together?"

"How does my time with Croc Harry affect my friendship with you?"

Horace sulked and refused to answer.

"Tell me how," Beatrice said.

"It doesn't affect anything," Horace said quietly.

"My dear Horace, you're still my friend. And so is Croc Harry. If you want my respect, don't try to cut off my friendships. It's not what friends do."

Horace sniffled. "All right," he said. "He can be your friend." Horace forced a smile. He turned and hopped away.

Beatrice could see that Horace was in a bad mood, but he'd get over it.

She watched Horace hop slowly. He was in no hurry to leave her. As he hopped, Beatrice could hear him muttering, "I am not jealous. Not jealous. Not jealous at all. Have no time to waste on a crocodile. He's a big fat weptile and can't even hop. No time to waste on him! Matilda won't teach speckled wabbits, but I need my lessoning. I must change her mind. Change her mind. Change her mind."

Soon, Beatrice would return to teach at the Argilia Rabbit Academy and find out more about why the speckled rabbits were disappearing. Perhaps she could find a way to change Matilda's mind. But first, it was time to look for Croc Harry. She had to find clue number 4. If she failed to do so, she'd spend the rest of her days in Argilia.

CHAPTER 12

Croc's Honour

"Harder!"

Beatrice turned away from the deep waters and looked at her left shoulder, where Fuzzy, the tarantula, perched. Beatrice's throwing arm was killing her. She had already pulled back her slingshot twenty times to send stones flying across the water.

Beatrice was hoping that Croc Harry would show up, since she had to find the fourth clue. While she waited, what better to do than test her newly repaired slingshot?

"You're not half bad with that slingshot," Fuzzy said.

"I need a break," Beatrice said.

"We're little beings, you and I," Fuzzy said, "and little beings in a big forest are at a disadvantage. We can't afford to take breaks."

The waters ran deep in this section of the Argilia River.

Still no sign of Croc Harry. On the surface, Beatrice could see the reflection of six geese flying overhead. They squawked as they flew. "No landing here," the head goose called out. "Not safe. Not safe at all. Did you catch sight of that foolish girl by the water?"

Beatrice frowned. So now birds were judging her? How irritating! But she didn't have much time to consider the matter. She studied the river and rubbed her sore shoulder.

"If you keep working out," Fuzzy said, "you'll put some pop in your bicep. And then nobody will mess with you. Shall I coach you? I am an excellent coach!"

Beatrice just wanted to have a little conversation, practise with her slingshot, relax and wait for Croc Harry.

"How about if we just palaver," Beatrice said. She was starting to speak like Croc Harry. Palaver was one of his favourite words.

"Let me tell you about tarantulas," Fuzzy said. "We expend a lot of energy to stay alive, so we have to stay fit. Don't I look fit to you?"

Beatrice smiled at the hairy arachnid. Fuzzy was twice the size of Beatrice's palm. Her fangs were an inch long. Beatrice realized that, like Croc Harry, Fuzzy was an ambush predator. Good thing Fuzzy was a friend. Nobody in their right mind would want a Blue Sapphire Tarantula to be their enemy.

Fuzzy yawned. "These are my usual sleeping hours, so I'm a bit tired."

"It must be exhausting to hitch a ride on my shoulder and let me do all the walking," Beatrice said with a grin. "Your poor aching legs!"

"Imagine if you had so many legs," Fuzzy said. "It's like walking on eight stilts. Hard cardio! Also, when it's time to defend myself or to eat, I've got to deal with biting. It's tricky, biting creatures that are much bigger than me. While I go on the attack, I have to be careful not to get crushed. Or get my legs broken."

"I had no idea," Beatrice said.

"We all have to eat," Fuzzy said. "I'm a let's-get-this-done sort of arachnid and have no time for aimless chatter. I save my energy for fleeing, biting and sucking up liquid flesh. So take it from me, one tiny being to another. You need to strengthen your throwing and slingshotting arm. Not everyone in this grand Argilia Forest will like you. You could be a touch less naive."

"Naive?" Beatrice hadn't heard that word before.

"It means believing everyone will be nice to you," Fuzzy said. "That's naive."

"You do take a dim view of things," Beatrice said.

"A dim view might keep you alive. When you are smaller than your natural enemies," Fuzzy said, "you must work harder, be faster and be smarter."

Fuzzy climbed down Beatrice's arm and leg, got onto the riverbank and did twenty push-ups. Her legs looked like hydraulic pumps. Up and down her body went, slowly and smoothly.

"I love calisthenics," Fuzzy said. "I also practise deep breathing. I have taught myself to hold my breath for up to five minutes. You should too. You never know when you might get stuck underwater."

Beatrice remained stuck on the idea of natural enemies.

"I don't believe I have any—" she began to say, but she stopped when she saw a dark colour circling and swirling under the water. Fuzzy was doing more push-ups, so she didn't notice.

Beatrice picked up a stone and hurled it with all her might. It travelled three-quarters of the distance across the river before dropping soundlessly into the water. With more practice, perhaps Beatrice would be able to throw a stone clear to the far side. Fuzzy had already said that stone throwing—speed, length and accuracy—were important, because you never knew when you might have to defend yourself. She might not always have time to pull the slingshot out of her Beasack, load it up and let the stone fly.

Even though her throwing arm was sore, Beatrice readied herself for one final pitch. Just as she cocked her arm, she spotted a nose and crocodile eyes cruising above the surface of the water. They advanced silently in her direction. Two eyes stared straight at her.

"Croc Harry, I've been looking for you," Beatrice said. "Stop trying to scare me."

There was no response. The eyes cruised closer.

In all the time she had known him, Croc Harry had never

attempted to spook her. She felt that she understood him. She knew how his mind worked. In some ways, she felt that she had always known him. But this was out of character.

"No more fooling around," Beatrice shouted.

The eyes approached the riverbank. They were ten feet away. Then six feet. Beatrice put her hands on her hips. "Stop it this instant," she said.

When the crocodile was only four feet away, Beatrice finally saw his body. He had different-coloured scutes on his back. Croc Harry's scutes were turquoise. But these scutes were brown. His eyes were menacing, hungry and full of evil intent. Beatrice jumped back.

The brown-backed crocodile shot out of the river.

Beatrice hurled the rock. It struck the crocodile in the right eye. He stopped for an instant, shook his head and gave out a bellow. Beatrice jumped to the side.

The giant croc swivelled in her direction. Beatrice had no more rocks. She tried to jump away, but tripped on a log and fell to the ground.

The croc belly-crawled in her direction and then got up on all four legs. As he opened his massive jaws, Fuzzy ran under and bit him on the belly. The giant croc hesitated and gasped.

"Who did that?" he called out. "Who just bit me?"

Fuzzy scurried into the bushes.

"Hurts like stink. But never mind. I have known worse." The giant croc trained his eyes on Beatrice. He took two more steps toward her and opened his jaws.

Beatrice would have used the slingshot, but it had landed beyond her reach when she had tripped and fallen. Her hand tapped the riverbank, but she could not find it.

More colours began to appear close to the surface of the water. Turquoise. Beatrice recognized those scutes. Croc Harry shot out of the water. He flew right past her.

"Get back, Beatrice," he said. She had seen Croc Harry playful, and she had seen him tossing rabbits into the back of his mouth like popcorn, but she had never seen him murderous.

Beatrice knew that she should run, but she was transfixed. Could Croc Harry beat this giant crocodile? Could she help him? She got up, picked up another stone and retrieved her slingshot. Perhaps she could put out the bad croc's other eye. But there was no time.

Croc Harry clamped his jaws around the attacking croc's throat. Croc Harry pitched and swivelled and bit down hard. The two crocodiles grunted and wrestled on the rocks. They sent stones and twigs flying. The riverbank shook under the thrashing of two enormous reptiles. The brown-backed croc looked bigger and more fierce, but Croc Harry was not giving up. He wasn't just fighting for his life. Beatrice could see that he was fighting for her life too.

Croc Harry kept wrestling. He was on top, and then underneath, and then back on top, but he never released his enemy's throat. The other crocodile thrashed his tail and cracked the trunk of a tree on the riverbank. Croc Harry dragged his adversary underwater. The water roiled and gushed. Croc Harry hauled his enemy out of the water and shoved the creature back down again. When he lugged the enemy croc back up onto the riverbank, Croc Harry tore a massive chunk from his belly.

The attacking crocodile slumped on the rocks, motionless except for shallow breaths.

"You shall pay for this," the croc said, gasping. "Impeding my meal. Taking the side of a human. Humans are our enemies. Look what they did to you."

"Nobody attacks my friend," Croc Harry roared.

The brown croc gasped on the rocks of the riverbank. One eye was nothing but a bleeding hole, and the other eye was closing.

Croc Harry crawled up to his face.

"Are you the girl's only enemy here in Argilia?" Harry asked.

"There was the snake, but it was foiled."

"Who sent you?" Croc Harry said. The enemy croc refused to answer. Croc Harry bit the giant croc's bleeding belly and gave it a shake. "Who sent you?"

"Put me out of my misery," the dying croc said.

"I have never seen you in Argilia," Croc Harry said. "Why are you here?"

"If I tell you, will you end my suffering? My insides are torn. You are a fellow crocodile. You owe me an honourable death."

"I will respect your wishes if you speak the truth," Croc Harry said.

"I will answer three questions," the dying croc said, "if you promise to end my suffering immediately."

"Croc's honour," Croc Harry said, touching the tip of his tail to that of the dying croc.

"Let's get this over with," the dying croc said.

"What do you have against this child?"

"She might be the one. Some say she could become the future leader of our sworn enemy. Our mighty leader wants to turn her."

Although Beatrice could not keep her hands from shaking, she walked right up to the dying croc's face. "I am no one's enemy," she shouted. "What did I ever do to you?"

"You just wasted a question," the dying croc said. "I do not speak to our enemy."

Croc Harry brought his mouth right up close. "Today, what was your plan?"

"I was sent to threaten the girl, kill you and deprive the child of a friend, which was meant to weaken her resistance and open her brain up to the giant. I swear allegiance to the giant. Three questions. That is all. Honour your promise."

Croc Harry seized the neck of the croc, clamped down on it and gave a mighty heave. The enemy croc flipped over and lay completely motionless.

"Is he dead?" Beatrice asked.

Croc Harry brought his face beside that of his enemy. He waited a moment. "Yes," he said.

"Couldn't you have asked more questions?" Beatrice said.

"We touched tails," Croc Harry said. "I promised him an honourable death."

Beatrice began to walk along the riverbank to put as much distance as she could between herself and the dead croc. Croc Harry high-limped beside her.

Beatrice took a long look at her rescuer. He had a gash on the right side of his belly. Beside the cut, there were also some strange markings. They looked like bits of words, but they were split up like puzzle pieces and impossible to read.

"Shall I stitch you up?" Beatrice said.

"I don't think the other crocodiles would respect me if they saw a little girl sewing me up."

"Lie still and stop fussing," she said.

Beatrice removed a sewing kit from her Beasack.

"What do you keep in that bag?" Croc Harry asked.

"Bit of this and a bit of that. Stop talking."

She threaded the needle and began sewing back and forth across his torn flesh. As she tightened the threads to close the wound, she noticed the markings on his belly growing closer. They were almost forming words.

"What are these markings on your belly?" she asked.

"No idea," he said. "I can't see my own belly."

"Does it hurt when I pull the stitches tight?" she asked.

"It hurts some."

"Hang on. I'll be quick."

Beatrice kept sewing to pull the crocodile flesh back together. The leather felt soft and cool.

"No wonder people in books love their crocodile leather purses and wallets," she said. "So soft. I should have taken some and made a purse."

"That's not funny," he said.

"It's a little bit funny."

"I save your life and you joke about crocodile leather purses? Some vegetarian!"

Beatrice chuckled. She checked to make sure that Croc Harry's wound had closed. She stopped and stared. Now that her stitches had pulled Croc Harry's belly back together, she saw a pattern of dark lines. In the lines, she found clue number 4. It was just a few words: *Horace is in danger.* She studied the flesh more closely. There, under the stitching, three more words had been fit together: *He belongs to you.*

Beatrice stood up. "I have to go," she said.

"Let me accompany you," he said.

"You are truly a gentlecroc. You may walk with me toward the Rabbit Academy, but don't get too close. You'll create mass panic."

"No need. I can only eat so many."

"How many?"

"Not counting the ones you saved using decrockestation, I have only eaten a few in the last weeks."

"Horace tells me that speckled rabbits have been disappearing."

"I only eat what I need. What do you take me for? A pig?"

"A pig has higher intelligence, but you are an unapologetic

carnivore," Beatrice said.

"Hey! I may be a carnivore, but I'm of high intelligence too. You'll never find a pig with my vocabulary."

Beatrice felt a wave of sympathy when she noticed Croc Harry shuffling painfully beside her. When he walked, he could not lift his left legs quite as high as his right.

"About that conversation you had with the giant croc on its death bed," Beatrice said.

"Death *rocks*. We had the conversation on its death rocks."

"Okay, fine. But what did all that mean?" Beatrice said.

"Don't know," Croc Harry said.

It was a strange and ugly feeling, knowing that someone wanted to hurt her. It made Beatrice wonder if she had done something wrong. She realized that it was difficult to feel good about herself when someone hated her. Difficult, but important!

"That croc had evil intentions," Beatrice said. "It's not a nice feeling."

"I had evil intentions when I saw that crocodile going after you."

"I put out one of his eyes," Beatrice said, "and I don't even feel bad about it."

"You should have put out both eyes," Croc Harry said. "Can't you throw two stones at once?"

"Humans don't do that," Beatrice said.

"How do you know?" Croc Harry said.

Beatrice suddenly found a tiny remembrance in her brain. It was like a little puzzle piece announcing itself, sliding from across a table. What she suddenly remembered was the game of baseball.

"I have seen baseball," she said. "In fact, I have played baseball. I can only remember three things: I have been a pitcher, I have played shortstop and nobody ever throws two balls at once."

"I know about baseball too," Croc Harry said.

"How would you know?" she asked.

"I'm not sure," he said, "but I do."

Beatrice was about to cross the giant oak tree that had fallen over the Argilia River like a natural bridge. She said that she wanted to make the rest of the journey alone, as she had thinking to do.

"I hate being alone," Croc Harry said.

"Why?"

"Because I start thinking about how bad I am."

"You *are* a carnivore, but you can't help that. You are not bad. You saved my life."

"If you do a lot of good things," Croc Harry said, "does it erase all the bad you did before?"

"Not sure," Beatrice said. "But it makes you a better person."

"But I can never change what happened before," Croc Harry said.

"Before what?"

"Before I was a crocodile."

Beatrice took a step back, examined the crocodile and rubbed her chin.

"Croc Harry, are you thinking straight? Did you get a concussion in that fight?"

"No concussion. I am not sure, but I believe that I have not always been a crocodile."

"I don't understand," Beatrice said.

"I don't either," he said.

"Maybe we will figure it out together," Beatrice said.

"Maybe," he said. "Wait here."

Croc Harry disappeared into the river. Beatrice looked upstream, where she saw movement near the surface of the water, and then she saw him fly out of the water, over the fallen oak tree and back into the river. Moments later, he came back up onto the riverbank.

"No predators in the water. Safe to cross."

"Thank you."

"Could we be friends for life?" Croc Harry asked.

"I hope so," Beatrice said, "although I do want to find my way home."

"Me too," he said.

Croc Harry swam as easily as a fish, but on land, he seemed to be hauling hundreds of pounds of sadness.

Croc Harry turned toward her and rolled onto his back, his flesh neatly sewed and gleaming in the sunlight. "Will you sit out on the branch under the tree house and palaver with me over breakfast tomorrow?"

"Yes. And thank you for . . . for your intervention this morning."

"What you call an intervention," Croc Harry said, "I call a fight to the death." He turned back over, slid under the water and disappeared.

CHAPTER 13

Straight Answers

Beatrice could not find Horace. She checked by the river. Beside the outhouse. Inside the outhouse. Under the three-fruit tree. In her tree house. Even under her bed. No sign of him.

Beatrice called out for him until her voice grew hoarse, but there was still no sign of the furry creature. She didn't think that Croc Harry would eat the rabbit, but she was so desperate that she asked anyway.

"I can't believe you thought that I would eat Horace, after all that I have promised," Croc Harry said.

"I didn't mean to offend you," Beatrice said. "I'm just worried."

"Well," Croc Harry said, "I have not seen him or eaten him, either. He is the most annoying rabbit in the history of the Western hemisphere. And the Eastern Hemisphere too. But I do hope that you find him intact."

"Intact," Beatrice muttered to herself as she ran off to continue her search. She, too, hoped that Horace was *intact*.

* * *

The skies opened up. Beatrice let the rain pour down on her. She welcomed the warm shower, but it soaked and matted her hair and left it hanging uncomfortably on her neck. She didn't have much time to fix it, but she had a quick plan. She ran to the bend in the river, picked a ripe avocado hanging from a low branch and ran to the tree house. She peeled the avocado. She was a bit hungry, so she ate most of it. Delicious! She mashed up the rest, mixed it with some water, rubbed it in her hands and combed it through her wet hair. Finally, the combing was easy. And painless. Once her hair relaxed, she pulled it into a bun behind her head. What a relief to get that sopping wet hair off her neck. She slid a slender stick through the bun and tied it with twine. She ripped up a T-shirt and wrapped half of it around her bun and tied a bow at the bottom. She turned her head to look in the mirror. Not bad. Not bad at all. Beatrice told herself that if she ever had a daughter who put her hair together so quickly, she would tell her that she was both clever and beautiful.

Beatrice climbed down from her tree house. The rain subsided as quickly as it had come. The clouds parted, leaving room for the sun. Beatrice raced to the open meadow and looked high in the sky.

"I'm here," she called out.

No response.

"Ms. Rainbow, are you there?"

Still no response. It was hard to be patient when Beatrice had so much to do. She counted slowly. She got to one hundred. Still nothing. Two hundred. Still no show. Beatrice kept counting. At exactly 333, the skies turned bright blue and seven colours banded together in a giant arc in the western skies.

"Are you there yet, Ms. Rainbow?"

"I am," came the voice Beatrice found so calming. "Can't you see me?"

"I wasn't sure if it was you," Beatrice said.

"There is only one rainbow in Argilia," Ms. Rainbow said. "And you have met her."

"So," Beatrice said, "I've looked high and low but can't find Horace."

Ms. Rainbow shimmered and glowed and seemed even more radiant than before.

"You have not yet faced the second test."

"Well, what is it?"

"You shall know if you pass it."

"How will I know?"

"I'll give you a sign."

Beatrice threw her arms up in the air. She shouted at the

top of her lungs. "I mean COME ON! Why do I have to do all of this? I don't even care right now about leaving Argilia. Just let me find Horace."

"Patience," Ms. Rainbow said. "There have been some doubts about your leadership abilities, but you are dispelling them."

Beatrice put her hands on her hips. "What doubts?"

"Never mind about that. If you pass the test, you will be eligible to hunt for the final four clues."

"Isn't this a dialogue?" Beatrice said. "Don't I get to ask questions?"

"Not every situation allows for dialogue," Ms. Rainbow said.

"How come you get to be in charge?"

"You will decide your own destiny. If you find the last four clues, you will be eligible to attempt to leave Argilia."

Beatrice waved her arms in the air. It was impossible to get straight answers from a curved rainbow. "Attempt?"

"Leaving is dangerous," Ms. Rainbow said. "Success is rare."

"When do I get to know what all of this is about?"

"In due time. If you live."

"May I ask one more question?"

"No. I have to go. Focus, Beatrice. You are in danger. When the time is right, be ready to leave."

With those final words, Ms. Rainbow let out a loud pop and disappeared in a flash.

"Tests," Beatrice muttered. "Doubts!" Beatrice did not doubt herself and saw no reason why anybody else should either. She would keep her Beasack packed with food, the hatchet and the slingshot. She would be ready to go in a moment's notice. But first: Horace!

CHAPTER 14

Aren't You The Little Saint?

Matilda waited on a throne of grass outside the entrance to the Grand Warren Underground Castle, home of the Argilia Rabbit Academy.

She nibbled on a carrot top, tossed down a rotten bit and made a flicking motion with her paws at a speckled rabbit who was there at her pleasure.

"Servant, pick that up," she said.

The speckled rabbit retrieved the rotten carrot top and held it expectantly.

"It goes in the garbage," Matilda said. "Over there."

The rabbit ran off to leave it in a garbage pail.

"These speckled rabbits," Matilda said to Beatrice, who had come carrying her Beasack with Fuzzy hidden in a pocket. "You have to tell them everything."

Matilda spoke without looking at Beatrice. She was counting bunches of carrot greens.

Beatrice studied the speckled rabbit. He was the skinniest bunny she'd seen in Argilia. He stood on his hind paws, ready to pop the rotten food into the garbage. As soon as Matilda turned away with the carrot greens, the speckled rabbit swallowed the bit that he was supposed to throw out. He caught Beatrice's glance and brought a paw to his lips. She understood the sign. It meant "Don't tell on me." Beatrice brought a finger to her own lips, while Fuzzy scrambled to the ground.

"Good luck, Fuzzy," Beatrice whispered.

"Not to worry," Fuzzy said. "I'm so pliable. I can go anywhere and not be seen. I can squeeze into spaces. Spying is one of my great powers."

"Thank you for agreeing to do this," Beatrice whispered. "Please be careful."

While Matilda was counting carrot greens, Fuzzy ran past her and slipped into the rabbit castle.

Matilda put down the carrot greens and turned to examine Beatrice.

"You are a sturdy little brown thing," Matilda said.

"I am not a thing, and I have a name," Beatrice said. "It is Beatrice."

"Talk about sensitive," Matilda said.

"The guard. That speckled rabbit. Does he live here?"

"Heavens to Betsy, no," Matilda said. "I get them to do odd jobs. The things our own rabbits won't do. For one week's work, I give them a bit of celery, a red pepper and some carrot tops."

"He looks hungry," Beatrice said.

"Not my concern. Or yours. You are here to work."

Beatrice was afraid to bring up the matter because Matilda kept dismissing it. But she had no choice but to speak up. "Are any speckled rabbits being mistreated here?"

"If there's any hint of mistreatment," Matilda said, "I'll look into it."

"Maybe I could investigate," Beatrice said.

"Why would I allow that?"

"I would give you an honest report."

"There is nothing wrong with my Academy," Matilda said.

"After I teach, just give me a little tour."

Matilda stood back and rubbed her furry brow. She said that if a tour was all Beatrice wanted, she could arrange it after class.

Fuzzy crawled out of the rabbit warren, inched close to Beatrice and climbed up her leg and arm.

"Inside," Fuzzy whispered. "Three rooms to the right, there are some speckled rabbits. Locked inside. And more in another spot, six rooms to the left. Word inside is that many other speckled rabbits are being locked up and left to die."

"Thank you," Beatrice said to Fuzzy. But she said it too loud.

Matilda's ears pricked up. She took hold of a large book and hopped closer. "Ew, is that a tarantula? Kill it! Kill it right now!"

Fuzzy raced to the ground.

"No," Beatrice said, "she's my friend."

"Nonsense!"

Matilda held the big book directly over the tarantula and dropped it just as Fuzzy raced for cover under a pile of carrot tops. The book crashed to the ground.

"Did I squish him?" Matilda said.

"Fuzzy is a girl, and I hope not."

Beatrice crouched to look under the carrot tops. No sign of Fuzzy. She ran ten steps to the left and then to the right, checking under twigs, branches and bushes. No sign of Fuzzy. She ran forward and backward to check again. Still no sign of the Blue Sapphire Tarantula. Beatrice struggled to keep from sobbing. She ran back to Matilda.

"Why did you do that? She was my friend. You could have hurt her badly. You could even have killed her."

"Hopefully the latter," Matilda said.

"How could you?"

"What? It's just an ugly spider."

"She's not ugly. She's my friend."

"You have poor judgment in friends. She's not even a mammal. Not even warm-blooded."

"Who cares? She never hurt anyone unless they deserved it."

"She bit me, once," Matilda said, "so today I got her back. Mark my words. Any creature that is bright blue or speckled is not to be trusted."

Beatrice felt a flash of anger run through her blood. Her

face was warm. She felt insulted. She wanted to cry and scream and shout, all at the same time. But she took a breath. This was no time to lose self-control. She would keep looking for Fuzzy later. For now, she had to get things done. She intended to keep Matilda talking. This would give Fuzzy more time to escape, if she was still alive, and it would help Beatrice learn more about the Academy. What was happening to the speckled rabbits? And was Horace in danger?

In the dictionary, Beatrice had read about the word *ruse*. A ruse was something you did so you could learn about something else.

"Could you pay me before I teach?" Beatrice asked.

"No way," Matilda said. "Not happening. As a matter of fact, this conversation is making you late for class. As a warning, you shall lose half your payment for today's class. Next time, arrive early."

Beatrice considered her situation. She tried to define it. In her tree house, she had read the definition of *situation* in her dictionary. It meant what was really happening, including the big picture. As far as Beatrice could see, this was the situation: Matilda was trying to dominate her. If Beatrice allowed it to happen, the problem would just get worse.

Beatrice summoned her firmest voice. "Matilda," she said.

"You may address me as Your Excellency, the Highest of the Head Rabbits."

"Matilda," Beatrice repeated.

"Such insolence," Matilda said.

"Just the other day, I used decrockestation to save some bunnies."

"Not my bunnies. They must have been the speckleds."

"The rabbits could have died."

"No need to save them. Letting them perish in a croc's stomach would have meant fewer speckleds to chase out of Argilia."

"I would help any rabbit in a pickle, and those five rabbits were in trouble."

"Aren't you the little saint?" Matilda said. "I must say, however, that I am impressed you mastered the decrockestation technique. Perhaps you can teach that to our rabbits."

Beatrice turned to leave. "Goodbye," she said.

"You said you would teach here!"

"I cannot accept any reduction to my salary. To do this job, I require ten bags of carrot greens, six celery stalks and one red pepper. Today!"

Matilda stood up on her hind legs, waved her front paws as if to lecture Beatrice and then seemed to change her mind. She sighed and rested her front paws on her hips.

"Fine," Matilda said. "Fine. Fine. You may have it all. After you teach."

Thunder crashed through the air like a drum roll. The rain came down in torrents again. The wrap fell off Beatrice's hair, and her bun fell apart. But in that moment, Beatrice didn't care. She had pressing issues to resolve.

The storm faded in a flash, just as magically as it had appeared. The clouds split, and the sun poked between them. Beatrice looked to the far side of the sky. There, for an instant, Ms. Rainbow appeared. She flickered on and off. Three times. And then Ms. Rainbow disappeared without a word.

That was it. Beatrice knew that she had passed the test. She turned back to face the entrance to the Rabbit Academy.

"Strangest storm I have ever seen," Matilda muttered. "Let's get in before it rains again."

Beatrice tied up her hair again as she followed Matilda, who seemed to be studying her. Guessing her thoughts.

"May I remind you," Matilda said, "this warren is my kingdom and it is for purebreds. You are not to allow any speckleds into class. They come from the other side of the mountain, and that is where they belong."

"In my books," Beatrice said, "a bunny is a bunny is a bunny. They all have the same needs."

"Poppycock!" Matilda said. "The needs of the speckleds are not my concern. Enough debate. The class awaits."

Beatrice crawled through the door of the warren, which opened up into a majestic castle with corridors and lanterns and bowls of water. Up ahead were many classrooms, but they were locked like prison cells. She walked through a meandering corridor. She passed a locked door to a room on her right. Beatrice heard frantic hopping in the room. From inside, a familiar voice rang out.

"This is wong," the voice said. "Wong, wong, wong. Let me out. I demand my fweedom. I demand my lessoning."

Beatrice stopped.

"Horace?" she called out.

But she did not have a chance to hear the answer, because Matilda and five of her helper rabbits pushed Beatrice farther along and into a classroom of twenty chattering bunnies who fell suddenly silent.

"Anyone who fails to listen and to pay utmost respect and attention to our special visitor, Miss Beatrice of the Tree House, will enjoy a flogging at the hands of my servants. Is that clear?"

"Yes, Your Excellency," a chorus of bunnies erupted. They all had the same grey fur.

"Miss Beatrice, you have one hour, so mind your minutes."

Matilda exited. The bunnies sat at their tiny desks with pencils and paper.

"Miss B," one bunny in the front row said, raising her paw in the air. "Is it true that you rescued five bunnies?"

Beatrice turned to face the entire class. "Are you all aware of this incident?"

"Yes, Miss B," the entire class called back to her.

"Miss B," the student in the front continued, "is it true that you used decrockestation to get them out?"

"Yes," she said.

All twenty opened their mouths and said wow at the same time.

One bunny at the back of the room piped up. "It's good to know that technique, but those speckled bunnies should have stayed home."

"Their warrens were flooded," Beatrice said. "They had no food. What if this had happened to you?"

Another bunny said, "Why can't we share our food? We have plenty, and they need help."

The door flung open. Matilda appeared. "Fifty-six minutes left. Stick to the lesson!" She slammed the door shut.

Beatrice told the students to take notes while she reviewed crocodile basics:

Weight: easily 700 pounds.

Length: up to 17 feet.

Teeth: 69, and replaceable. If one falls out while tearing flesh from bone, it will grow right back. Crocodiles can grow as many as 1,000 teeth over a lifetime.

Dental hygiene: relies on plovers and other toothbirds for flossing.

Stomach acid: can burn through bone and disintegrate a baby antelope or a piglet in a matter of hours.

Life expectancy: 40 years or more. Some say a crocodile can live forever.

Languages: Crocodiles have the gift of the gab. They lure their victims into conversation right before spraying spittle on them and swallowing them.

Speed: fast on land, faster in water and fastest when

bursting out of the water to seize a tasty bunny on the rocks.

Thermal regulation: The body temperature of a crocodile goes up and down. They suntan to warm up and go into the water to cool down. They have solar panels on their backs. The scutes, or mobile bony scales, on their backs hold the heat of the sun and help keep the crocodile warm even after the sun goes down.

Tears: Crocodiles cry. Whether they feel emotion and cry out of sadness is a matter of debate. But they definitely cry, usually when they are on land and their eyes get dry. The tears rinse out a third eyelid called a nictitating membrane. They are salty and full of minerals. Butterflies are known to drink them.

Truthful: A crocodile is never truthful when it intends to eat you. At other times, a crocodile can be surprisingly honest.

The rabbit at the back of the room raised his paw again.

"Miss Beatrice," he asked, "is it true that you can wrestle a croc and beat him?"

"No, I am not good at wrestling."

"But," the rabbit continued, "a big person can put down a crocodile, right? If he knows how to shut that croc's mouth and keep it shut?"

The class burst out in laughter.

"Let's get back to basics," Beatrice said.

When the lesson ended, Matilda came to fetch Beatrice and took her to her office. She sat at her desk, opened a big drawer and counted out the food that Beatrice was owed.

"I love teaching your rabbits, and I feel that I can save many of their lives," Beatrice said.

"Wonderful," Matilda said.

"But I cannot teach again unless you release the speckled rabbits you have locked up."

"I don't know what you are talking—"

Beatrice put up her hand. "Release them, or I will not come back." Beatrice was expecting a fight. She was anticipating an argument. She was thinking about what to say next, and how she would argue her point. But suddenly, Matilda put her head in her paws and began to sob.

"It is so stressful here, so much to do. All these rabbits to feed! Sometimes I don't know what gets over me, but I feel meanness coming out. I wasn't born mean, but now I am horrid. I don't know where it comes from. Something makes me hate all speckled rabbits, and then I hate myself for hating them. I don't know how I will manage. So many responsibilities managing a warren, but I don't expect you to understand." She stopped sobbing and said it again. "No, I don't expect a little girl in a tree house to understand a single solitary thing."

Beatrice walked over to Matilda and put her hand on her head.

"I know it is difficult."

"You have no idea. Sometimes I feel my mind is not my own. I don't know what's wrong with me."

"You will have better days," Beatrice said, "but today you must release the speckled rabbits."

To Beatrice's astonishment, Matilda straightened, gave Beatrice her food, took a key from her desk drawer and said, "Come."

They walked back along the long corridor. Matilda unlocked the third door on the right. Horace Harrison Junior the Third and four other rabbits spilled out of the locked room.

"She told us we could study here," Horace shouted, "but when we got into the classroom, she locked us in."

Matilda hopped straight up. Her fur stood on end, as if she had received an electric shock.

"Go," Matilda shouted. "Go before I change my mind and lock you up again. Don't come back asking to study here. Or else!"

For once, Horace had nothing to say. He hopped with the others as fast as he could along the corridor and out the door of the warren.

Beatrice was thinking again. It was too soon to leave. What about other rabbits that might be in jail?

"I would like to take that tour now," Beatrice said.

Matilda held her head in her paws. "My headache is killing me. It's like someone is breaking into my brain. He's already in there, and starting to take over. What can I do?"

"Free the other speckled rabbits," Beatrice said.

"Take it and get out," Matilda said, shoving the key in Beatrice's hand.

Beatrice ran to the sixth classroom on the left and unlocked the door. Twenty-five speckled rabbits, all looking like they had not eaten for days, limped toward her.

"Go, go," Beatrice said. The speckled rabbits limped and hopped out as fast as they could move. Beatrice stumbled back to the room where Horace had been held captive.

There she found clue number 5, written on the wall: *The brain is your best tool. What do you read to sharpen it?*

Yes. That was it. Beatrice was on her way to finding the second half of her clues. Maybe she would escape Argilia. Maybe she would make it home. As for finding the next clue, this one seemed obvious: Beatrice would have to find it in her dictionary.

Beatrice spun around. She meant to interrogate Matilda about where other speckled rabbits were locked up. Surely, there were more. But Matilda had vanished.

Beatrice walked outside. The speckled rabbits had all run away. Matilda was still nowhere to be seen.

The last thing Beatrice wanted to do was to return to that rabbit warren. But she needed to understand more about Matilda. She needed to understand why Matilda was so angry. What was overtaking Matilda's brain? Perhaps it was the same thing that had been threatening Beatrice during her nightmares.

Beatrice remembered hearing that Matilda had not always been angry. Perhaps Matilda's better side had gone missing. Perhaps she had forgotten how to be good. Beatrice did not like Matilda, but she decided not to hate her either. Instead, Beatrice would try to understand her. Maybe Matilda would stop being so angry. Maybe this could save some speckled rabbits. Maybe visiting the warren again would help Beatrice understand where she came from, why she was in Argilia and why someone was trying to enter her brain when she was fast asleep and stuck in a looping nightmare.

Beatrice felt that her life was one huge puzzle and that she had not yet been able to fit the pieces together. She felt an overwhelming need to lie down and sleep. Searching her dictionary would have to wait until the next day. She would not even bother with dinner. She would climb up into her tree house, pull the ladder up behind her and get into bed. She hoped that she would not dream. She did not want to have any dreams at all.

CHAPTER 15

Mundane Impediments Like Geography

The next day, Beatrice climbed to the highest branch in her tree and crawled to the far edge. She checked to see that no animal was crawling, walking or hopping below. She dropped a coconut. It missed the rock she was aiming for and made a soft thud as it landed on the earth. She pulled a second coconut from her Beasack, took better aim and dropped it. Coconuts were awfully hard to break, but she heard the second one crack on the rock.

Beatrice scrambled to the ground, picked up the cracked coconut, pried it open with a stick and emptied the water into a pot. She sat at the base of her tree, poured some of the coconut water onto her hair and tried combing it out, but it didn't work. The ends of her hair snapped and broke, and untangling it became even harder. Her hair was a royal mess.

It was attracting sticks and small bits of leaves. She didn't like appearing messy, even if there were no other humans around to see her. She didn't want to look uncombed or messy even in the eyes of alligators, rabbits and tarantulas. A girl had her pride!

Beatrice washed out the coconut water and then tried what she had done before. She peeled an avocado and mashed up a bit of it. She rubbed it into her hair. Once she could pass the comb through her kinks, she divided her hair into sections. First in half, then in quarters and finally in eighths. Working with an eighth at a time, she split each one into two strands of hair. She twirled them around and around her fingers until they were united into a single, hanging twist. She didn't know where that knowledge came from, but the memory of what to do seemed imbedded in her fingers. She worked quickly. Eight twists sufficed. They would be practical. She wouldn't have to fuss about her hair every morning.

As she finished arranging her hair, Beatrice felt a tickling on her leg. She looked down. Fuzzy!

"You're alive!" Beatrice said.

"Somewhat."

"Are you hurt?"

"My leg snapped off," Fuzzy said, "but I am still in the land of the living."

Beatrice felt a wave of sadness grip her chest. She couldn't bear to think of her friend in pain.

"I sure would like to help you," Beatrice said.

"It helps to know that you're here," Fuzzy said. "It also helps to know that you're collecting your clues, and that if you keep going, you might get out of here."

"I want to get out of here," Beatrice said, "but not without you."

"In the land where you come from, maybe girls and tarantulas are not allowed to be friends."

Beatrice felt so sad that she could barely speak. But she refused to cry.

"So what will you do?" Short sentences, without too much emotion, were the only ones that Beatrice could manage without sobbing.

"I had a good meal recently. That snake who nearly bit you offered up some delicious juices. Snake juice is nutritious. Delectable too."

Beatrice gently petted Fuzzy's back.

"I like it when you do that," Fuzzy said. "Without someone like you here in the wild forest, I don't get many opportunities to have my back stroked."

Beatrice kept petting the Blue Sapphire Tarantula.

"I must go away for a while," Fuzzy said.

"No. Stay here with me."

"I have to heal. Best way is to crawl under a log or go into a burrow and wait to moult."

A sob burst out of Beatrice like water fleeing a dam. "Sorry," she said.

"It's okay," Fuzzy said. "I don't mind you crying. In the

animal kingdom, it's not often you see someone sobbing over a tarantula."

"Are you in pain?" Beatrice asked.

"It's not the first time I've lost a leg, and it won't be the last. I can manage. But you're my friend, so I wanted to say goodbye."

"No goodbyes," Beatrice said. "Can we just say that we'll meet again soon?"

"If you wish," Fuzzy said.

"I wish there were a way to never lose your friends."

"You don't lose friends," Fuzzy said. "Not if they are true soul mates."

"What do you mean? You are going away and I don't even know if we will see each other again."

"But you carry me in your heart. Friends and books are like that. If you love them, and if they love you, they stay with you regardless of mundane impediments like geography."

"Mundane impediments like geography?"

"It just means it doesn't matter where you are, or where I am. If we are friends, we are joined. We are together."

Beatrice stroked the soft, furry tarantula. Her blue was almost purple—the colour of the leaves of a violet flower.

"I wouldn't have found my first clue had it not been for you," Beatrice said.

Fuzzy did not reply. She was purring. It was a soft vibration radiating from Fuzzy's back.

"And although you are indeed so very much smaller than me, you saved my life first. You saved my life before Croc Harry fought the giant croc."

Fuzzy limped away and then turned to face Beatrice.

"It's not always about the one with the biggest muscles or the fiercest jaws," Fuzzy said. "Sometimes you can save a life without a lot of fanfare and without anybody even noticing."

It was Fuzzy's right hind leg that was missing. Beatrice noticed the torn flesh as the Blue Sapphire Tarantula disappeared into a thicket of bushes.

As soon as Fuzzy left, Beatrice let out another sob. Why could Beatrice not remember her own family? If she stayed alive and healthy, perhaps her memory would return.

Beatrice told herself that this was not the time to give up or despair, or to let her guard down. Beatrice had to be strong to find clue number 6 and to figure out how to leave the place she loved before it became a hateful prison.

The tree house was a satisfactory temporary home. It kept out the rain. It had a bed, food supplies and books. But living alone in a cabin high up in a fig tree was not, Beatrice concluded, an ideal home. Home, in her opinion, would include other people. Living all alone could only serve one purpose, which was to make her stronger, capable and more confident, and never afraid to solve her own problems. If the time came to live among her people, Beatrice would be ready.

* * *

Her dictionary had 1,761 pages. It was so big that she had to pick it up with both hands. How on earth was she to locate clue number 6 in such a gargantuan book? She held it on her lap and flipped it open. She looked under A for Argilia, B for Beatrice and H for help, but found no clue. She looked under C for crisis. No clue there either. She stayed with C a little longer and moved her finger up the page. There it was. A dictionary definition of the term *clue number 6:*

If you are looking for clue number 6, you have just found it. If you seek to return to the Queendom, you must use traditional means. You will need a partner. One of you will have to be a strong hiker, and the other an excellent swimmer. As for finding clue number 7: look for a heart-shaped stone deep inside the belly of the beast. Also, educate yourself in these very pages about teleporting.

Beatrice flipped to T. She found *teleporting* on page 1,071.

Teleporting is the means by which certain humans and other animals arrive in Argilia. As a bio-experiment, teleporting can only handle one human being at a time. If you are an intelligent, incisive and promising human, you will have made it this far and want to escape Argilia. But teleporting as a technology only works one way. You can be teleported into Argilia, but you cannot teleport out. Few humans have ever managed to leave Argilia and return to the Queendom. But it is possible. Perhaps you will be one of the few.

Beatrice had much thinking to do. So she came from a place called the Queendom. It did not ring a bell. She had no memory of it whatsoever. She looked under Q in the dictionary, but there was no entry for Queendom. First, she had to locate clue number 7 deep inside the belly of the beast.

CHAPTER 16

Six Out of Ten

Beatrice sat on her tree house branch and let her legs swing freely. It felt like riding a bicycle in the sky. She ate her last bites of oatmeal and looked down at her big friend. Was it a strange thing for a girl to be best friends with a crocodile? Well, who cared? They were friends, and that's all that mattered.

As Croc Harry rolled over to bask in the sun, Beatrice could see that the stitches were holding fast in his lower right side. When he yawned, Beatrice saw a loose tooth. It must have been loosened in the fight with the giant croc. The wiggling tooth made the crocodile seem less fearsome. It almost made him look human.

"You have a loose tooth," Beatrice said.

"It won't come out," Croc Harry said. "There is nothing more aggravating. Say, how's it going with your clues?"

Beatrice explained that clue number 6 had instructed her to search for a heart-shaped stone in the belly of the beast.

"I swallowed a stone like that this morning," he said. "It looked just right for grinding rabbit."

"You have eaten more rabbits?"

"A growing boy's gotta eat."

"You're not growing anymore!" she said.

"I might decide to grow some more. It's one of the few things in our relationship that is out of your control."

Beatrice laughed. It was true. She did like to control things. How else was she to feel good about living in a forest that was surely not her true home?

"Anyway," Croc Harry said, "I indulged in a little snack because I did not want to show up hungry for our palaver. I can hold back my digestive acid a little longer. The rabbits are just sitting around in there right now. I can hear them chattering. In fact, they won't shut up."

It occurred to Beatrice that a crocodile couldn't possibly know the terror of being trapped inside another crocodile's belly, awaiting death by stomach acid and gastroliths. But she didn't have time to educate him because there was another pressing matter at hand.

"I have to get that heart-shaped stone," Beatrice said. "Without it, I may never get back home."

"How?"

"Normally, my palatal valve stays shut when I am in or about to go in the water. I will open it to let you in. Then it will close. But I will open it back up to let you out. Just give me a holler."

"What if you don't hear me?"

"Knock three times on the ceiling of my stomach. I will feel the vibrations in my scutes. Just three light thumps, please, because nobody likes to have their stomach punched. It's especially unpleasant to get socked from inside your belly. Or kicked. I get that from time to time."

"Once I get in there, I hope to get out fast."

"There are some things I have been meaning to talk to you about," Croc Harry said. "Weird dreams have been coming to me, flooding my mind even when I am awake. I am not quite sure what they are or what they mean."

"Me too, Crockers. It is awful, isn't it?"

"I think I once did something wrong. In a previous life. I think I am paying for it."

"I wonder what it all means?"

"Change is coming," Croc Harry said, "and nothing will ever be the same."

"I have business to conduct in your belly," Beatrice said. "Focus, Crockers. Open wide. Wider. Come on. Wider! Open that thing wide enough for you to swallow a baby hippo. Come on. Open that bad boy. Open it. Open. You can do it!"

Croc Harry unhinged his jaw and cranked open his mouth to an astounding width. Beatrice knew this was her chance. She stood on the branch, lifted her arms above her head, pointed her hands together and dove into Croc Harry's mouth. She slid over his vast tongue. She held herself firmly in a line to avoid his teeth, which looked like stalagmites and stalactites as she flew past them. She crashed through the space left open by his palatal valve. She found herself in a stomach chamber with four speckled rabbits who were shivering and huddled together.

"Are you an angel?" the biggest rabbit asked. A bit of his fur was torn, but other than that, he appeared unharmed.

"No, I am Beatrice."

"Are we dead?"

"No, but you will be if you keep talking. Quick. Help me find a heart-shaped stone."

They only had a few minutes before Croc's stomach acid would reach them. It would burn them up like liquid fire. She picked up one gastrolith. Round. She tossed it to the side and examined another. She ordered each rabbit to start picking through a mound of gastroliths.

"How about if we forget the stone and get out of here?" the biggest rabbit said.

If Beatrice did not find that clue, she would never find her way out of Argilia. She would never meet her people. She would never be able to step into a baseball game. If she ever got back to playing baseball, she would walk up to the first smiling woman she saw and ask, "Excuse me, but is there any chance that you might be my mother?"

Beatrice turned over four stones. She found nothing. Another ten stones. Nothing. She turned to the three smaller rabbits, but none of them had found an unusual stone. She turned to the big rabbit, who said, "Is this what you are looking for?"

It was a stone of unusual colour: periwinkle. About the size of her palm. Round near the far edges but with a cavity midway along the top. She reached out for it.

"What will you give me for it?" the rabbit said.

Beatrice had no time for this. She hated being pushy, but this big rabbit was a nincompoop. He was endangering their lives with idle talk. So she reached out fast and snatched the periwinkle, heart-shaped stone out of his paw.

"Follow me, now."

Beatrice thumped the ceiling of his belly and shouted, "Let us out now, Crockers!" He did not respond. She led the rabbits as she ran along a watery trench. She called out again, but still received no response. A line of acid began creeping toward them. Just steps away, the acid was beginning to incinerate the hindquarters of a baby antelope.

"Croc Harry," Beatrice shouted. But still no reply.

She reached up with both hands and pulled down his palatal valve as hard as she could. It took all her strength to hold the valve down as the four rabbits scrambled out.

"Keep running but watch the teeth," she called out. She climbed over the valve just as the steaming acid began to melt the heels of her running shoes. She flew out of Croc Harry's mouth as fast as she could.

"Run, run, run," she shouted. The rabbits disappeared without even turning to thank her.

Beatrice put the stone in her pocket and climbed her tree house ladder. Once she was at a safe height, she called down.

"Crockers, what was that?"

"I would advise you not to go diving into my stomach again," Croc Harry said.

"Duly noted," Beatrice said.

"My stomach was demanding to eat you," Croc Harry said, "even though my mind said no. My mind said 'open that valve' but my stomach would not listen. My palatal valve is not behaving."

"Don't worry," Beatrice said. "I'm safe now."

"But I *am* worried," he said.

"It's about more than your palatal valve, isn't it?"

"Exactly. Every day, I have the growing sense that I was bad in a previous life. Very bad."

"Nonsense," Beatrice said. "Let's see about that heart-shaped stone."

Beatrice examined the rock. It was not actually a rock. It was a locket. It seemed familiar. Like something she had held long ago. She pried it open and pulled out a tiny plastic bag in which she found a handwritten message. In purple calligraphy.

Dear Beatrice, it said. *Read this when you get out.*

She *was* out. She would never have wasted precious seconds reading a note when the stomach acid was rising like a mortal tide.

Croc Harry rocked nervously from side to side. "I'm not feeling good about the note," he said.

"Why?"

"What if it makes you decide to stop liking me?"

"I like you sufficiently," she said.

"Maybe you will change your mind? That's the problem when someone really likes you. One day they might decide to stop."

Beatrice dropped a twig on Croc Harry's head. "Enough of that nonsense," she said. "You're good. I like you enough. You're a solid six out of ten."

"I would feel better if you'd climb down from that tree and sit with me," he said.

Even though Croc Harry had not managed to help her escape from his own belly, Beatrice did not even hesitate. She climbed down the rope ladder and patted Croc Harry on the scutes. They were hard and bony.

"I wouldn't say no to a belly scritch," he said.

"Roll over."

Croc Harry rolled onto his back and stretched out his arms and legs like a dog. He hummed while Beatrice scratched his belly, avoiding the wound and the stitches.

She lay down beside him on her back and stretched out her arms, lifting the letter up so that Croc Harry and she could both read it.

"Could you read it aloud?" Croc Harry asked.

"Don't you know how to read?" Beatrice said.

"Of course," Croc Harry said. "But if it says awful things

about me, I'll be listening to your voice. I'll find that sooth-ing. Maybe if you're the one who is saying it, it won't hurt so much."

Beatrice gave Croc Harry a reassuring pat. If he had a hand, Beatrice would have held it.

Just then, he swivelled around to look her in the eye. "Hey," he said. "Did you just say I was a six out of ten?"

CHAPTER 17

The Only Family She Had

Croc Harry opened his mouth to pant. He wasn't hot. He was nervous. He expelled anxiety with every rapid, shallow breath. Beatrice sat beside him with the locket in her hand. She didn't know where or how, but it seemed to her that she had seen that locket before. Yes. That was it. The colour was unmistakable. Periwinkle. A soft, gentle, almost unnatural shade of blue mixed with violet. The locket had once sat on her dresser. Beatrice searched her mind for memories of the dresser, or of her bedroom. Nothing came to her. Nothing at all. Just the locket.

Croc Harry asked her to read the message in clue number 7 to him.

Beatrice used her most soft and gentle voice.

Dear Beatrice and Croc Harry, the note began. *If you are reading this, it might seem something of a miracle that you are still both alive. You are each alone in Argilia Forest. Croc Harry, you are without a congregation. Beatrice, it has been a long time since you have spoken with another human being.*

Beatrice tried to remember a time when she had spoken with another human. She had a distant, glimmering, micro-memory of an older, wiser person with a playful voice—was this her mother?—laughing as Beatrice ran her fingers across a dictionary page.

For his part, with his mouth still wide open, Croc Harry began to moan. Tears sprang from his eyes. Two butterflies landed on his face, drank his tears and flew away.

"Croc Harry, are those just crocodile tears? Are you faking it?"

"These tears are real. They come from my lacrimal glands—the same ones that make your tears."

"Why are you crying?"

"Beatrice, you must forgive me. I have done something wrong. I can sense it in my dreams. I did something bad that brought us both here."

"Relax, Crockers," Beatrice said. "We are both here, right? We are not doing so badly in Argilia. We both get a good night's sleep, even though you sleep with one eye open."

"At least I don't snore," Croc Harry said.

"I don't snore," Beatrice said.

"Yes you do," he said.

"How would you know?" she said.

"I hear you every night," he said.

"How is that possible?"

"At night, after hunting, I often come to sleep under your sitting branch. I like to make sure that nobody bothers you. I don't sleep very well, but it helps me relax to hear you snorting and snuffling like a little piglet."

"Wrong!" Beatrice said. "That's not me snoring. It's Horace."

"How come he gets to sleep in your tree house?"

Beatrice sucked her front teeth in disapproval.

"Don't tsk me," Croc Harry said. "I can tsk you too."

"Yeah?" Beatrice said. "Let's see you try."

Croc Harry tried over and over to suck his teeth. But his tongue remained stuck on the floor of his mouth. He couldn't do it.

"Could we please get back to the letter?" Beatrice said.

"Yes."

You are both in great danger, so the two of you must embark on a journey. We have reports that the rebels, who are led by the giant, are trying to crack the code and enter Argilia. We do not believe that they have succeeded, yet. But if they do, they may try to enter and poison your minds. They may try to occupy Argilia and use it as a springboard to attack the Queendom.

The rebels will be coming from the south. So you must travel north. Follow the Argilia River down-

stream. Follow the North Star. Begin your journey, and you shall find your way. Time is of the essence. Beatrice, pack up some oatmeal and accoutrements. Croc Harry, eat your last meal. Navigate carefully. Avoid danger. Help each other. When you come to a white house with a purple door, you will know that it is safe to enter. If you detect any humans before reaching the house, avoid them with all of your ingenuity.

To find clue number 8, study the night sky. When it sends you a message, it will be time. You must leave Argilia the next morning.

"I could go now," Beatrice said. "I have already eaten."

"So have I," Croc Harry said. "I had the munchies last night."

"Crocodiles get the munchies? What did you have?"

"Baby antelope."

"You are incorrigible," Beatrice said.

"And you are imporridgeable," Croc said.

"That word is not in the dictionary," Beatrice said.

"It's in my dictionary," Croc Harry said.

"You own a dictionary?"

"It's all up here," Croc Harry said, "in my capacious brain."

"Right, Mr. Fancy-Pants," Beatrice said. "So what does it mean?"

"You can't live without porridge. You need your porridge and will not be denied. Imporridgeable."

"I do rather enjoy a hot bowl each morning, if it is suitably topped with raisins, brown sugar, milk and a few other niceties."

"I travel with nothing but a full belly, but you appear to be different. You carry stuff. Humans are so impractical. They carry too much stuff. Shoes. Clothes. Knapsacks. Too much trouble, I say. Are you and all your stuff ready to go?"

"When the time is right, I'll be just as ready as you!"

Beatrice said she had business to tend to, but that she wouldn't tarry.

"Where are you going?" Croc Harry said.

"I'm going to see Killjoy," she said.

"Why?"

"I have to ask her a few things. And we have a journey ahead of us, so I want her to do my hair."

"Hair is a waste of time," Croc Harry said.

Beatrice liked Croc Harry. She trusted him deeply. But when he asked the foolish question about whether she had been born brown and when he said that hair was a waste of time, Beatrice wondered if he would ever truly understand her. If, from time to time, annoying comments were to erupt from his mouth, Beatrice felt that she owed it to herself—and to their friendship—to reject his nonsense and stand up to him.

"That's easy for you to say," Beatrice replied. "You're a reptile. Bald and forever hairless."

"I still say fussing about hair is an exercise in vanity," he said.

"What's vanity?"

"It means useless self-love," he said.

Beatrice smacked him with her palm.

"That didn't hurt, but I felt it," Croc Harry said.

"Good. You'll feel it more if you make me mad. You're a crocodilian, so you know nothing about this. So let me inform you."

Croc Harry yawned. "I'm listening."

"If you lost all of your teeth—even the intimidating ones that sit outside your lips when you close your mouth—would worrying about that be an exercise in vanity?"

Croc Harry opened his mouth wide to display his sixty-nine teeth. "My teeth serve a function. They put sustenance in my belly."

Beatrice turned, kicked some stones furiously and turned back to face him. "Sustenance? What, pray tell, is that?"

"You know, nourishment, nutrients, food, all that."

"Well, my hair provides sustenance too," she said.

"How?"

"On cold days, it keeps me warm. In the sun, it protects me from head burn. And at all times, it puts sustenance in my psyche."

"Psyche?" Croc Harry said. "What's that?"

"You know," Beatrice said, "nourishment for my true nature, nutriments for my personality, food for my spirit— all that."

"All right," Croc Harry said. "You can have your hair."

"Well," she said, poking him with her foot, "thanks for your permission."

"Can we be serious for a minute?" Croc Harry said.

"I *was* being serious."

"Can we be serious about something else?"

"Yes," she said.

"I'm anxious about you leaving me right now. What if something happens when you are all alone?"

"I'm alone most the time," Beatrice said. "I'll be just fine."

"How can you be sure?"

Beatrice put a hand up to her hair. "Because I have sustenance, my true nature, personality and spirit will keep me safe."

"Very funny," Croc Harry said. "But if you don't come back soon, I will come looking for you. Not to bother you. Just to make sure you are okay."

Beatrice felt the warmth of friendship tingling on her arms. But she could not resist teasing Croc Harry. "What are you, my protector?"

"I *am* bigger."

"And I *am* smarter. So I'm just as much your protector as you are mine."

"I guess that's fair," Croc Harry said.

CHAPTER 18

A Little Nap on Such a Soft Bed

After her first meeting with Killjoy, Beatrice had learned that the dentist grew furious if you missed an appointment or arrived without payment. In that case, the tailless lemur cancelled the appointment. You had to pay for the visit you missed, and you couldn't come back for one year. Although she was not known to have a single friend, Killjoy received a constant flow of customers. After she fixed your teeth, she would do your hair. You were expected to pay for everything. The teeth. The hair. The conversation. Once, when a customer complained about having to pay for conversation, Killjoy famously replied, "It's not idle chatter. For that, go talk to yourself while brushing your teeth. Do you feel better when I fix your teeth, do your hair and listen to all your troubles? Yes, you do! This is not just chatter. It is talk therapy. So pay up!"

Beatrice had been looking forward to returning to ask Killjoy about the clues. Who was leaving her these messages?

As she walked along the far side of the Argilia River, a territory in which she was less familiar, Beatrice passed through a grassy meadow and came to a pond. The water was as still as glass. She bent over and saw her reflection. Her hair was a disaster! Her twists had come undone. Why had nobody told her that her hair was tangled and wild, punctuated with bits of leaves and a broken stick? She tried to run her fingers through it, but they got stuck in the kinks. This would not do. Even if her friends were crocodiles, rabbits and tarantulas, she couldn't walk around Argilia looking like this. Beatrice backed away from the pond and continued her walk.

She passed under a tall canopy of pine trees and entered into a kind of daydream. She felt an urge to lie down and sleep. Killjoy would be seeing patients all day, and Beatrice did not have an appointment until sundown. She yawned. She had time. The thick bed of brown pine needles looked soft and inviting.

Beatrice lay down and used her Beasack for a pillow. She held her slingshot in one hand and slinging stone in the other, just in case she awakened to danger. But what danger could there be on pine needles? What harm could come of a nap on such a soft bed?

Soon, she was fast asleep.

At first, she dreamed of her tree house and of different flavours of oatmeal. There was oatmeal with butter and maple syrup, and oatmeal with brown sugar and blueberries. They were very distinct sorts of oatmeal breakfasts. Beatrice dreamed that she was testing new variations each day.

However, her dream tumbled into a nightmare. A fire under her oatmeal pot was burning out of control. Beatrice had no water to put out the fire, and she could not get out of the tree house because someone had locked it from the outside. As the blaze intensified, the lock outside the door doubled in size. And then the giant's voice came at her again. What frightened Beatrice the most was that sickly sweet way he tried to sound like an uncle or an old friend.

"Beatrice, open the door. Open the door to your brain, and all this will get better, and you will escape the burning tree house."

"No," she called out.

"Open up before you roast."

"No," she repeated. Beatrice felt a slight change in the nightmare. She felt that she could control the nightmare, even though she was still in it. It seemed possible for her to stand up to a bully. She knew what she had to do. She felt no fear.

"Final warning," the giant said. "If I have to break down that door, it won't be pretty."

In her dream, Beatrice had heard enough. She got out of her bed and walked right through the door, as if it were made of papier mâché. On the other side, she entered the brain of the man who had been pursuing her. Strangely, being inside his brain allowed Beatrice to see him clearly.

He was very tall, with a huge stomach and the broadest shoulders, thick legs, a bald, shining head and eyes that stared out at the world accusingly. He could tell that Beatrice stood in his brain.

"Hey!" he shouted. "I'm the one who invades brains. You're not allowed. Get out!"

Beatrice understood that he could do nothing about it. He was powerless to expel her from his brain. Beatrice hummed loudly, just to irritate him. He groaned. She explored the hallways of his mind. She poked into memories, looked into his past and could see the world through his eyes. She even knew his name because she was in his brain.

"Hello, Brian," she said.

"No trespassing," he said. "Get out.

Brian was a towering giant. His feet were so big that his toes stuck out of the ends of his shoes. If, instead of occupying his brain, she had been standing in front of him, he could have crushed the bones in her fingers.

Beatrice could see that the giant ruled over a land of hatred. There was no mingling allowed between species. Different people and animals were all taught to hate each other. Beatrice could see that some groups of people were kept hungry and imprisoned in camps, and let out only when they were forced to dig, shovel, build and cook for the rulers in the Giant's Land.

Standing in the giant's brain, Beatrice could even see his thoughts and memories. He used to live in the Queendom, but he didn't live there anymore. He and the people in his world were locked out of Argilia, but he was trying to break in. The giant had read dozens of books about ways to influence other people. He had learned that a person having a nightmare left a door open to their brain. If the giant could walk through that door, he could step in and make the person afraid. If they were terrified, he would be able to lead them, he believed. He would take control of their thoughts and use them as a stepping stone to enter Argilia. Once he gained control of Argilia, he would be able to take back the land from which Beatrice had come.

Where was it, Beatrice wondered. *Where was this land?*

The giant's brain looked like a dusty library that nobody visited. It was lined with shelves holding boxes. Beatrice looked at shelf after shelf, covered in cobwebs and dust bunnies. One shelf was labelled "Things I Hate." It held several boxes. Inside one were the words NO RESPECT. The capital letters looked like they were shouting. Inside another box were the words PEOPLE WHO TOOK MY JOB. A third box was labelled THE QUEENDOM: WHERE I ONCE LIVED. AND WHERE BEATRICE LIVED. Beatrice tore it open and looked inside. She hunted for any box that might explain who she was, or if she had a family. But she found nothing. Nothing at all.

"Stop fishing for information," he said. "Get out of my brain."

She was almost done. She walked down one more hallway. It was covered in cobwebs. It needed sweeping in the worst way. But twenty steps down this corridor, she could see Matilda, the head rabbit. The giant had cracked open the door to Matilda's brain. He already had one foot in it. No wonder Matilda was becoming increasingly hateful—the giant was manipulating her thinking.

Beatrice ran back through the cobweb-filled brain corridor. She got one more look at him. Biceps the size of melons. Bushy eyebrows. A sneer on his face. This man had no love in his heart. He governed with hatred.

Perhaps she could defend herself better if she understood why he was so unhappy. She kept on with her search. Rifling through the boxes of his memories, Beatrice saw something that made her shiver. Years earlier, the giant had worked in a circus. People bought tickets to watch him wrestle crocodiles. He proudly showed off the scars on his arms and face. He boasted that a surgeon had removed a crocodile tooth from his thigh. The giant knew exactly how to take down a crocodile, and he took pleasure in the fight. However, when a new queen came to the throne, she banned crocodile wrestling in the Queendom. The giant lost his job. He was required to take a test. He did not do well. He was told that he would no longer be allowed to use his wrestling skills. His new job was to work on an assembly line, building solar panels. He did not like building solar panels. He was not good at fine motor skills. What he liked was working in a circus as a famous crocodile wrestler. But that was no longer allowed.

His own people used to be in charge, but now others ruled the land under the reign of the new queen. He began a rebellion, escaped arrest and had to flee the Queendom. Now he was living in the Contested Lands, gathering recruits and planning to attack the Queendom.

Beatrice had enough information. Soon, it would be time to exit the nightmare and return to her life, awake in Argilia.

"I told you to get out of my head," the giant said.

"I can see why you are angry," Beatrice said.

"Get out."

"But there is no need to hurt people."

"I said get out," the giant said.

"Make me," Beatrice said. "See, you couldn't get into my brain but I got into yours."

The giant stomped his foot. He stomped the other foot.

"Don't you ever try breaking down the door to my brain again, "Beatrice said, "because I'm not letting you in."

"I don't need that anymore," he said. "I know what you look like, and I'm coming after you."

"You have no idea what I look like."

"Black hair, brown eyes, brown skin, about the height of a pipsqueak, freckled face, messy hair, maybe eleven years old. Believe me now?"

Beatrice was shocked. She had no idea he could see her in there.

"You think you're safe in Argilia," he said, "but I have my ways to get you. And if you dare to leave, I'll get you for sure.

Some thought you might be a leader. But your test results weren't so perfect either. And now you spend your days in a tree house, eating porridge? A fat lot of leadership you're showing!"

Beatrice swallowed. She nearly cried. She nearly shouted. She detested being told that she was useless, especially because she feared that it was true. And what was this about her not doing a test perfectly. What test? Let her take it over again! She'd show him. However, this was not the time to argue. This was not the time to give the giant any bit of information that he could use against her.

The giant kept at her. "Instead of petting bunny ears, why don't you come over to my side? You could be my assistant! You could have influence. Nobody would care that you are brown. We have the science in the Giant's Land. We have the means to lighten your skin. One painless needle, and you could look like me."

Brian was raising his hands in the air and shouting. Beatrice wasn't sure what her own home in the Queendom looked like, but she knew what she did not want, and what she would never accept. She liked the colour of her own skin. She liked the way she was. She would never live in a land that tried to change her.

Brian kept hollering and stamping his feet. She observed him coolly. He was having a temper tantrum. Inside his own home, he was throwing chairs and smashing plates, but he could not hurt her, because she was inside his head. Perhaps

Beatrice could learn from this. If she ever met him in real life, perhaps she could use his own anger against him. This, she was sure, was what Fuzzy would have advised her to do. But it was time to stop listening. Beatrice could not stay a moment longer in that poisonous brain.

"Goodbye and good riddance," she said, and she walked right through the door and out of his head.

Beatrice woke up in a terrible sweat on the pine needles in the forest. There were pine needles stuck to her cheeks and arms. She was trembling. The last light of the day was fading. She had dropped her slingshot and stone. She put on her Beasack and held the slingshot in one hand and the stone in the other. It was time to visit with Killjoy.

CHAPTER 19

The Navel of the Universe

Beatrice arrived half an hour after sunset. Killjoy was saying goodbye to her final patient of the day—a chimpanzee who had eaten too many bananas and developed a cavity.

"Rinse your mouth with clear spring water tonight," Killjoy told the chimp, "but no meals until tomorrow." The patient nodded and departed quietly.

A stream of clear water ran nearby. Killjoy kept a soft bed of grasses for patients who liked to lie down and recover. She had a bag of tools—ropes, twine, tweezers, pliers, knives and scissors—that she cleaned in boiling water between patients. She had a handwritten schedule of each day's patients and kept it nailed to a tree.

"Beatrice," Killjoy said, "you are my only human patient. Thank you for waiting until the end of the day. Soon it will be dark, but the moon will be full. It promises to be a cloudless night, so I trust you will be able to find your way back home without hiccups."

Beatrice reached into her Beasack and gave Killjoy a giant bowl of raspberries.

"Thank you, child," Killjoy said. "Now what brought you halfway up Argilia Mountain to meet me? Is your mouth well? Have you been flossing? Shall I take a look?"

"I brush and floss, yes. I came to ask if you could do my hair. And answer some questions."

"The hair, for sure," Killjoy said. "What would you like?"

"I want to look strong," Beatrice said. "I want my hair to say, 'Don't mess with me.' But I don't want it falling apart on me while I travel. So I'll have cornrows."

Killjoy washed Beatrice's hair. She cut up an avocado and brought out a tin container of coconut oil.

"Hey," Beatrice said. "Where'd you get the coconut oil?"

"Not telling.

"Ah, come on. I could have used that, before."

"Sorry. I'm the only hairdresser around, and it's a secret."

Killjoy mashed up the avocado and mixed it thoroughly in a wooden bowl. She added a dollop of coconut oil and mixed it all again. She rubbed it into her palms, warmed it up and slid it into Beatrice's hair, giving her a head massage as she worked. Beatrice closed her eyes. The head rub felt good. Perhaps this was what it would feel like to return home and have someone take care of her hair.

"I have found seven clues," Beatrice said.

Killjoy had been working behind Beatrice, but she walked around to look in her eyes.

"Seven already?" Killjoy said. "Not bad. Lucky, I suppose."

"Why do I have to chase down all these clues?" Beatrice asked.

Killjoy returned to standing behind Beatrice as she worked. "That's a vague question. Can you offer anything marginally more specific?"

Marginally more specific, Beatrice thought. Killjoy always spoke as if she had been born in the middle of *The St. Lawrence Dictionary of Only the Best Words, Real and Concocted* and had spent years promenading among the letters until she emerged with the best vocabulary in Argilia.

"I want to go home. Why all this rigmarole?"

"What makes you think I can answer that question?" Killjoy set a comb into Beatrice's hair. She began pulling it back, breaking up all the knots. Beatrice flinched. Killjoy tugged even harder at Beatrice's hair.

"Ouch," Beatrice said.

"Aren't you little miss tender-headed," Killjoy said.

Beatrice knew that she couldn't proceed until her hair was detangled, so she took a deep breath and let her continue. She worked for several minutes.

"I need to find clue number 8," Beatrice said. "It's supposed to be in the night sky."

"Wait for the stars," Killjoy said. "Lean back. I have corn-rowing to do."

"That hurts," Beatrice said. "Couldn't you go more gently?"

"Do you want cornrows or not?"

Beatrice took another deep breath and tried to stay quiet while her scalp stung. Eventually, it grew numb.

Killjoy handed her a mirror. "What do you think?"

Beatrice gasped. Her hair was gorgeous. Tight, thin, strong braids swam across her scalp in rows. Best of all, the hair would hold fast, no matter what she did. She wouldn't have to worry about it, think about it, or pay any attention to it at all until . . . until . . . until she was out of Argilia. If she managed to leave.

"My hair looks lovely, so thank you," Beatrice said.

"Not bad," Killjoy said. "Not bad at all."

"But we have to get down to business now," Beatrice said. "I must find that clue tonight."

"Does the world revolve around you?" Killjoy said. "Since when are you the navel of the universe? The only one who is searching?"

Beatrice turned around to face Killjoy. Speaking as gently as she could, she said, "So what's your story?"

Killjoy lifted up her palm. "I don't matter. Promising, talented girls who know nothing at all matter, but do I? No, I do not. I'm never getting out of here."

"Killjoy," Beatrice said, "what—"

Killjoy patted Beatrice's shoulder. "Forget it. I shouldn't have said that. Would you like to see my moves?"

"Sure," Beatrice said.

"I don't usually let people see me do this," Killjoy said, "because I like my privacy. But a girl's got to move. And you're all right. So watch this."

Killjoy stood tall on her two hind legs and bounded across the forest floor. Killjoy flew up and down, and left and right. She bounded like her legs were full of springs. With a simple hop, she took off vertically and spun three times in the air, like a figure skater. She spun so fast that Beatrice could no longer distinguish between Killjoy's black and white splotches. She was neither, and she was both. Then, she took three big hops and leapt well above Beatrice's head, landing high up in a tree. Then she jumped back down, did a backflip, and hopped to a table with a pitcher and two glasses. Killjoy poured lemonade into a glass, held it in her hand and bounced back to Beatrice without spilling a drop.

"You're quite the dancer," Beatrice said.

"I dance to be whole," Killjoy said. "And to unite my colours. I can be not just Black, or white, but I can be both. Plus, I like to work on my moves. Passes the time when you live alone."

"Why do you live alone?" Beatrice asked.

"Well," Killjoy said, "why do *you* live alone?"

"I had no choice in the matter," Beatrice said. "It's just how I came to be here. All alone."

Killjoy's perfectly round, bright blue eyes stared right at

Beatrice. She said nothing, but stared and stared and kept on staring. Beatrice could feel what Killjoy was communicating. *Same here, girl. Same here.*

Finally, Killjoy broke the silence. "Care for some lemonade? Made it myself. It has a splendid mixture of water, lemons and sugar. It is the perfection of alchemy."

Killjoy handed the lemonade to Beatrice, who took hold of the cold glass and drank the lemonade. In her dictionary, Beatrice had read about alchemy, the seemingly magical process of combination. She searched for a compliment to match Killjoy's vocabulary.

"It is stupendous. Truly superfactionous. It also happens to be quite tasty."

"Thank you," Killjoy said. "It can lead to cavities, so brush and floss when you get home."

Beatrice asked for the mirror again. She studied her cornrows. They made her look smart. Like a girl who had vision. Like a girl who was independent and knew how to take care of herself.

Beatrice put down her lemonade, reached into her Beasack and handed over clue number 7.

"Now I have to find clue number 8," Beatrice said. "The final clue. Can you help me find it in the night skies?"

"Have more lemonade."

"Come on, Killjoy. Tell me something I don't already know."

"Stay for a while," Killjoy said. "The evening has just begun."

Beatrice explained her nightmares, including the one she had in the pine forest.

Killjoy listened attentively. She used a flashlight to peer into Beatrice's teeth. "Do you mind if I inspect your teeth while we talk? I feel more purposeful when I am working. And when I am purposeful, I listen better."

As soon as Killjoy put down the flashlight and took her hand out of Beatrice's mouth, Beatrice asked what it meant that she had walked into the giant's brain.

"It means that you are indeed extraordinarily intelligent and full of empathy. It means you have the possibility of becoming a leader. I can see why the giant wants you. He wants you to help him lead his own people."

"If the Giant's Land is what the world of humans looks like," Beatrice said, "I am not leaving Argilia."

"The Queen will be hoping that you return to her Queendom. But it won't be easy."

"How do you know about all of this?"

"I have many patients. People tell me things. Other humans have been here before. Like you, only one at a time. But I am not at liberty to tell you about that."

"A giant is trying to get into my brain."

"You must keep him out."

"Why is all this happening?"

"In time, you will learn."

Beatrice begged Killjoy to tell her if she had a family.

"Can't help you there."

"Then tell me about the Queendom," Beatrice said.

Killjoy said she had heard that in the Queendom, people were tested in childhood. They were tested for health, strength, manual dexterity, empathy, intelligence, social vision and leadership. Once you were tested, you were streamed. According to your score on the test, you were trained to become a labourer, high worker, manager, director, artist, entrepreneur, educator, high educator, leader, high leader, highest leader or King or Queen.

"Is there any choice in the matter?" Beatrice asked.

"Apparently not," Killjoy said. She said that people had choices a long time earlier, but they kept fighting wars and burned up all the fossil fuels, and when the new world had emerged, the Queen made up her own rules.

Many different people lived in the Queendom. Of different sizes, shapes, colours and physical abilities. Some men loved men, some men loved women, some women loved women, and none of this mattered. Some people were neither men nor women. All of that seemed fine, and people got along, but they were tested and streamed.

The opportunities to study and learn and work depended on your test results, and you were tested only once. This made some people angry. They complained that they had been forced to do work that did not suit them. A civil war began. A long and nasty war. The giant and his people fled and were plotting to take back Argilia.

"What is this place called Argilia?" Beatrice asked.

"It was created one decade after teleporting was invented."

"Is Argilia a land of the dead? A graveyard for people teleported from the Queendom? Am I dead?"

"No, child, you are not dead. But you nearly died. In the Queendom, if you are considered important and you nearly die before your natural death in a war or an accident, and if nothing can be done to save your life in the Queendom, you can be teleported to Argilia. You won't remember anything . . ."

"Unless you are exceptionally intelligent," Beatrice added.

"Exactly, unless you are among the brightest and most promising ever, and then you might be able to recover a few memory fragments. But you are sent here to have a chance to regain your health. If you are able to live in peace with the animal kingdom, it might be possible for you to return. Chances are slim. Believe me, I know."

"What do you mean?" Beatrice asked.

"Let's focus on you," Killjoy said. "Your travels will be dangerous. The giant and his people will look everywhere for you. If they catch you, they will harm you. Grievously."

"So was I important in the Queendom?" Beatrice stood a little taller.

"You were only a child but deemed to be of some promise. Why do you think that nobody has eaten you in Argilia?"

"I take care of myself," Beatrice said. "Even Croc Harry tried to get me."

"He was just fooling. If he had wanted to have you for breakfast, it would have been done, lickety-split. He is a fearsome hunter. His stomach acid burns through bones just as easily as you, say, digest spaghetti."

Beatrice retrieved a memory. A plate of spaghetti Bolognese on a kitchen table. A chair for Beatrice. She couldn't see anyone else at the table. The Bolognese was covered with freshly grated Parmesan and four leaves of fresh basil. On the table, near her knife, sat the periwinkle locket. It went where she went.

Beatrice returned to the conversation with Killjoy. She wove her fingers together and brought her hands to her face. She rested her chin on her thumbs.

"Why was I only of 'some promise'?"

"Back in the Queendom, you failed a test."

"What test? Why?"

"I am not sure. But as a result, there were doubts about you."

"And here I am, proving myself," Beatrice said.

"Doing a better job than some of us," Killjoy said.

"What is that supposed to mean?" Beatrice asked.

"Nothing."

"All right," Beatrice said, "tell me this. Is Croc Harry stronger than the giant?"

"Hard to say," Killjoy said. "Croc Harry is more noble and powerful, but as far as fighting goes, the giant is more skilled."

"Is the giant more intelligent than me?" Beatrice asked.

"He has more knowledge, but you are more clever."

"So he is not to be underestimated," Beatrice said.

"The difference between the giant and you can't be measured in degrees of intelligence," Killjoy said. "The difference lies in how you use it. He uses his intelligence to make people afraid. How do you want to use your smarts?"

"To do good things for animals and people," Beatrice said. "Also, I'd like to give that giant a big fat smackdown."

Killjoy retrieved Beatrice's glass and hopped back to the lemonade table. "Good luck with that."

"All these problems in the world . . ." Beatrice said.

"As soon as you become aware of the world's problems, you have to help deal with them."

"Talk about pressure!"

"Don't mention it. Why do you think they call me Killjoy?"

Beatrice sat back and looked up. The stars were coming out. She could make out the Big Dipper.

"Would you fancy a cup of mint tea with a pincho of honey?" Killjoy asked.

"What is a pincho?"

"It is a little bit. A smidgeon. Just the right quantity to give your mint tea a taste of personality."

Beatrice knew it had to be the same as a smackerel in the books about Winnie-the-Pooh.

Beatrice took hold of Killjoy's hand.

"What did you mean about knowing how hard it is to get from Argilia to the Queendom?" she asked.

Killjoy pulled her hand back. She turned away to fuss with

the teapot. "Tea is ready," she called out.

"I'll take a pincho," Beatrice said.

They spent an hour drinking tea with a pincho of honey and watching the stars grow brighter.

CHAPTER 20

Drama King

The sun had set over the Argilia River. The stars shone against a darkening sky.

"Watching the stars is like watching water rushing over rocks," Beatrice said.

"Or like being mesmerized by logs burning in a fire," Killjoy said.

"You could watch all day," Beatrice said. "Or all night."

Killjoy sat in silence. They remained quiet for a while. Finally, Beatrice said, "So what do you do when you are up all night?"

"I have what you call a hyperactive mind," Killjoy said. "Things bother me. It is hard for me to stop thinking about them. So I dance to relax. To forget. To stop thinking so much. To make use of my fabulous legs."

"Show me how to dance," Beatrice said.

Killjoy took her by the hand. They stood in a patch of open meadow. Killjoy came up to Beatrice's waist, but when she stood on her hind legs and began to dance, she soared above Beatrice. While she leapt up and down, Killjoy wailed in a high, wavering pitch. Beatrice suddenly remembered the sound of trumpets. She remembered learning to play. She remembered blowing into the instrument and hearing sound come out like a wounded beast. Killjoy sounded like that when she wailed, but made it sound good. Killjoy made it sound like she had something to say.

Beatrice hopped from one foot to the other. It did not feel natural. It did not feel easy.

"No, girl," Killjoy said. "Like this." Killjoy bent her knees slightly and shot up in the air. "Spring from both feet," Killjoy said. "Leap high. Spring like something has been bottled up inside you and now you are going to dance it out."

Beatrice hopped. She hopped hard. She hopped fast. She hopped from left to right and bent her knees and flew straight up as high as she could. She would never bounce like Killjoy, but it felt good to jump up and down. It felt good to use her own legs until it felt like they had filled up with lead. As she danced, Killjoy joined her, hopping along with her, and took her hands. Soon, Beatrice was gasping for air.

"I need a break," Beatrice said. She could barely get the words out.

"Remember," Killjoy said. "Night is the time to dance. If the stars aren't watching, why bother?"

They sat together and sipped more tea.

For a time, they stared at the Big Dipper, pointing out the long handle and the four corners of the scoop.

"Who was the first person to see those stars and call them a dipper?" Beatrice asked.

"Or the first lemur," Killjoy said. "Although I personally am short, I spend much of my life high up in trees. Lemurs live closer to the sky than humans. So in all probability, it is likely that we saw the stars first."

"Imagine being so high up," Beatrice said, laughing, "that you could grab the Big Dipper and take a drink."

"Wouldn't that be something," Killjoy said, "to reach up in the heavens and take a gulp. I bet they serve lemonade."

Beatrice took Killjoy's hand and gave it a squeeze. "I wonder if my own people are studying the Big Dipper at this moment? Right now. Just like us. I wonder what they are like? Are they short, like me? Are they book people? Do they rifle through dictionaries the way I do? Do they have brown skin like me?"

"Beatrice," Killjoy said, "your people are Black."

"What do you mean? I'm not Black. I'm brown."

"Black isn't just a colour. It's a people. A shared history. A sense of belonging."

"But I have no history and I belong nowhere," Beatrice said.

"Did I just cornrow your hair?"

"Yes. And you did a fine job."

"Then just take my word for it," Killjoy said. "You belong. You're Black. Be proud of it."

Beatrice was not sure how she could belong when she did not even know where she came from. But dancing with Killjoy gave Beatrice reason to believe in her own identity, even though she had been taken from her homeland and she was not sure what or where it was.

A twig cracked. Stones rolled on the walking path. Beatrice heard a grunt.

"We have axes," Killjoy shouted, "and we will use them!"

"Axes?" Beatrice whispered.

"Shhh," Killjoy whispered. "He's coming."

"It's me," Croc Harry called out. "I hear you two palavering. I have never met a dentist who takes an axe to the office. But no worries. I'm not hungry."

Croc Harry high-walked right up to them, lay down on the dental-recovery bed of grasses and opened his mouth wide.

Killjoy said, "May I draw your attention to the sign on this tree? Perhaps, in the darkness, it escaped your notice. Allow me to read it for you: 'No eating the dentist or her patients.'"

"Not here to eat," Croc Harry said. His words were slurred. He was not enunciating properly.

"Why are you sneaking up on us?" Killjoy asked.

"I am not sneaking. I made noise. I let you know I was coming. If I wanted to eat you, I would have waited in the path for you to walk into my jaws. My loose tooth is killing me. Could you pull it?"

"I can vouch for the fact that Croc Harry was duelling recently," Beatrice said. "In fact, he saved my life."

"How gentlecrockish," Killjoy said. "Anyway, I decline to perform dental surgery in conditions of caliginosity."

"Could you say that in English?" Croc Harry said.

Beatrice put her hand on Croc Harry's head. "It just means darkness. Caliginosity is darkness."

"Whatever," Croc Harry said. "I need this tooth out, now."

Beatrice couldn't resist teasing her friend. "Croc Harry, that tooth can't represent more than one-millionth of your body mass. How bad can one measly millionth hurt?"

"It hurts so much I can't think of anything else. I have a one-track mind. It is shouting, 'Tooth, tooth, tooth. Get that tooth out.'"

Beatrice patted his scutes. There had to be a softer part of a crocodile to pat in a friendly way. Next time, she'd ask him to roll onto his back so she could pat his leathery belly.

"Due to caliginosity," Killjoy said, "I decline to reach into the jaws of a crocodile. Make an appointment to return in conditions of luminosity."

Beatrice could see that Croc Harry was at the end of his rope. She didn't want to make him angry.

"Luminosity means light," she said quickly.

"I know what luminosity means," Croc Harry said. "Enough with the 'osities.' I need help now."

"I'll do it," Beatrice said.

"Not with my tools," Killjoy said.

"Do you have twine, and can you tie a half-decent knot?" Croc Harry asked.

"Roger that," Beatrice said and opened her Beasack.

"I do not condone substandard dental procedures," Killjoy said.

"It's the third tooth in, on the top right," Croc Harry said.

Beatrice asked Killjoy to shine a light on the tooth. With the flashlight beaming, Beatrice could see the tooth, which was the length of her own index finger. She reached in to touch it.

"Wobbly," she said. "I'm going to use my expandable ruler. I don't want you clamping down on my hand by accident, or in pain."

"Just end my misery, would you? Honestly, I am entirely disastroflated."

"You made that word up," Beatrice said. "Croc Harry, you're such a drama king."

Beatrice removed the steel ruler from her Beasack, placed it inside Croc Harry's giant jaws and expanded it fully until it was pushing firmly against the top and bottom of his mouth.

"This is unprofessional," Killjoy said. "Very unprofessional."

"Killjoy, hold that light steady," Beatrice said. "Croc Harry, say, 'Aww.'"

"Why should I say that?" Croc Harry said. "It doesn't make any difference."

"Say it anyway," Beatrice said.

"You are not a trained dentist," Killjoy said.

"Hold that light, Killjoy. At this moment, I'm the tooth doctor. Say it, Croc."

"Aww," he moaned.

"Feel any better?" she asked.

"No."

"Scissors," Beatrice said, holding her hand out. Killjoy handed her a pair.

"Twine," she said, and Killjoy handed her the string.

Beatrice cut the string. She made a loop in the middle, which left the ends of the string loose. She slipped the loop over the wobbly tooth and tightened the knot.

"Ouch," Croc Harry said.

"Steel yourself," Beatrice said. "I'm going to tug on the count of three."

"Do it."

"One. Two." Beatrice yanked hard before she got to three. The tooth held firm.

"Ouch," Croc Harry said. "Double ouch. Owee! You didn't even wait till three."

"I was trying to save you discomfort."

"Yeah. Thanks for that."

Beatrice peered deeply into Croc Harry's mouth. She examined the tooth. It was sharp enough to slice through the thickest cardboard. It was more than two inches long! Part of the root still clung to the gum. Beatrice got set to put her arms and back and legs into the next effort.

"Hang on, Croc. I can get it out but this is going to hurt."

Killjoy said, "Never advise a patient of pain to come. Imagination exacerbates the experience of pain."

"How about we all stop talking and get down to business?" Beatrice said. She tightened the knot and sat on the ground inches from Croc Harry's mouth. She placed her feet on either side of Croc Harry's jaw. "Killjoy," she said, "shine that light steadily and brightly."

Killjoy stood directly behind Beatrice, holding up the flashlight.

Beatrice sat on the ground like a rower in a boat. Knees bent slightly, she reached into Croc Harry's mouth, grabbed the twine—one end in each hand—and suddenly rowed back hard and fast. She gave a mighty tug. She could hear a little pop like a firecracker exploding. She fell all the way back and saw the tooth fly out of Croc Harry's mouth. It twisted and turned and sailed up and away into the moonlight.

"Ouch," Croc Harry said. "You got it that time, and there she goes."

"A total and complete violation of gravity," Killjoy said. "Only a highly promising future leader can make a tooth fly like that. Child, you are one of the chosen ones."

Beatrice stared as the tooth entered the heavens. It kept flying and shining against the blackened sky. The twine trailed behind like a runaway leash. Finally, the tooth splintered into fifteen marvellous pieces that tumbled around and around chaotically until they suddenly aligned. In a straight line, the heavenly tooth splinters formed the letters B E A T R I C E G O H O M E.

The words shone like the world's brightest magic. They remained visible for a few unforgettable moments just below the handle of the Big Dipper. Finally, each little letter shifted and drifted and slid away to mix in with all the other stars in the galaxy.

"Did you see that?" Beatrice said.

"Yes, I saw that," Croc Harry said.

"I didn't see a thing," Killjoy said. "Maybe you're imagining it."

"I feel no more pain, not even a bit," Croc Harry said.

"And I feel no more doubt, not even a bit," Beatrice said. "It is time for me to go home. Even your tooth says so."

"I'm going with you," Croc Harry said.

"Lucky ducks," Killjoy said.

Beatrice spun around to thank the dentist. "Thank you, Killjoy. And I know you saw that message."

But Killjoy had turned to face a pot of soapy water. She scrubbed her dentistry tools with furious intensity. In the dark, Beatrice could only see the lemur's busy hands and her black-and-white back.

"We're all done here," Killjoy called out. Her voice broke. She took a moment to compose herself. Still, she kept her back to Beatrice and Croc Harry. "You best get going."

CHAPTER 21

Not Sharing You With Anyone Else

In the morning, Beatrice prepared to leave the place she had called home ever since she'd awoken in Argilia. There was nothing to organize in her tree house, because she had kept an immaculate room. The bedsheets were tucked firmly into the corners. The jars of oatmeal and accoutrements were lined neatly on a dusted shelf. The books were all arranged, from A to Z, in perfect order on her bookshelves. She picked up her Beasack and found a floppy, purple sun hat on a hook behind the door. It had a dark stain inside. She had no idea where that came from. But it didn't matter. The hat was comfortable, and nobody could see the stain. She put the hat on her head. She looked around the room where she had lived—the only place she could remember living—and said a silent goodbye.

It was no time to get emotional. Life carried on, and she had things to do. She closed the door behind her. As she climbed down the rope ladder for the last time, she remembered that she had worn the hat before. She'd worn it when she left a house full of people and crossed the street and began walking somewhere. Who had been with her? Where had she gone? She could not recall. Something awful had happened. It had sent her spinning endlessly through chambers of darkness. Then she had awoken one sunny morning on her bed in the tree house in Argilia Forest.

"Ready?" Croc Harry was waiting at the base of the fig tree.

"Ready."

"I'll take the river," he said.

"And I'll take the path," she said.

"Stay close," he said.

"Not too close." She chuckled.

"Not to worry," he said. "I've eaten enough antelope to last me for a while."

"I never did turn you into a vegetarian," she said.

"I have developed a taste for apples," Croc Harry said, "but only as dessert. Don't ask me to be what I am not."

"I hope you are content, then," Beatrice said.

"I am strangely dissatisfied," Croc Harry said. "I do not belong here, and I want to find out why. But I do fear that I have done something terribly wrong."

"You are the only crocodile I know with a guilt complex."

"I am the only crocodile you know. I am the only crocodile you will ever want to know. The only one who will protect you."

"What makes you think I am not here to protect you?" she said.

Croc Harry panted. Tears formed over his eyes again.

"You're not crying, are you?"

"No. That's just my nictitating membrane."

Beatrice watched as the two butterflies came back. They drank his tears. Before flying away, one of them sang out, "Salty. Better than potato chips. Splendiferous. Thanks, Crockers."

Just a moment into their journey, Beatrice asked Croc Harry to wait for her by a bend in the river.

"Where are you going?" he asked.

"You keep asking me that," she said.

"I'm starting to worry about you."

"I am going to see Matilda, the head rabbit."

"Why?"

"To save her brain."

* * *

Two soldier rabbits stood as sentries at the Argilia Rabbit Academy. They instructed Beatrice to wait outside the warren door. They disappeared inside. In a few minutes, they opened the door from inside and threw Horace Harrison Junior the Third out onto the grass.

"If you try to sneak into another classroom, we'll put you in the dungeon and feed you to the crocodiles," one soldier rabbit said.

Horace stood up, dusted himself off, and said, "Fat chance. The only cwocodile awound here is my fwend."

Beatrice stopped him. "Horace, why did you come back here?"

"I don't care if I go to jail. I'm not giving up until Matilda teaches all wabbits."

At that moment, Matilda opened the door and stood outside the warren. "I ought to lock him up. We have enough rabbits as it is. I have to feed and educate my own rabbits. There are only so many carrot tops to go around."

Beatrice walked up to Matilda, put her hand on her shoulder and said, "Surely, we could figure out how to get enough food for everybody."

"Speckled rabbits are not like us," Matilda said. "They should stay where they belong."

Beatrice opened up her palms. "But Matilda, they're just rabbits. They have a few spots on their fur. How exactly are they different from you? It's not really about the speckled rabbits at all, is it? You're angry. You're afraid. This is not the way you really want to be, is it?"

Matilda put her paws to her eyes. "No! I hate the way I

feel. These days I seem to loathe everyone. Even myself. I feel that something . . ."

". . . has taken over your brain?" Beatrice finished the sentence.

"Yes," Matilda said, "yes. It wasn't always like this."

"Has someone been speaking to you in your dreams? Trying to get into your mind?"

"Yes! Exactly!"

"You can resist," Beatrice said. "You don't have to let him in!"

Beatrice took Matilda's paw in her hand. "Have you locked up other speckled rabbits? Are they suffering?"

Matilda pulled her paw back. She sat up as if an electrical current had jolted her. "Go. You must all go. If you and the speckled rabbit don't leave immediately, I will lock you up. Go. Go. Go."

"I am leaving Argilia," Beatrice said, "but one day I hope to come back and drive that giant out of your brain."

"Please free me," Matilda said, "because this is torture." But right away Matilda lowered her voice and told the guards, "If they don't leave on the count of three, lock up these intruders."

Beatrice could see that Matilda was unwell. Her own mind was at war with herself. It felt wrong for Beatrice to leave. But she could do nothing more to help Matilda. Not at this time.

"One," Matilda said.

Beatrice reached out to shake Matilda's paw, but Matilda refused to budge.

"Two," Matilda said. The soldier rabbits stood on their hind paws and got ready.

Beatrice nodded at Matilda. She smiled. It was better to smile than to hate. And she began to walk away.

Horace hopped beside her. Two steps forward, three hops up, then two steps forward again. Then he hopped up and down wildly. He looked like a yo-yo.

"Take me too," Horace said. He kept up his wild hopping. "No ifs, ands or buts about it."

Beatrice couldn't imagine leaving without Horace. She felt like she had known that silly bunny forever. She sighed and looked up at the white strands of clouds in the otherwise blue sky. The strands pulled apart, swirled around and disappeared. Then the sky was nothing but bright sun against a blue canvas.

"Of course, I'm taking you," Beatrice said.

Horace was too small to give a hug, so he hopped up to Beatrice's arm and wrapped his legs around her bicep. "You're taking me. You're taking me. You weally are!"

Beatrice smiled. "Count on it," she said. "But have you seen Fuzzy?"

"No," he said, "and I'm not sharing you with anyone else!"

As they walked away from the Academy, Beatrice asked each rabbit she passed if they had seen Fuzzy. Nobody had seen her. Beatrice choked back her tears and reminded herself that she still had Horace and Croc Harry. She thought about what Fuzzy had said when they last spoke: *Friends are like books. You carry them with you forever, regardless of mundane impediments like geography.*

CHAPTER 22

Emotional Neglect

Beatrice walked all day along the Argilia River, which widened as it went. Just a few feet away, Croc Harry swam with his eyes just above the water. Horace hopped along. No one had any idea of what dangers might lie ahead. After many hours, they had to cross the rushing river. Beatrice saw that the path continued on the far side of the water. She crossed on the back of Croc Harry. She offered to carry Horace in her arms.

"No need," Horace said. He bounded up toward the water's edge, did a giant hop and a skip, and then he jumped right over the river. Beatrice had never seen such an energetic hop. That rabbit was part bird.

Beatrice did not know exactly where they were going or how they would reach the Queendom, but for the first time since awakening in Argilia, she knew where she was supposed to go. Nothing could stop her. Whoever had set up those clues did not know about everything that was happening in Argilia. Brian, the giant, was already sending in enemy crocodiles and snakes. He was poisoning the mind of the head rabbit. Soon, he would pass right through the body of Matilda, penetrate Argilia, take control of other animals and attack the Queendom. Beatrice had to get home to tell people what was really happening. She had to find somebody to help her stop the madness. And she had to find her mother and father and siblings, if they were still alive. If they still remembered her.

Now that she was on the move, Beatrice wondered if she would ever again live like she had in Argilia. On one hand, the forest had been closing in on her like prison doors. On the other, she had been completely free to do as she wished. Wake up when she wanted. Eat when she wanted. Bicker with Croc Harry when she wanted. Stroll over to visit with Killjoy and get her hair done when she wanted. Build her vocabulary when it pleased her to do so. But now life was changing. She might be escaping a possible prison, but she might never be so free and independent again. Now that Beatrice had been living with nobody telling her what to do, or when to do it, Beatrice was not sure she was ready for civilization. Nothing would be the same. Beatrice trembled as she walked. She wondered if something might leap out from the dense forest and attack her. She kept the slingshot ready.

Beatrice did not want to look like a target, so she kept moving and frequently shifted to the left or the right. She told herself that she was not alone. Croc Harry and Horace were travelling with her. Croc swam smoothly and soundlessly, swishing his tail gently, never lifting more than his eyes and ears above the water. Horace made more noise. The word *quiet* was not in his vocabulary. He chattered at her, asking her over and over to lesson him, because, he said, no self-respecting speckled rabbit should go without a fine education.

Once, when Beatrice was ignoring him because she was lost in thought about how she had come to Argilia, Horace got fed up.

"Emotional neglect," he called out. "You are subjecting me to emotional neglect and that is wong, wong, wong."

He picked up a long branch, held it straight out ahead of him, charged forward on his hind legs, planted the stick down hard in the ground and pole-vaulted himself way up over Beatrice's head. She watched him disappear in the highest branches of an ancient cedar tree.

Horace climbed down, dusted himself off and said, "Do I have your undivided attention?"

Croc Harry lifted his entire head out of the water, opened his mouth and bellowed, "Tell that no-good, pole-vaulting, yip-yapping rabbit to settle down or else."

"Or what?" Horace called back. "Speak to me, Cwockers. I am here. Wight here. Speak to me."

"Or I will toss you back into my belly and make you sleep on my gastroliths."

Horace did a giant hop, landed on Croc Harry's head and hopped back onto the riverbank. He did a little dance on his hind legs. He swivelled his hips and pumped his arms in the air.

"Fat chance, Cwockers," Horace sang out. "Fat chance, baby."

Croc Harry charged out of the water while Horace was still admiring his own dance moves. He snatched Horace into his mouth, flipped his head back and hurled the rabbit head over paws through the air. Horace landed right back in the cedar tree.

"Who's da king?" Croc Harry bellowed. "Who's da King Croc?"

Beatrice smiled. She kept walking. They would catch up. They were her friends. They were going on a big hike, or as Horace called it, "embawking on a giant pwomenade." They were friends, fellow travellers, and they felt like family. As far as Beatrice knew, they were the only family she had. But what would become of her family once they left Argilia?

CHAPTER 23

Popping Socks

As Horace hopped and Croc Harry swam, Beatrice walked for miles beside the Argilia River. She passed through a corridor beside an endless row of giant cedars. Five times taller than her fig tree in Argilia, the cedars seemed to have been standing guard for a thousand years. Numbers began rolling through her head. Discovering new words made Beatrice feel awake and alive, but juggling numbers helped her stay calm.

She guessed that, on average, the women in her family line would have been about twenty years old when they began to have children. If the cedars were indeed a thousand years old, that meant that Beatrice's last fifty female ancestors—mother, grandmother, great-grandmother, great-great and so on—had lived and died during the life of the one ancient cedar that shaded her now as she walked. If it had eyes, that one tree would have seen fifty of Beatrice's ancestors come and go. And it would now be watching over her. Beatrice patted the cedar's rough bark and leaned her entire body against the tree. She tried to hug the tree. Beatrice was aching to hug and to be hugged. But the tree couldn't hug her back.

She did not know where she was going or what awaited her, but Beatrice intended to honour her ancestors—the greats, the great-greats and all the rest. Forward to the Queendom was the only path she knew. For the time being, her job was to take good care of her friends. She found it strange to be in charge of a brooding crocodile and a high-flying rabbit, but she did feel responsible for them.

Passing under the ancient cedars made Beatrice feel purposeful and peaceful. The air tasted sweet. Beatrice believed that no matter what bad things might happen to her in the future, none of them could happen here. The trees were like the arms of her parents, she imagined, keeping her safe as long as she walked under them.

Where were they, and who was she? What would become of Croc Harry and Horace?

Although Croc Harry had once nearly eaten her, since then he had become her steady companion. How could she not learn to care for someone who showed up at her tree house every single day and called out to her to palaver over breakfast? When you shared the breakfast hour and had a conversation every day, how could you not want to have that friend in your life forever?

"Croc Harry," she called out, "what if nobody was out there to care for you?"

"I take care of myself," Croc Harry said.

"What if you had nobody to talk to? Nobody to watch cooking oatmeal? No toothbirds to clean your teeth?"

"I would slide deep into the deepest river and never come up again," he said.

"Were you unhappy before I came to Argilia?" she said.

"I have no memory of when I came to Argilia or when you came, exactly," he said, "but ever since I met you, I've just known that life wouldn't be right if you were not here."

Horace hopped up and down. "Is this not a three-way discussion? What about me? I was unhappy, too, you know. Why do you think I keep hopping? I get sad. Hopping keeps me busy, so I can't be sad."

"We love you too," Beatrice said, "but you're a pest. As for how well you are walking—or hopping—through an unknown and possibly dangerous forest, I am giving you five out of ten."

Croc Harry gargled huge mouthfuls of water, which was his way of chuckling, but Horace jumped up and down again.

"Not funny. I do not accept five out of ten. I am a twelve out of ten."

"If you want those extra seven points," Beatrice said, "you have to earn them. You start with a five."

"Then how about this?" Horace hopped, did two backflips and landed on his hind paws with his forepaws outstretched. "Do I get points for that?"

"You'll have to work harder than that," Beatrice said.

"Then how about this?" He hopped even higher. Horace hopped so high that he cleared the treetops, swivelled in the air to see everything beneath him and came back down. "Huge waterfalls ahead. Cwockers cannot swim it. How do you like them apples? Now do I get a twelve out of ten?"

"We shall see," she said.

They kept on moving north, Croc Harry in the river and Beatrice and Horace on a riverbank path. Croc Harry resembled a giant goldfish—but turquoise instead of orange, and many times bigger. Beatrice ran another number in her head. If a goldfish weighed half a pound and Croc Harry weighed 700 pounds, that meant that Croc Harry was 1,400 times bigger.

Croc Harry stopped swimming and began to tread water. "Something is coming up," he called out. "The vibrations in the water are changing. The water is slowing down and there is about to be a big, big . . ."

"Croc Harry, stop!" Beatrice called out.

Just two crocodile lengths ahead, the water slid over a cliff and plunged onto rocks far below. No crocodile or mammal could survive the drop.

"What did I tell you?" Horace shouted. "Get out of the water or you will become cwockodile mush."

Croc Harry paused, holding himself almost vertically in the deep water, swishing his tail to stay in one place.

"You look so innocent, treading water," Horace told him.

"Get out now," Beatrice said.

Croc Harry climbed out. "Water is so much better as a medium for long-distance travel," he said.

"Hush," Beatrice said. The path zigzagged down a long hill bordered with spruce and oak trees.

"Stay here while I investigate," she said.

"But I'm supposed to be looking after you," Croc Harry said.

"You?" Horace said. "Who saw the waterfalls first? Who just earned a twelve out of ten?"

"Hush, silly one," Beatrice said.

Croc Harry yawned. "Well, I haven't slept in ages, so if you don't mind, I'll catch a little shut-eye while you look around."

Croc Harry rolled over on his side and fell into a deep, uneasy sleep. Horace napped beside him. Beatrice ran all the way to the bottom of the path, where she saw water flowing at the foot of mammoth waterfalls. Then she hiked back up to tell her friends what awaited them.

When she arrived at the top of the trail, Beatrice found Croc Harry thrashing wildly on the ground. The only way she could wake him was to throw water on his face.

"Croc Harry, please wake up!"

Croc Harry came to his senses.

"I'm here, Beatrice. I'm here."

"You had me worried. What were you doing there?"

"I was asleep."

"Asleep? Crockers, you were thrashing as if you were fighting for your life."

"Must have been a nightmare."

"Do crocodiles have dreams?"

"Apparently."

Croc Harry said that in his dream, he was not a crocodile. He was a tall young man with a gun. He was approaching a horse and buggy at an intersection. Something went wrong. Terribly wrong. Then he was travelling for a long, long time through a dark tunnel. That was the last thing he remembered before the life he now knew.

Beatrice gave him a hug and said she was glad that he was out of his nightmare.

The three of them began the long downhill journey. They had to navigate sixteen switchbacks. As they neared the end of the downhill trek, Croc Harry's forearms and hind legs were so heavy and tired that he could barely move.

Sometimes, to distract him, Horace did backflips and called out, "You can do it, Cwockers. You can do it. I believe in you."

After two hours, they reached the bottom.

"Easy-peasy," Beatrice said.

"Exhausting," Croc Harry said. "I was so tired dragging my seven hundred pounds down those switchbacks that I thought I would pop my socks."

"Croc Harry, you don't wear socks."

"Doesn't matter. I thought I would pop them anyway."

"What does it mean?"

"It means I thought I would bite the dust. Kick the bucket. Die."

"Don't go popping any socks on me, Crockers. We have a journey to make."

"No sock-popping if I can help it."

"I can wear socks," Horace said. "What about me?"

"Don't you go popping socks either," Beatrice said.

"I like you lessoning me, Beatwice," Horace said. "Today's lesson. New word: *Pop socks*. Synonyms: *kick bucket, bite dust, die*. Antonyms: *steady the bucket, spit out the dust, live*."

Beatrice didn't correct Horace, because she found herself staring at two massive waterfalls that cascaded down into a huge pool at the foot of the cliffs. It looked like the most beautiful swimming hole in the world.

"Shall we swim?" Beatrice said.

"What about me?" Horace said. "I want to play, but wabbits don't swim."

Beatrice asked him why not. He said a rabbit's centre of gravity was too low for swimming.

"I'd sink like a stone," he said.

"You'd sink like a rabbit," Croc Harry said. He offered to let Horace hop up and down on his back. So Horace used Croc Harry as a trampoline until he got tired. Then he hopped back onto the banks of the river and went to sleep.

Croc Harry slid into the deep, cool water and Beatrice

joined him in the depths. The afternoon sun was sinking. The air was cooling. They had travelled together all day and had seen only squirrels, birds and worms. Beatrice swam to the edge of the pool and pulled herself up onto the rocks. She picked up a few and pointed to a log floating in the distance.

"Do you think I can hit that log?"

"Give it a try," Croc Harry called.

Beatrice pitched the rock as hard as she could. It smashed against the log. Then she practised with her slingshot.

"Hey," she said, "are you two hungry?"

"Nope," Croc Harry said.

"Not me," Horace said.

"Well, I'm famished," Beatrice said. She found a clearing in the woods, just twenty steps from the river. She built a fire and made oatmeal.

"Don't you get tired of that?" Croc Harry asked.

"Nope. I could eat it for breakfast, lunch and dinner. Bit of cinnamon. Some raisins. Dollop of brown sugar. Perfection. Want some?"

"Still digesting my antelope."

The fire burned down, and Croc Harry rested on his back a safe distance from it. "It's a bit like the rays of the sun," he said. "Aids in my digestion."

Beatrice lay down on the grass but she had no pillow. She shifted around but could not get comfortable.

"Come over here," Croc Harry said, "and use me as a pillow."

Beatrice curled up near the foot of his tail and put her head on his soft, leathery underside. Horace crawled onto Beatrice's tummy. They all fell into a deep sleep.

CHAPTER 24

One Hundred Percent Not Dead

H ow did you two sleep?" Beatrice said.

The sun was shining in the early morning sky. Beatrice had already made a fire, eaten and packed up her bags of oatmeal, cinnamon, raisins and brown sugar. She cupped water from a stream to brush her teeth. She slipped on her runners. She checked to make sure that her Beasack contained all of her essentials: slingshot, hatchet, sewing kit, apples, oatmeal and accoutrements.

Horace was still snoring. But Croc Harry had been awake for hours. When he felt safe and secure and was in a thinking mood, he lay on his back with his forearms and legs in the air. He held a branch in his jaws and rolled his head from side to side, rolling the branch around in his mouth and humming. He looked like a giant, elongated, furless dog asking to have his belly scratched.

"Morning Beatrice," he said.

"What are you doing?" she asked.

"Dental hygiene," he said. "And pondering."

"What are you thinking about?" she asked.

"Not much," he said. "Life. Death. Where we come from. The state of the universe."

She reached down to tickle him on his exposed leather belly. "Lighten up, Crockers."

Usually, he wiggled his arms and legs and emitted a happy bellow when Beatrice rubbed his soft belly. But this time, he remained motionless. He dropped the stick. He flipped over so that his back was up, his belly down and he was ready to travel.

"I had the strangest dream," Croc Harry said. "I swallowed an orange seed."

"Yuck," Beatrice said. "I hate that."

"So do I," Croc Harry said.

In his dream, the orange seed took root in his belly. It began to grow into a small tree. "It was impervious to stomach acid. Impervious, I tell you. And that's no small potatoes. My stomach acid can incinerate a hippo femur. In my wilder days, I even tried to eat one or two hippos. Those fellows are right nasty. Let me tell you, a big hippo can fight. The babies are easier to tear apart."

"Babies! You're mean."

"Just telling it like it is, Beatrice. Your bestie is a carnivore. Get used to it. It's in my CNA."

"What's CNA?"

"It's like DNA. A genetic code, for crocs. It stands for crocksy-ribonucleic acid."

"Aren't you full of vocabulary and science today!"

Croc Harry continued to describe his dream. The orange tree in his belly turned out to be the fastest-growing tree or plant known to crocs. It grew faster than bamboo. It grew two feet each day. In his dream, the tree trunk snaked out of his nostrils and expanded into a six-foot tree rising straight out of his head. In his dream, he became the biggest crocodile in the world: twenty feet long and one thousand pounds, and he needed all of that size to support the weight of the tree.

In the orange tree nested monkeys, birds and squirrels. Horace had moved into Beatrice's house, which was lodged at the very top of the orange tree, and Croc Harry was responsible for carrying them all to safety. From a lookout on the roof of the tree house, Beatrice and Horace kept watch as Croc Harry swam along the surface of the water. They warned him about rocks, waterfalls and other crocodiles. He had to take great care to avoid other predators. Now that he had an orange tree and family on his head, he could no longer fight. He wouldn't even be able to do a death roll.

"A death roll?" Horace asked.

"It's my wrestling move to kill big prey or to fight other crocs. I take them by the neck, and I roll over. It hurts and it takes a huge amount of my energy to roll all the way over and haul a crocodile or antelope with me, but this is how I rip them apart so I can swallow them in large parts."

"No death rolls in your dreams." Beatrice giggled. "Heaven forbid!"

"Well, it was a problem in my dream, because it was my job to defend you. And to usher you to safety."

"And here we are, ushering each other to safety. Are you ready to go? I have a feeling we will find the house with the purple door today."

"What house?" Horace asked.

"The seventh clue in the locket," Beatrice said. "It told me to look for a white house with a purple door."

"I'm just about ready," Croc Harry said. "I have not met with a single plover recently, so would you terribly mind brushing my teeth?"

The crocodile did not have the physique for complete dental hygiene. His arms were too short. To brush his own teeth, he'd need a giant toothbrush that reached out from his arms and made a U-turn into his mouth.

Beatrice pulled the hatchet out of her Beasack and cut a small branch off a spruce tree. She soaked it in water and rubbed toothpaste into it.

"Open up," she said.

Croc Harry unhinged his mighty jaws and opened his mouth wide. Wide enough for a baby hippo. Beatrice inserted her expandable ruler, because even though they were now officially friends, she still did not like venturing into his mouth without the protection of the ruler. What if he sneezed, for example, and clamped down accidentally right when she was in there?

Croc Harry had nearly seventy teeth, and Beatrice scrubbed each one of them with the spruce branch.

"Don't spit till I get out of here, okay?"

"Can I gargle?"

"No! Wait!"

Beatrice retrieved the ruler, stepped away from Croc Harry and tossed the mangled spruce branch in the river. Croc Harry swam into the waters to rinse out his mouth. Then he climbed back out and spat.

"I have never seen you spit before."

"Well, then, watch this."

Croc Harry closed his palatal valve, took a huge mouthful of water, lifted his head well above the water and began to gargle. As he gargled, he yodelled. Up and down the musical scale he went. "Yodel-ay hee-hoo," he gargled. "Yodel-ay hee-hoo."

Beatrice bent over in laughter. "Don't ever do that again in public," she said. "It's an offense against all good taste. It's an offense against humanity."

"Beatrice, as a proper King Croc, it is not my job to worry about humanity. That's on you!"

They laughed together and set out on their journey. Soon, they came to a section of the forest that was so thick and full of thorns that the path was no longer negotiable. The thorns scratched Beatrice. Both of her legs started bleeding. The path was totally blocked, and she was facing a wall of thorns. She was about to bring out her hatchet to clear a path for herself, but it looked useless.

Horace took a giant hop up in the air. He sailed up for six, ten, fifteen feet, and then came back down, landing as softly as a cat. "Nothing but more thorns," he said.

Beatrice calculated that she could use her hatchet to hack away at them for hours and still not make much progress. She saw something bright to her left. A sign. Hammered onto a huge spruce tree.

"What's up, Beatrice?" Croc Harry called out.

"Hang on a second."

This was no note with friendly purple calligraphy. It was a sign with large, black, typed letters.

This is the northern border of the Argilia Forest. Electric Gate Ahead. No animals, reptiles, birds, insects or humans allowed across the border. You are at the far edge of an experimental zone operated by the Queendom of Carolina. If you are lawfully inside it, you will be protected and allowed to have vocalized communications between living species. It is unlawful to attempt to enter or leave the Argilia Forest. Do not touch the gate. It is electric. It has enough voltage to terminate an elephant. If you are an elephant, or anything smaller, you will be electrified.

"Croc Harry," Beatrice called out. "We have an issue here."

Croc Harry swam over to the edge of the river. He listened to Beatrice's report and said, "I have examined the river carefully. It is deep, and the current flows too fast for a human. You have the most comical manner of swimming. What is the point of water travel without a tail?"

Beatrice climbed onto Croc Harry's back, swung her arms around his neck and let her feet trail in the water on either side of him. Horace looked for something to hold on to.

"Get in my sack," Beatrice told him. "I'll zip it up." He climbed in. She zipped it up carefully.

"You comfy in there?" she asked.

"Yes," he said. "As warm as pie."

She found herself travelling across the surface of the water without moving her arms or legs. She felt Croc Harry's powerful tail swishing back and forth underwater. He felt as strong as a horse. She remembered that too, now. She had known the strength of a horse, and she had felt it gallop. Travelling on the back of a crocodile was much smoother. It felt like gliding over water. Beatrice imagined that this was as close as she would ever get to gliding on the back of a mermaid. But then again, she never knew. If there were talking crocs and high-flying rabbits and lemur dentists in Argilia, perhaps there were mermaids too.

Beatrice feared that the electric gate might extend into the water, but they passed out of the forest of Argilia uneventfully.

Croc Harry swam until the thickets of thorn bushes finally ended and Beatrice could see a path on the other side of the river, again.

Croc Harry pulled over to the side of the river.

"I'm good to walk now." She got off his back.

He said nothing.

"Thank you for the ride, Crockers. You are smoother than a horse."

He said nothing.

She got back onto his back and hugged her arms around his neck, and only then could she make out his words, vibrating through his body. "I can't talk to you anymore, but I seem to be able to think through my skin."

"Can you still understand me?" Beatrice asked.

"I will always understand you, Beatrice. But you shall only understand me if you are on my back and hugging my neck or standing right beside me and touching some part of me."

"Then we must swim again one day, but at this moment, I prefer the independence of my own locomotion," she said.

"Now you sound like Killjoy."

"Perhaps I should pull another tooth and see if we get another message in the sky."

"That sort of thing only works once," Croc Harry said.

"Okay, Crockers, swim safely."

Beatrice had been desperate to undertake this journey home. But now that she was outside Argilia, she was already missing it. She felt that she had only begun to touch the magic of the forest and know its many creatures.

Horace Harrison Junior the Third thrashed in the Beasack. She let him out. She asked him how he was doing, but could not hear any answer. He hopped onto her back and put his arms gently around her neck. Only then could she make out his words.

"I nearly got seasick in there," he said.

"I can't hear you anymore, unless you are on my back with your arms around me," she said, "or unless you are touching me in some way."

"Wait," Horace said. He climbed down. He stood on the ground and tried to hop. He could only manage small hops. Three feet here, maybe four feet there if he gave it his all. Horace couldn't bounce up way above Beatrice's head anymore. He couldn't fly up toward the sky. Horace Harrison Junior the Third was no longer part bird. He hopped back up onto Beatrice's back and put his arms around her.

"No more pole-vaulting for me," he said.

Beatrice, however, was starting to see things more clearly. She was remembering a bit better. Once, she had lived in the Queendom of Carolina. She had a brother. Something had happened. Something awful. She had nearly perished. She had to be teleported. What had happened to him? She wasn't sure.

Horace hugged her, gently, around the neck. Beatrice, in turn, wrapped her arms around Croc Harry's neck.

"Horace, can you hear me?"

"Yup yup yup," he said.

"Crockers, can you hear me?"

"Roger that," he said, "but only when you are on my back."

"Guess what?" she said.

"What?" they both said together.

"We have left Argilia and lost its magic."

"Can you still lesson me?" Horace asked.

"Hold on tight, and we'll give it a try."

Croc Harry began to swim, keeping an eye on Beatrice and Horace on land. Beatrice walked alongside the river in this strange new place, whose name she now remembered. It was called the Contested Lands. Horace rode on her back, with his arms around her, and Beatrice distracted him with a lesson.

"Five times seven," she said.

"Thirty-five. Give me something hawder."

"Twelve times twelve," she said.

"One hundred and forty-four. Come on, Beatrice, give me something good."

"Seven thousand, three hundred and ninety-nine times eight," she said.

"I have no idea. I need more lessoning. What's the answer?"

"Fifty-nine thousand, one hundred and ninety-two."

"How do you do that?"

"I don't know. It's easy."

"Not easy for me," Horace said.

"You just break it down. Multiply eight times seven thousand. Multiply eight times three hundred and ninety-nine, which is just like multiplying eight times four hundred, except you get eight less. Add the two sums together. And there's your answer: fifty-nine thousand, one hundred and ninety-two."

"Beatwice," Horace said.

"Yes."

"You're weird."

"I like you too, Horace."

"Sometimes you annoy me, but even then I don't stop liking you."

"That's the nicest thing I've heard all day."

"How about all month?"

"Don't push it," she said, laughing.

"I feel like I have always known you," Horace said.

"I know what you mean," she said.

They continued their lessoning for an hour. And then Beatrice made him get back down and hop independently. They had a challenging journey ahead, and she had to conserve her energy. In his dream, Croc Harry had felt responsible for all those living in the tree that had grown out of his belly. But this was no dream. They had left Argilia, and Beatrice now knew that she was definitely, absolutely, one hundred percent not dead, nor were Croc Harry or Horace.

It was her job to keep them all alive. She would have to be smart. She would have to be ready. She stopped for a moment to open up her Beasack. She thought she detected the tiniest movement in her bag. No. Nothing. She must have been imagining things. She took out her slingshot. There. That felt better.

CHAPTER 25

A Piece of Her Mind

Thump thump thump.

When Croc Harry wanted Beatrice's attention, he smacked his tail against the water. She would never want to be hit by that tail. It cracked down and sent waves crashing over the riverbank.

Beatrice put Horace in her Beasack, stepped into the water and climbed onto Croc Harry's back.

"What's up, Crockers?"

"Something is up ahead. I hear voices."

"If you let me out, Beatwice," Horace said, "I could participate in this conversation."

"Not safe right now," Beatrice said. "Get ready to hold your breath. We may have to go under."

"I might have something to say about this," Horace said. "I am not fond of deep water. I am not at all an aficionado."

"Aficionado," Beatrice repeated. "Very good, Horace. Your lessoning is taking hold."

"I mean it," he said. "I am not a fan of this at all. You do not have my support. You do not have my approbation. You do not . . ."

Beatrice patted the rabbit's bottom, which was resting on the bottom of her Beasack, and said, "Easy, Horace. Easy."

"But hopping helps calm me down!" Horace said.

"Concentrate on your breathing," Beatrice said. "Crockers, the voices you are hearing—are they human voices?"

"Yes. If I have to take a dive, can you hang on tight?"

"Is anybody consulting me on this?" Horace called out.

For good luck, Beatrice rubbed the periwinkle locket in her pocket. "You'll have to trust me," she said. She squeezed her arms right around Croc Harry and lay her cheek flat against his head.

"For how long can you hold your breath under water? Twenty minutes?" Croc Harry asked.

"Crockers, that's ridiculous. I can barely last twenty seconds."

Horace shouted, "I can only do fifteen seconds. I wefuse to drown. I have lessoning in front of me. Great lessoning."

Croc Harry asked Beatrice to lie low. He kept his entire body submerged except for his eyes, nostrils, ears and Beatrice. On Beatrice's back, Horace lay flat in the Beasack.

Croc Harry swam silently for a minute, his tail swishing slowly and purposefully under water.

Up ahead, Beatrice saw a cluster of humans eating a picnic

on the riverbank. Mama humans, daddy humans, adolescent humans and baby humans.

"I wonder if they are my people," she murmured.

"Not a chance," Croc Harry said.

"How do you know?"

"They have guns, and you do not. They are white, and you are not."

Beatrice said they were not exactly white. They were more like beige, with a tincture of tan colouring.

"Deep in my bones," Croc Harry said, "I believe that you are not from gun-toting people. I seem to remember that."

The people on the banks were all standing and pointing. Beatrice could hear them shouting.

"Look," a man called out. "Over there. A Black girl is floating down the river."

Beatrice looked to her left. And to her right. Was there a Black girl? Where? Now the man was pointing directly at her. Beatrice suddenly remembered what Killjoy had said.

"I see her too," another man called out. "Is she dead?"

"She might be," the first man answered. "She is not moving."

"She's moving," the second said. "I just saw her lift her head. She looked right at me. That Black girl is floating on a crocodile."

Beatrice liked herself and was proud of the way she looked. She wanted to find out who her people were and to whom she belonged, but she detested the sound of the men calling her Black. There was no love in their voices. There was nothing but hatred. Who were they to comment on her skin and assign her a colour? The men spoke of her as if she looked like burnt toast. These people could not see properly. They certainly couldn't see *her* properly. If she ever had a moment with them, she'd give them a piece of her mind. In all of her time in Argilia, she had never lectured or spoken angrily to or lambasted a single animal. But she felt up to the task. She would lambaste those people up and down, just as thoroughly as she might paint a wall. Painting. She remembered that, too, now. Once, she'd painted the entire wall of her bedroom. Purple.

"Quick," the first man said. "I'll take the rowboat. After I scoop up the girl, you shoot the croc."

"Take a breath and hang on tight," Croc Harry said.

"Horace, take a big breath now," Beatrice said.

"This is an imposition," Horace said.

"Hush up and hold your breath."

"And did I ask for a big sister?" he said.

"Take your breath now, Horace. That's an order. Sisterly enough for you?"

She heard the rabbit inhale deeply. She did the same.

A man started rowing toward them.

Croc Harry slid deep into the water, with Beatrice's arms around his neck. Suddenly, they dropped much deeper in the water. Beatrice felt her ears pop. Croc Harry's tail swished back and forth with steady strokes as they shot forward.

They rocketed through the water. She could barely hold her breath. Beatrice counted slowly: one thousand, two thousand, three thousand, and when she got to twelve thousand, she tapped his head. She thought her lungs would burst. He shot up to the surface of the water. She could hear shouting far behind her.

"There she is," a voice shouted again.

Another human voice said, "If you see that Croc, put a bullet in his head."

Horace panted heavily. "I can't see those people," Horace called out, "but I don't like them. Also, it is soaking in this bag. I hate when my fur gets wet. Hate it hate it hate it."

"Shush," Beatrice told him.

"I am sick and tired of you telling me to—"

"Hang on once more," Croc whispered.

"Keep quiet, Horace," Beatrice said. "And hold your breath."

Down dove Croc Harry.

His tail swished even harder than before. They sped by fish, frogs and rocks. When he came up for air, Beatrice told him that she had barely been able to hold her breath or hang on. Horace was gasping so heavily that he couldn't speak.

There was still a distant sound behind them, so he dove again, swishing, swishing and swishing, until Beatrice suddenly saw no more fish or frogs or rocks. Everything went black. She was floating, floating, floating . . . Then she could hold her breath no more. She saw the air bubbles leave her own mouth and she began to choke as the water poured in.

She tried to swim but seemed unable to move, and then she was moving again, but not of her own locomotion. Something was under her back, supporting her very gently but lifting her powerfully to the surface, and then they breached the water and she began to cough. Still she was being lifted out of the water and onto the riverbank when she noticed she was in Croc Harry's mouth. Somehow, his teeth were not tearing at her. He eased her out softly on the rocks. The rocks were a lot less friendly than the inside of Croc Harry's mouth.

"You lost consciousness. Did I hurt you?"

"Not a scratch. How is Horace?"

"About time you asked," Horace said. "Let me out of this bag."

Beatrice unzipped the Beasack. Horace tumbled out. He hopped up and down five times, showering the riverbank with water. He leaned against Beatrice while she lay beside Croc Harry.

"Are the people gone?" Beatrice asked

"They are, for now. But we must keep moving," Croc answered.

Beatrice said she could not believe that even after being transported in Croc Harry's mouth, she didn't have a single cut in her skin.

"Crocs can tear apart hippos," Croc Harry said, "but we also have gentle mouths. I have seen female crocs crack their own eggs and carry their babies into the water."

"I admire the way you swim," Beatrice said.

"I can't say the same about humans in water," Croc Harry said. "Your arms and legs are like toothpicks. How do you expect to outswim a shark or a killer whale if you are using toothpicks for locomotion?"

"We don't try to outswim predators," Beatrice said. "We just race each other."

"If you raced every fish in the ocean, you'd finish dead last," he said.

Beatrice sat up and slapped her forehead. "I remember swimming. I was in a race. I stood at the edge of a pool with a cap on my head and got ready to dive in the water."

"Why would you bother with a cap?" Croc Harry said.

"The cap pins your hair close to your head," she said. "I placed second in that race. I also recall being in a buggy pulled by a horse."

Horace climbed onto Beatrice's lap. "Was it a black buggy?" he said.

"Yes."

"Four doors?"

"Yes, how did you know?"

"I was there, Beatwice. I was there too."

Beatrice tried to make sense of her memory. Where had she been? And how could Horace have been there with her? She had no idea. She tried, but in that moment, she could not retrieve any more memory fragments. All she knew was that it felt like she had spent all her life listening to his adorable and annoying voice.

They continued their journey, Beatrice and Horace on foot, and Croc Harry in the water, trying to see what else they remembered. But none of them had any more recollections. As the light began to fade, Beatrice started to look for a dry, flat, open space in the forest where they could build a fire and spend the night. The river grew so shallow that Croc Harry could no longer swim.

"Come with me along this path," Beatrice said.

They continued on the trail until Croc Harry was exhausted. His arms and legs were not built for hours of strolling on land.

"Shall I carry you?" she asked.

He said nothing. She asked again. Still no reply. She forgot that he could no longer speak, so she climbed on his back and said it again.

"Very funny," he said.

Horace could no longer make any spectacular hops. He could hop laterally, and he could hop forward, but only a few feet at a time.

"I am feeling mortal," he said, "and it's not a good feeling. In Argilia, I hopped like an Olympian. Here, I am an ant. Pinned by the merciless force of gwavity."

Beatrice hugged the rabbit. "Oh, poor you," she said. "So terribly pinned. I don't know how you can bear it."

"Shaddup," Horace said, wriggling in her arms.

"Look!" Beatrice said. She pointed. She got down on Croc Harry's scutes and gave him a hug too. There it was, at the top of a hill. A small white house with smoke emerging from the chimney, and a purple door.

CHAPTER 26

Life in a Cage

It was a white, rectangular, single-storey house with purple shutters covering all the windows and a purple door with no window but a mysterious, voice-activated lock.

A note, in purple letters, was neatly attached to the door.

If you are not B, HHJ the T, or CH, please go away. This is private property. The door will not open for you. If it is you, B, HHJ the T and CH, please each say your names now.

All three of them spoke in turn.

"Beatrice."

"Croc Harry."

"His Majesty the King Horace Harrison Junior the Third,"

Horace said, "and by way, you big old door, it's nice to be able to speak without touching all the time."

The door remained shut.

"Stop that," Beatrice said to Horace. "This is serious."

"Just thought I'd try it out for size," Horace said.

"Your name is long enough. Say it properly. Don't waste my time," Beatrice said.

"You never spoke of time in Argilia," Horace said. "You're changing."

"Do it, Horace, or I shall not carry you for one more step in my Beasack."

Horace hopped back up to the door and said his name: "Horace Harrison Junior the Third."

A mechanical, recorded voice called out, "Voice recognition accepted."

"How does it know our voices?" Beatrice asked.

"From before," Croc Harry said. "It remembers us all, from some time before."

"How do you mean that it remembers us?" Beatrice said. "What do you remember?"

"Nothing yet," Croc Harry said.

The lock unlatched. The door swung open. "On this property only," the automated voice called out, "you will be able to communicate as you did in Argilia."

"Hello," Beatrice called inside. There was no answer. She called louder. Still no answer.

She prepared to step in.

"I'll go first," Croc Harry said.

"But it's dark in there. How will you see?"

"I see better at night than most animals. That's why I sometimes hunt at night."

He was still panting from the long walk up the hill, but he pushed up onto his legs and high-walked inside.

"Is there room for you in there?" Beatrice called out.

"Plenty. This house was designed for a croc."

Beatrice stepped in. She found a light switch and flicked it. It was a huge open room. There was plenty of room for a crocodile to enter and turn. There was a back door too, with a little sign in blue: *Crocodile bath ahead.* Beatrice peered outside. She saw a little pond, just big enough for a large crocodile to bathe in, and, next to it, a pen full of chickens.

"You're not hungry, right?" Beatrice called inside.

"Still working on that antelope," he said.

"Good. There's a bath for you outside, but don't touch the chickens."

"Don't be telling me what to snack on," he said.

"Except for the chickens in that pen, you can go snack on anything you want."

"Hmmph!" he snorted.

To the side of the room, there was a pile of fresh hay, with a big tunnel dug into it. Horace crawled into it.

"Ah, perfection," he called out. "There are carrot tops in here. I'm going to eat them. Anybody have any objections?"

"Knock yourself out," Beatrice said.

Beatrice heard Horace chewing. He was the loudest eater in or out of Argilia. And then he began to snore. The entire house rose and settled with his raucous breathing. Beatrice felt some relief that Horace had fallen so quickly asleep. No doubt about it, he was a high maintenance rabbit.

Inside, there was a small single bed pushed up against one wall, with white bedsheets and a purple pillow. Beside the single bed was a bed of hay that ran nearly the entire length of the room. There was a writing desk with a lamp, and three dozen books on a bookshelf beside the bed, and a small refrigerator. Beatrice could hear it humming.

She could remember the last time she had heard the hum of a refrigerator. She had taken something from it. Sliced mangoes. She had eaten them and licked her fingers and headed outside to a black buggy with a toddler seat. She had travelled for some time in the buggy. The buggy and someone else and Beatrice were being pulled by two beautiful Clydesdale horses whose lower legs resembled big white socks. Beatrice saw that fragment of memory clearly, but she did not know who was with her, who was driving the buggy. Here, in the white house with the purple door, she prepared to open the fridge.

"I have a feeling I know what's in there." Beatrice had already grown accustomed to holding Croc Harry when he spoke, so she crawled onto his back.

"What?" Croc Harry said.

"Sliced mangoes."

"Who would bother slicing a mango and putting it inside a refrigerator when you could just pull a ripe one off a tree and bite into it?" Croc Harry said.

"Not every person has a mango tree standing next to them," Beatrice said.

"Just open the fridge."

Beatrice opened it. On the top shelf, closest to her, sat a dozen slices of fresh mango in a glass bowl. She also saw a glass jug of milk, some fresh blueberries, fresh raspberries, dried cranberries, a dozen apples and water. On the big jar of water were the words: *Drink this water. Do not drink the river water. It is not potable.*

On the kitchen counter, she saw small bags: cinnamon, brown sugar, ground almonds and oatmeal. They were all neatly identified, in the usual purple calligraphy.

"Somebody has been looking out for me," she said.

"And providing you with antiscorbutics," Croc Harry said.

"So what is that, Mr. Fancy-Pants?"

"Fruit with Vitamin C to keep your teeth from falling out and your gums from rotting. Whereas I don't have to worry about my teeth falling out. They fall out all the time, and then they just grow right back."

"Except when they don't fall out, and you have to call on me to send one up to the heavens."

Croc Harry laughed, which involved squeezing his tail up toward his head and releasing it several times, while panting quickly. This made Beatrice laugh and fall off Croc Harry.

"What are we supposed to do here?" he said.

"You go have a bath out back," Beatrice said, "and I'll look around. Come back in fifteen minutes and we'll compare notes."

"And I can't even eat a single solitary chicken?"

"There are twelve chickens in that penned area, and I expect to see twelve after your bath."

She opened the back door, and Croc Harry stepped out. She looked all over the counter and on the doors and inside the fridge and under the beds—both of them. There were no notes for her.

She stepped outside and saw Croc Harry lounging in the pond. She looked in the pen. The wire covering the pen had been torn off. No chickens inside. Not a single one.

"Croc Harry!" she said. He didn't answer. "Croc Harry, get out of that bath right now."

He lunged out, which frightened her. She stepped back, but he wasn't aiming for her and his jaws were not open. He had been lunging for the door. He high-walked inside and lay down on his croc bed. She came after him, locked the door and said "Did you eat those chickens?"

She lay beside him.

"No," he said.

"Then where are they?"

"I ripped down the fence and let them go. No animal should be put in a cage. If I get to live, I fear that will be my fate. Life in a cage. Outside Argilia, there will be nothing for me to do except sit in a cage and wait to die. I will be useless."

"Crockers," Beatrice said, "you are useful to me. Even if you weren't useful, you'd be my friend. You help me and I help you. We take turns."

"I can't help you much in this house. I don't even belong in a house. I belong in water and mud and high grasses and the comfortable spot under your fig tree."

"We won't be here forever. You shall help me again. I'm not alone, right? You are with me, right?"

"When you know who I am, you won't love me anymore."

"What do you mean?"

"I don't know, exactly. But that is what I fear."

Beatrice suddenly remembered a blinding flash of light. But what had she been doing, whom had she been with and what had happened next? She had no memory of that.

Beatrice and Croc Harry came to an agreement. He would not worry about not being useful, and she would not be angry with him for something he may have done before they met in Argilia. He would do his best to forget about hunting for a few days, forget about protecting her and relax and sleep and digest his antelope and wait for her to root around the house. She would keep the doors locked and the windows shuttered, and they would both be as silent as could be and she would try to find the clue that was surely waiting for her in purple calligraphy.

Horace hopped out of his warren and onto Beatrice's shoulder.

"And you shall not come to any agweements without consulting me. I am here too, you know. I am equal in this equation. I . . ."

Beatrice snatched him in her arms, gave him a big hug and told him to hush.

"We know you're here, Horace Harrison Junior the Third."

"I love love love it when you say my whole name," Horace said.

"I'll do it whenever I have an hour to spare," Beatrice said.

"But could you add the word *esquire*? I like the sound of Horace Harrison Junior the Third, Esquire."

"Not on your life," Beatrice said.

"Then lesson me some more. Wead me a book. I want my vocabulary to exceed that of Cwoc Harry."

"That will never happen," Croc Harry said.

"It will," Horace said.

"It won't," Croc Harry said.

"It will. Did you know my brain is bigger than yours? I weigh eight pounds, and you weigh seven hundred, but I have more gwey matter."

"If your brain is so big, spell hypercrocksterfabulation," Croc Harry said.

"Is that even a word?" Horace asked.

"It refers to crocodiles inventing big stories," Croc Harry said, "which, I'll have you know, takes brain power."

"Did he make that up?" Horace asked Beatrice.

"I'm staying out of this. Both of you hush. The mangoes

in the refrigerator are for me to eat. And the thirty-six books here are for me to read. Hush and let me get to work."

Croc Harry rolled over to his side. Beatrice laid on her back and rested her head against Crocker's leather belly. Horace curled up in a ball on Beatrice's tummy.

Croc Harry whispered to Horace, "I won't even ask you to spell crocodiliosis."

"What does it mean?" Horace asked.

"It is what happens when a crocodile sprays his digestive juice on your skin. And I can assure you that any condition that ends with 'iosis' is not good."

"Is that twue?" Horace asked.

"I'm staying out of this," Beatrice said.

"Cwoc Harry, I'm asking, is that twue?" Horace said. "I like knowing what is real and what is concocted."

Croc Harry did not reply. Slowly, steadily, evenly, Beatrice grabbed the first book on the shelf. To silence her travelling companions, Beatrice began to hum. She hummed louder and louder until they finally got the message.

CHAPTER 27

Teleportation Now

The shelves beside Beatrice's bed contained only books that she had read before her time in Argilia. *The Hobbit. Beezus and Ramona. Henry and Ribsy. The Lord of the Rings. Brown Girl Dreaming. Harry Potter. The Wind in the Willows. Charlotte's Web. The Little Prince. Anne of Green Gables. Sugar Plum Ballerinas. The Reluctant Journal of Henry K. Larson. The Stone Thrower.* How strange! Although she could recall only the tiniest fragments of that life, she remembered the details of every single book. The stories came back to her with images as clear as the sun and the stars. They greeted her like old friends.

Beatrice lifted Horace off her lap, wriggled away from Croc Harry and stood up. She opened the first book. Perhaps she'd find a message waiting inside.

On the title page of *Charlotte's Web*, she saw sixteen

words that stunned her. In purple calligraphy. *From the library of the one and only Beatrice Stackhouse, Valencia County, the Queendom of Carolina.*

She began by examining all of the books on the top shelf. She opened the next book. And the next one. And the one after that. The same sixteen words in purple ink appeared on the title page of each book. She flipped through the books, turning every page of every tome, but there were no other clues or messages.

She said the words aloud: *Beatrice Stackhouse, Valencia County, the Queendom of Carolina.* She hoped they would trigger some memories. But nothing came back to her. Nothing at all.

On the second shelf beside Beatrice's bed, there was only one book. The cover was blank. No words appeared on the spine. Inside, the book appeared to be blank, except for the first page, which said: *In the event that he self-extricates from the forest of Argilia, Harold Crocton is hereby entitled to a limitless, five-year supply of reading material from the Orangetown Library, Valencia County, the Queendom of Carolina.*

Beatrice dropped the book.

Croc Harry had been resting patiently on his bed of straw, with his big eyes staring at Beatrice. She turned to look at him. He had tears in his eyes.

"Croc Harry, are you crying?"

No response.

She lay down on top of him and wrapped her arms around his sides, and said it again, "Were you crying, Croc Harry?"

"Just a bit of glandular production," he said.

"You were crying. I knew it. Do you know what I saw in there?"

"Yes. Beatrice Stackhouse and Harold Crocton. Those are our names. Or they were *once* our names."

"Who was I," Beatrice asked, "and who were you?"

"It can't be a happy story," Croc Harry said.

"Does it have a happy ending?"

"We are still here, and we are still together," Croc Harry said.

Horace hopped onto Beatrice's back. "Can't we make our own ending?"

"We shall see," Beatrice said.

On the third shelf beside her bed was one last book.

"Shall we read it together?"

"No," Croc Harry said, "Let's go back home. Back to Argilia. I'll swim in the river, you'll make oatmeal in your tree house, Horace can jump to the rainbow and back and we can palaver in the sun."

"Don't be afraid," Horace said. "I'll take care of you."

Croc Harry gave him a look. His nictitating membrane opened and shut. Another tear appeared. A butterfly fluttered at the window, but it could not get in. "I wish you could," Croc Harry said.

Beatrice gave Croc Harry a hug and a smile. "I'll build a fire."

Although she was still lying on his back, with her arms around his side, Croc Harry said nothing.

Beatrice got up, drew the hatchet from her bag and began splitting logs into kindling. She placed six thin sticks of kindling one way in the fireplace and then another six on top in a perpendicular direction. Beatrice put two logs on top and another log in the other direction on top of the first two. The fire was ready for lighting. A box of matches sat on the mantle. She lit the fire. It roared to life.

She noticed a box to the side of the fireplace. She opened it. Inside was a stack of old newspapers. *The Carolina Enquirer.* She picked out the very first paper. She saw a photo of a face on the front page. It was a close-up of a young girl with brown skin, a slight smile and a bottom tooth missing. Her hair was pulled back in eight perfect cornrows. They gleamed in the sunlight against a smooth scalp. Beatrice was looking at herself. Her mouth fell open. How could this be? She turned to call Croc Harry and Horace and saw that they had been right beside her, watching the whole time. They had seen everything.

"Wead it to us," Horace said.

Croc Harry flipped over onto his back. Beatrice lay down beside him. Horace nestled in between them. Beatrice stretched out her arms to hold up the newspaper so that they could all read together.

"Read it aloud," Croc Harry said. "I'll feel better hearing your voice. It will remind me that you are still alive."

"'The Carolina Enquirer, page one, November 23, 2090,'" she began. "So now we know the date."

"No, we don't," Croc Harry said. "We know when it happened. We don't know how much time has passed since then."

"When what happened?" Beatrice said.

"Are you sure we can't go back to Argilia?" Croc Harry said. "We can sneak past those humans. We can get by the electric gate."

"We are not made for walking backward," Beatrice said. "I only have eyes in the front of my head."

"Then read it, please," Croc Harry said, "and hold me tight."

Beatrice began by reading the headline: "'Girl and boy shot, gunman injured, in church invasion.'" She continued, "'With death imminent, controversial teleporting to the ancient forest of Argilia.'"

"Beatrice," Croc Harry sobbed. "I remember now. I am so, so sorry. I am sorry to you, too, Horace."

Horace had no means to calm his friend, so he hopped up and down on his back. "We'll work it out, Cwockers," Horace said.

"You know what happened, don't you Horace?" Croc Harry asked.

"I do," Horace said. In an unusually quiet voice, he added, "I am furious, but still, I'm kind of weady to forgive you. Maybe."

Beatrice dropped the newspaper. She looked at Horace.

Then at Croc Harry. She was utterly bumfuzzled. "I don't remember anything," Beatrice said.

"That's because you were hurt the most," Horace said.

"I still don't understand," Beatrice said.

"Read on," Horace said, "and you will lesson yourself."

Beatrice picked up the newspaper and continued reading.

Beatrice Stackhouse, her brother Horace Harrison, their parents and 200 other people in the African Methodist Episcopal Church in Orangetown, Valencia County, had been listening to a pastor—a woman named Geneviève Edwards—on Sunday, November 19, 2090, when a 25-year-old white man named Harold Crocton burst into the church with a stolen gun. He fired a shot into the ceiling and shouted out that it was a robbery and that every person should throw their wallets and purses into the aisle.

Nobody moved. Crocton fired into the ceiling once more. Screaming broke out, but the pastor calmed people down. She tossed her own purse down into the aisle. "No need for heroes, just do what he says," Geneviève Edwards called out.

Parishioners tossed their valuables into the aisle. A police officer burst into the church. Two others followed right behind him. Shouting erupted. Crocton spun around. He shot at an officer and missed. The bullet shattered a stained-glass window. The officer fired at Crocton. His bullet missed Crocton but passed through the arm of the eight-year-old named Horace Harrison Junior the Third. Horace screamed and fell into the aisle. His 12-year-old sister, Beatrice Stackhouse, jumped out of her seat.

The pastor yelled at her to sit back down. Eyewitnesses report that Beatrice ignored her pastor and took two steps toward her brother. She called out to him. But just as the name Horace left her lips, Crocton fired at the officer. He missed. His bullet struck Beatrice in the abdomen. It knocked her back. Clutching her belly, she fell near her brother. Beatrice ignored the trail of her own blood and kept crawling toward Horace. The officer fired again and hit Crocton in the chest. Crocton crumpled. His gun clattered on the floor.

Beatrice Stackhouse and Harold Crocton each sustained grave injuries. The loss of blood was massive. Neither was expected to live. Horace Harrison received an injury to his arm, but was expected to survive. They were airlifted by battery-powered, short-haul helicopters to the Valencia Central Hospital. Doctors fought to keep each of them alive, but the vital signs of the girl and the man were diminishing.

To save their lives, the Queen of Carolina invoked the Argilia Forest Escape. Teleportation was the only way, she claimed. The rules were that if teleportation was invoked, all injured parties had to be sent away together. Critics said the Queen wasted the forest magic on three lives—two of whom were children and one of whom was a criminal—when it had been intended to be used to resolve issues of war. Critics also noted that teleportation was meant to be reserved to save the life of a leader, but that Beatrice Stackhouse had not received the 90 percent grade required to qualify for Queendom Leadership Training. The Queen countered that the child had come very close, with a grade of 88 percent, and had fallen short only because she had been taking care of her own mother, who had become very ill. The child was a natural leader, the Queen said, and insisted that she would not stand by and let a potential leader die.

Since traditional medicine would not save the girl's life, the only solution was to dispatch all three injured parties to the magic forest. It was well known that there could only be one human at a time in Argilia, so Beatrice remained a girl. Horace Harrison was transformed into a speckled rabbit, and Harold Crocton into a King Crocodile. As for whether they will be able to reconcile and return together to the Queendom—that was anyone's guess.

Beatrice finished reading. She was exhausted. She still could not remember her family or what she'd been doing during the first twelve years of her life except for reading and horseback riding. But she did remember that she had heard a loud popping sound in the church and the burning hole in her belly. She had fallen to the ground near her purple purse, out of which spilled her favourite periwinkle locket. She worried that her younger brother might die.

She remembered thinking, *If only one of us can survive, let it be him. He is only eight. Let him have more years.* She remembered thinking about their different names. She had the last name of their mother, and he had the last name of their father. Crawling toward her brother on the floor and trying to call out to him but not finding the breath, Beatrice had wished they had exactly the same last name, so nobody would doubt that they were siblings.

Beatrice recalled a team of medics gathering around her at the hospital. A doctor called for a scalpel. A nurse wheeled in a stand equipped with a bag of blood. Beatrice could sense that her own spirit was readying to lift out of her body. The medics stood aside for Queen Arthuria, who strode up to the operating table and called out, "As Commander-in-Chief, I invoke teleportation this instant. Save the child!" Beatrice's memories ended there.

"I knew it was bad," Croc Harry called out. "I knew it was awful. You will hate me now. I will leave this instant and go back to Argilia."

"Stay," Beatrice said.

"Why? You'll never want to see me again."

"We have a journey to make."

"You have a journey," Croc Harry said. "For me, it's over."

"You, too, have a life to live."

"But I may die."

"You will not die," Horace said. "I forbid it."

"We have all survived," Beatrice said. "We have to get back to the Queendom. We have things to do, and people to help."

"Don't you want me to go away forever?" Croc Harry asked.

"We stay together," Beatrice said.

"But I have to ask," Horace said.

"What?" Beatrice said.

"I am addwessing Cwoc Harry," Horace said.

Croc Harry glanced over at the rabbit. His eyes were wide and watering again. It seemed that he anticipated Horace's question.

"Why the gun?" Horace asked.

"I was angry," Croc Harry said. "Angry, hungry, and I didn't know what to do. I had no work. They classified me a low labourer, even though I had a good brain. Once you got classified, you couldn't change it. I felt trapped. Couldn't find a job. I was sick and tired of seeing all the other people get jobs and education and . . ."

Horace put his paw in Beatrice's hand. Beatrice squeezed it tight.

"But why the gun?" Horace said.

"I needed food. I was lost in my anger. I went to the church to steal. I thought it would be easy money. Then it all went wrong. I started shooting. I never stopped to think about who might be hurt."

Croc Harry's eyes kept watering.

Beatrice got up and took a few steps back.

"I'm so very, very sorry," Croc Harry said.

Beatrice now knew that Horace Crocton had nearly killed her. She was sad about all the people who were hurt that day. Her parents and the other churchgoers would never forget the terror of seeing Beatrice and Horace fall. But she had survived. Now she was safe. She felt no anger. What good would it do to hate Croc Harry now?

It took Beatrice a moment to find the right words. "Had it not happened," she said, "I would never have learned how to glue shut the mouth of a crocodile."

"And I," Horace said, "would never have leapt halfway to a wainbow."

"And I might never have had any friends," Croc Harry said. "Before Argilia, no person ever read to me."

The fire burned low, and they all fell into a deep sleep.

CHAPTER 28

He Didn't Know a Thing About Her

Early in the morning, while listening to Croc Harry breathe heavily in his sleep and to the steady, happy snoring of Horace Harrison Junior the Third, Beatrice felt her foot trembling. She could not stop it from shaking. She imagined it would comfort her to do something she had done a thousand times before, so she got up and made oatmeal.

She had thought that they would all be safe in the house. But as light began to seep through the dark skies and dawn broke, Beatrice became aware that the giant was trying to get into her brain again. She wouldn't let him. Being outside Argilia and closer to the Queendom of Carolina, Beatrice felt confident that she could keep the door to her brain shut and never let him in. However, he was still trying.

"So I know your full name now, silly girl," he said. "Beatrice Stackhouse."

"You do not have permission to use my name," Beatrice said, "and I am not silly."

"You're silly enough to have gone walking in my brain, which gave me a good look at you. I know you fled Argilia. Aren't you scared?"

"Not of you," Beatrice said, although she was.

"We're hunting for you."

"You're a hunter, are you?"

"Men do that work for me."

"Go away," she said.

Beatrice remembered what he looked like from the time she had inhabited his brain. She could not see him now, but she had heard enough of his voice.

"Go away," she said again.

"Make me," he said, taunting her.

Beatrice stood up. She shut her eyes and opened them again. She focused on what she had learned about her past and how she had come to leave the Queendom, and on all the animals she had met in Argilia. Soon, she was sure that she had driven away the voice of the giant. She was determined to close the door to his voice and keep him out of her head.

She put the slingshot in her pocket, carried a large bowl of oatmeal outside, moulded the food into a huge pile on a stump and took twenty steps. She pulled back her slingshot and let the stone fly. *Thwump.* The shot tore through a section of oatmeal, splattering it all over the bushes and trees. She formed another heaping ball of oatmeal, took thirty steps back, pulled back the sling, squinted with one eye and let it fly again. In that instant, Horace Harrison Junior the Third came out of the door and hopped toward the stump. Splat. Beatrice hit a bull's eye. The pile of oatmeal exploded. A hurricane of wet oats and raisins covered Horace's face.

"That's how you gweet your bwother in the morning?" Horace said.

She let out a giggle. "So sorry. Does your poor old fur need a shampoo?"

"You sound like a big sister. What are you doing?"

"Target practice," she said.

"You weally smashed that oatmeal," he said.

"Felt good."

"The oatmeal didn't stand a chance," Horace said.

"Somebody made me mad. I was thinking about what I'd like to do to him."

"What happened to that sweet Beatwice who was lessoning me in the forest?"

"She was a figment of your imagination."

"Fig. Is that from a fig twee?"

"No. Figment means an invention. That sweet girl was an invention of yours."

"So you are not sweet?"

"I can be sweet when I want. But I'm not in a sweet mood when people want to hurt me."

Horace hopped off to wash himself in a stream. Beatrice stepped inside to awaken Croc Harry.

"Come on, sleepyhead, it's time to go."

"We don't even know where we're going," he said.

"We have to keep searching."

"Last night," Croc Harry said, "we stopped reading after the newspaper account. You never opened the book on the bottom shelf."

Beatrice bent down, took the book, lay back down on Croc Harry's back and held the book straight out with her arms, so they could both read it.

The book was full of blank pages, except for the first page, in which she found, once again, the purple calligraphy, which began,

Beatrice, Horace and Croc Harry, if you are reading this, your journey remains urgent. You are outside the protections of the magic of Argilia Forest. You must pass all the way through the Contested Lands before you can reach the Queendom of Carolina. Powerful enemies oppose the constitution of the Queendom. The enemies are working on breaking the code and attempting to enter Argilia.

Beatrice put the book down and thought about the giant. "They have already broken the code," she said. "We have to report that to the Queen."

"If we ever get there," Croc Harry said.

Beatrice kept reading. The message said that Argilia had

been created to allow people who had been mortally wounded after grievous conflict to recover—as long as they made peace with each other and worked together to solve problems. The note went on:

You will have to take care of yourselves and each other. If you confront our enemies successfully, look for a hill so steep that it is named The Struggle. Find a castle with three purple doors. You must pass to enter my Queendom. Do not delay. Our enemies are bearing down on you.

* * *

It had become a hot, sunny day. After leaving the white house with purple shutters in the morning, they walked for hours. The thick forest gave way to a meadow with a long footpath bordered by strange-looking brown plants with big, bulbous heads. As they travelled along the path, one plant leaned toward Beatrice, opened up and nipped at her leg.

"Ouch," she said.

Horace hopped up and leaned against her. "What's that?"

"That plant took a bite out of me. Watch out. Don't touch it."

Horace bent over. He removed a chewing stick from his mouth and poked the plant. It opened again, grabbed the stick and pulled it right out of Horace's paws.

Beatrice stepped up and put her hand on the rabbit's back.

"Horace, we have no time for you to be making trouble. Let's go."

"Hey," Horace said, "that's my chewing stick. Give it back."

The plant swallowed the stick. Horace batted the plant with his front left paw. The plant opened suddenly and clamped onto his rear paw.

"Ow," Horace said. "Help. I'm being attacked."

Beatrice peered down. "Didn't I tell you not to touch that plant?"

"I'm being attacked," Horace shouted. "It is quite possibly fatal. Is this the time for a lecture?"

"Shush," Beatrice said. "You'll be fine."

"Help me!"

Beatrice took the hatchet from her belt. She hacked off the stem, near the top. Horace retrieved his paw, which was bleeding and bruised, but intact.

"You executed a most fortunate decapitation," Horace said.

"Walk more quietly and listen to my instructions," she said.

"Nag nag nag," he said.

"Say that again," Beatrice muttered, "and it will be the last time I save your toe."

After the meadow, the path re-entered the forest. Beatrice climbed the tallest cedar tree and saw a wide, north-flowing river in the distance.

When she came back down, Horace leaned against her left leg and Croc Harry, her right. "I wish I could climb too," Horace said. "I'd feel more useful."

"How do you think I feel," Croc Harry said, "slung low to the ground in an endless forest with no water in sight?"

"We'll get to the water," Beatrice said. "Carry on."

They continued through the winding woods. Occasionally, when the path was blocked, Beatrice had to use the hatchet to chop through fallen logs so that Croc Harry could pass. Croc Harry had the jaws to tear apart an antelope or a baby hippo, but he could not pass through a thicket of rose bushes or over a huge pile of logs.

Beatrice stumbled forward on the trail, with the rabbit and the crocodile labouring behind her. Beatrice rounded a corner. She came face to face with a man. A tall man with not a trace of kindness in his eyes. He had a quiver of arrows on his belt. He held a bow.

He was not the giant from her dreams, but he resembled him. Not as powerfully set. This one was very tall. Through a torn shirt, Beatrice could see the outline of his ribs. He looked like a hunter who had not been eating.

"You are the Black from Argilia," he said, in a flat, even tone. He raised his bow.

"Stop," she said. Where was Croc Harry? Hiding, maybe. She saw Horace go low to the ground and crawl, unnoticed, past the hunter.

"We were looking for you. There is a bounty on your head. My family and I will eat plentifully for a month if I bring you in dead. We will eat for three months if I bring you in alive."

"You have a family? Where are they?"

He removed an arrow from his quiver and inched it into the bow.

"Put that down," Beatrice said. "Let's talk."

His face was smeared with mud, and he wore army fatigues. His hair was matted and fingernails filthy.

"Why did you call me Black?" she said.

"You are all the same. Filthy. Trying to take over the world."

"How would you know what I'm like?"

"You can't fool me. I know what's up."

Beatrice sensed that if she could get the hunter to talk, maybe Croc Harry would save her.

"No, you don't," she told the hunter. "You just called me filthy. But I am clean and you are unwashed."

"I have poison in my arrow tip. Enough to knock you out. But you're a tiny little peanut. Maybe it will kill you. Guess we'll see."

"There is no need for violence. We can palaver."

"Your queen wants you back. But with you as our captive, we can negotiate. Our Master Giant prefers that we take you back alive."

"Please do not do this. There is another way."

The man did not listen. He had no capacity to listen. It was clear to Beatrice that he didn't care about her in any way. He didn't know a thing about her, but still he wanted to hurt her.

"I'm asking you to stop," Beatrice said. "Wait a minute."

The hunter refused to meet her eyes. He raised his bow, pointed the arrow low and shot.

Beatrice felt a searing pain in her left thigh. It was hot. Burning hot. The arrow was stuck in her leg. She was about to scream, but suddenly she felt sleepy. Her eyes became blurry. She saw the hunter retrieve another arrow. This time, would he kill her? He slid the arrow into place. He drew back the bow.

In that instant, Horace sank his front teeth into the hunter's Achilles tendon. The hunter let out a furious cry, whipped around and kicked. Horace went somersaulting through the air. The hunter turned back to Beatrice, who felt the whoosh of air as Croc Harry leapt right over her head. Croc Harry took the man's arm in his mouth, gathered him into a death roll and flipped him hard on the earth. His head smacked a log, and he lost consciousness. Croc Harry raced over to nudge Beatrice with his nose.

"He shot me," Beatrice said.

"I can fix you up," Croc Harry said.

"It's a poison arrow."

"Crocs have antibodies. We have antibodies as strong as any animal or reptile on the planet."

Croc Harry didn't warn her. He didn't tell her it was going to hurt. He instructed Horace to grab hold of the arrow and yank it hard. Horace did as he was told. Beatrice felt the arrow rip her skin, but her leg already felt numb, like it was no longer part of her. Beatrice was bleeding. She was trembling. She was hot. She wanted to sleep. Forever.

"Stay with me Beatrice," Croc Harry said, as he kept one of his legs against her shoulder.

Horace hopped up and down wildly, stopping only long enough to lean right against her ear.

"Beatwice. Beatwice. Don't die. Don't die. I insist."

Croc Harry nudged Horace gently with his tail. "Pick up that sharp rock, over there." Horace obeyed and came back with it to lean against the crocodile. "Scratch my underbelly. Hard enough to make me bleed."

"But . . ."

"Now!"

Horace did as he was told. He made the crocodile bleed. A small, steady stream of blood flowed from the cut.

Croc Harry held his bleeding cut against Beatrice's bleeding leg.

"Push her leg against my cut belly," Croc said. "Yes. Like that."

Horace pushed with all his might. After a minute, Beatrice began to move more easily. The fog lifted from her eyes. The pain faded.

"Feeling better?" Croc Harry asked.

"A lot," she said.

"Croc antibodies are the best," he said. "That's why we live so long."

"Could you please live forever?"

"No promises."

Within a minute, Beatrice felt entirely better. She pulled out her first aid kit and put a bandage over her cut.

"You'll be fine with my antibodies," he said.

"Shall I stitch you up too?" Beatrice asked.

"No, it's only a nick," Croc Harry said.

"You saved me," Beatrice said. "I owe you one."

"Don't mention it," Croc Harry said.

"Do mention it," Horace said. "Lay the love on *me*."

Beatrice rubbed his fur. "Hello, little brother," she said. Horace Harrison Junior the Third hopped all around her, drawing his front and hind paws together in the air, and then releasing them when he landed.

"What are you doing?" she said.

"It's a binky," Horace said. "I jump like that when I'm weally happy. You just called me bwother!"

Before they left, Beatrice examined the hunter and picked his pockets.

Croc Harry laughed. "Hey, you're pretty good at that. I used to be the best pickpocket in the Queendom, but I'm not much use with these short, stubby arms and legs."

In the hunter's pocket, Beatrice found a card. It said *Private Richard Colter, Mercenary, Eleventh Squadron, Anti-Queendom Liberation Army. Certified 100 percent Pureblood. Purity. Segregation. Supremacy.*

Beatrice put the card in her bag. Maybe it would interest the Queen. Croc Harry whacked the private on the head with his tail.

"That should keep him knocked out a little longer," he said.

"Thank you for not killing him," she said.

"My killing days are over," Croc Harry said.

They resumed their journey. Beatrice felt as strong and healthy as before. But after an hour, with the sun beating down on them and no water in sight, Croc Harry began to slow down. He panted heavily as he walked.

"Why don't you stick out your tongue when you pant?" she asked.

He did not answer. She remembered that she could only hear him if she was touching him. Life had been so much easier in Argilia, but now that she had to touch him before she could understand him, she felt their friendship deepening. They took a break, and she climbed on his back. Horace was exhausted and asked to be allowed to nap in the Beasack. She zipped him in.

"My tongue," Croc Harry said, "is stuck to the bottom of my mouth. It does not move."

"What a shame," she said. "No ice cream cones for you."

"How do you know about ice cream cones?" he said.

"I don't know," she said, "but the farther we walk from Argilia and the closer we get to the Queendom of Carolina, the more I remember things. Once I ate a double-decker ice cream cone with gummy bears on top."

"What flavour?" he asked.

"A towering chocolate scoop on top and an equally towering vanilla scoop on the bottom."

"Yum," Croc Harry said.

"If you're going to have an ice cream cone on the hottest summer day, towering is the only way to go. But you need a tongue, because when it melts, it starts to run down the cone. Gotta be fast to catch all those rivers of ice cream. There's a science to it. You divide your attention in a sixty-forty split."

"What does that mean?"

"Sixty percent of the time, you lick down from the top. The other forty percent, you mind your rivers and lick them up from the bottom before the ice cream runs all over your hand."

"What else do you remember about the towering ice cream?"

"I was eating it in the playground. I was standing at the bottom of a giant slide, taking my time and managing the sixty-forty perfectly. Three boys had been swinging on a horizontal bar. A man gave me a disapproving look, walked over to one of the boys and whispered something in his ear. The man walked off. Just before the boy left with his friends, he turned and called me a ragamuffin."

"What does that even mean?" Croc Harry asked.

"I'm not exactly sure," Beatrice said, "but I think it's just some mean way to talk about a person who is dirty or in ragged clothes. It made me feel awful. I had been liking the way I looked that day, but when I heard that, I just wanted to go home and cry. When mean boys come along, they are always in a gang. They always pick on someone smaller."

"I think, once, I was a mean boy just like that," Croc Harry said.

"Good thing you grew out of it," Beatrice said.

"I was angry," Croc Harry said. "I was not a person you would have wanted to know. But if anybody said an awful thing to you now, I'd have a bone to pick with them."

"If you were teeming with anger, it must have been a long time ago. Long before I met you."

"It was up until the moment that I hurt you," he said.

"Stop worrying about what happened a long time ago," she said.

"But I shot you," he said.

"You are going to have to let that go, Croc Harry," Beatrice said.

"I will make it up to you," he said.

"You already have saved my life twice," Beatrice said. "You are here with us. We are travelling together. That is what friends do. They do things together. They remember the things that they and only they have shared."

"So what else did those boys do?" he said.

"One of them said something about how I was chocolate, and that I couldn't have vanilla," Beatrice said. "It made me feel so ugly. But there was no way I would let them see me cry. The biggest boy knocked me down, snatched away the ice cream cone, shouted something about me being dirty chocolate and shoved the cone into my back. They all ran away. My mother came out of the store and found me on my hands and knees on the playground with ice cream all over my back. 'How on earth did you get that mess on your back?' she asked. But I did not tell her. I didn't want her to know what had happened. Didn't want to share my humiliation."

"You had no reason to be humiliated," Croc Harry said. "The boy shamed himself by acting badly."

"But haven't you noticed—when somebody does something bad to you, the natural instinct is for *you* to feel bad?"

"So what did you do?"

"Nothing. Mostly, I wanted to forget it, and I didn't want my mother to worry."

"Beatrice, wait," Croc Harry said.

"What?"

"You just remembered your mother."

"Yes!" she shouted. "I had a mother. She helped me get changed. She washed the dirty shirt. But I don't remember anything else about her. Not even her face."

"Nothing else?"

"One thing. She said, 'You wasted a ten-dollar double-scoop ice cream cone and you are quadruple silly, Beatrice Lucinda Stackhouse."

"So now you remember your mother and even your middle name," Croc Harry said.

"Yes!" she shouted again. And then she smiled. "I remember my mother saying, 'No other child in the history of the Queendom of Carolina has sullied her own back with chocolate and vanilla ice cream.' She had a laughing, playful voice.

'What's sullied?' I asked her. 'It's what you just did to your own shirt.' I also remember a bit of our game after that. We began walking. She held my hand. I looked at our fingers, intertwined. It was the first time I noticed that our fingers looked different. Mine were brown, and hers were white. I said, 'How about Neapolitan ice cream? Has anybody ever got that on their back?' 'Nope,' she said. 'Licorice ice cream?' 'Absolutely not.' 'Pistachio?' I asked. 'Never in the history of this planet,' she said. 'Mint chocolate chip?' 'An utter impossibility.' And so we carried on, as we walked home."

"Do you remember anything else?"

"Not for now."

"Those boys who took your ice cream cone. They sound like the hunter who shot you. There are people who do not wish you well, Beatrice."

"The hunter's identification card talked about purity and segregation."

"What do those words mean?" Croc Harry asked.

"I read about them in my dictionary," Beatrice said. "Some people think they are pure. They imagine that the people in their family are all from the same type. And they want to keep other people apart from them. They want the people they consider to be impure to be treated badly. But the whole thing is whack. It is ridiculous. The idea of purity makes no sense."

"What do you mean?"

"My dictionary explained it."

"What did it say?"

"I remember exactly. It said that maple syrup can be called pure, if you boil down the sap and don't add water to it. But blood can't be pure. Blood is blood. There are different types of blood, but no one type is better or more pure than another. People can't be pure, either. We have ancestors going back thousands of years. We are a mix of everything. Calling some people pure is just an excuse to treat other people badly. Some say that people of different colours should not mix. That they should be kept apart. Segregated. But that's just mean. And where does it leave me? I seem to be from people of different colours. I remember my mother's white skin, and I see my very brown skin. I bet that my father's skin, if I still have a father, is very dark indeed."

"I remember people who hate," Croc Harry said. "I was once one of them. I was so angry. I was living in the Queendom of Carolina and my heart was full of venom. Everybody else seemed to have everything. I thought I had nothing. It made me want to hurt people."

"Well," Beatrice said, "you got over it. So lighten up and keep going. Me strong like croc," she said, beating her chest. "Me strong with croc antibodies."

* * *

They walked for hours. Croc Harry panted and wheezed in the sun. They crossed a tiny stream and stopped to take a break. Beatrice scooped out water and dropped it all over his back.

"Getting hot," he said.

She climbed another tree and came back down. She climbed onto Croc Harry's back so they could talk while they rested. "It's just up ahead. We are almost at the water."

"My arms and legs are aching," he said. "I am not made for long-distance walking."

Beatrice laughed. "I don't know how you manage all the walking, with arms and legs like toothpicks."

Croc Harry didn't reply. He was still panting.

"Soon," Beatrice said, "you will be in the place where you can be yourself."

"Beatrice," he said. His voice grew low and sombre.

"What is it, Crockers? Tell me quickly, because we must keep moving."

"Do you know what a zoo is?"

"I have read about them."

"If I make it to the Queendom . . ."

"Of course, you will make it."

"If I make it, I do not want to be put in a zoo. I would sooner die."

"I won't let that happen."

Neither had any more to say, so they began to walk to the river. It looked like a body of water that could sustain a crocodile. It flowed as far as the eye could see, and it was too wide for Beatrice to throw a stone across. That, she decided, was the measure of a crocodile-friendly river. Long and deep and un-stone-throwable. Beatrice felt relieved that Croc Harry could finally be back where he belonged. In the water. Free. Able to draw in so much air in his nostrils that he could float effortlessly at the surface, then expel the air in an instant, close his palatal valve, and sink down into the depths, where he could hunt or hide or do flips for the fun of it. Beatrice wanted to find her way home, but equally, she wanted Croc Harry to be free and mighty in his own home. She also wanted Horace Harrison Junior the Third to find peace and love and confidence, and she felt grateful to feel him breathing heavily and sleeping deeply in the bottom of her Beasack.

CHAPTER 29

Nothing Wrong With Her Skin

Croc Harry swished strongly with his tail. Beatrice lay flat on his back, and Horace sat on hers. They slid smoothly over the water and entered a lake with deep, clear water.

"Could you do some flips with me? It might be our last bit of fun," Beatrice said.

"Ready?" he said.

"Excuse me," Horace hollered from his resting spot in the Beasack. "Have you consulted me about this play session? I'm opting out."

Croc Harry swam over to the bank. Beatrice unzipped her sack and let Horace hop out on land. Then she took a deep breath.

The crocodile dove down ten feet, and then tucked in his tail and did a total rollover. She held on fiercely as he spun her like a wheel and then straightened out and brought her to the surface for air.

She gasped three times and caught her breath. "More!" she shouted.

He dove down again, swished his tail mightily to speed back toward the surface and flew through the air like a dolphin. She took another breath before he nosed back into the depths.

For an hour, they gavotted and cavorted and amused themselves in the water. A school of brilliant orange fish stopped right there and watched them in the water, opening and closing their mouths in rapid succession to applaud the sight.

Finally, when Croc Harry reached the surface of the water again, Beatrice gasped for a minute and said that she couldn't hold her breath any longer.

"I kept busy in Argilia, but now that I'm out, it sure is good to play."

Croc Harry swam to the shore and climbed out to bask in the sun. Beatrice remained sprawled on his back.

"I haven't had that much fun since, well, I don't even remember," she said.

"Every child needs their fun," Croc Harry said. "It's a FUN-damental right. The necessities of life are food, shelter and fun."

"And books," Beatrice said.

"I seem to remember reading and loving books," Croc

Harry said, "but not recently. My arms are too short to hold a book."

"That's a real pity," Beatrice said.

"Short arms is the cause of crocohypo-literosis," Croc Harry said.

Horace hopped over to join them. "I hope you two are having fun."

"Do you have a problem with us having fun?" Beatrice said.

"You were splishing and splashing, and I was all alone twiddling my paws. And is cwocohypo-literosis even a word?"

"It is now," Beatrice said. "Look it up in the dictionary."

"I'm glad Beatwice left that dictionary in the tree house," Horace said. "It weighs too much for travel. And it took her attention away from me. So just tell me. What does cwocohypo-literosis mean?"

"It means that fewer and fewer crocs are reading these days," Croc Harry said.

Beatrice laughed.

"I hate feeling left out," Horace said.

"What if you perch on my shoulder and keep a lookout while I'm here on Croc Harry's back?" Beatrice said.

Horace climbed onto Beatrice's shoulder. "I'm top wabbit now. Yeah. Look at me."

They continued their journey downstream. After a few minutes of travel, Horace fell again into a deep sleep. Beatrice tucked him into her Beasack and still he did not awaken.

Croc Harry swam on for hours. Beatrice asked if he tired of swishing his tail in the water.

"Locomotion comes easily to me in the water," Croc Harry said. "And I want to get there too."

"Get where?"

"Wherever we are going. I want to get you there safely."

"What about you?" she said. "Don't you want to be safe?"

"My days are numbered," he said.

"Nonsense," she said. "Why can't we be friends forever?"

"In your memories, do you ever recall a girl and a crocodile being best friends?"

"I still don't remember much." But Beatrice did remember something. After she was shot but before she lost consciousness, she had wondered: *I did nothing to that man, so why would he shoot me? He must be very confused. I wish somebody had spoken to him. I wish somebody had helped him so he wouldn't go hurting people.* Beatrice decided not to tell that to Croc Harry. It would only make him feel bad.

At the far end of the lake, they entered another river.

"Humans ahead," Croc Harry said.

"I don't see anybody," she said.

"Do you know how far a mile is?" he asked.

"Yes. It is 1.6 kilometres."

"Exactly. I can smell blood a mile away. That's why I am such a good hunter."

"Should I get out and walk while you swim under them?"

"No. There are many humans. I can smell them. You cannot go onto the land. You shall have to hold your breath again, and this time, it will not be to play."

"All right." She awoke Horace.

"Can you hold your breath for thirty seconds?" Croc Harry asked.

"I will have to."

"What about you, Horace?"

"I will manage," he said, "but I hate getting wet and matted."

"Do you have any idea what swimming usually does to my hair?" Beatrice said. "But I'm cornrowed, so I can swim with impunity."

"What's impunity?" Horace asked.

"It means with no punishment," Croc Harry said. "With no consequences."

"Know-it-all," Horace said. He turned to study Beatrice's hair. "Humans have hairstylists," he said. "Wabbits don't."

"You don't need a stylist," Beatrice said. "You need a makeover."

"Hey. That's not funny."

"Shhh," Croc Harry said. "I'm about to save your bacon."

"Could we say that another way?" Beatrice said. "How about save your mangoes?"

"Save your carrots," Horace shouted.

"Save your oats," Beatrice yelled.

"Save your celery," Horace said.

"Quiet now," Croc Harry said. "Soon you will have to take a deep breath."

As they moved over the water, Beatrice could make out a boat, far ahead. As they drew closer, she could see two men in it, standing in the same army fatigues that the mercenary soldier had worn. But they did not have bows and arrows. They had rifles. They were scanning the river.

"There she is," one of the men shouted, "floating over there."

"She must be dead," the other said.

"Let's shoot her now," the first one said.

"No, if she is alive, we must take her back. Think of the reward! We will have houses and food if we take her back alive. Food for months!"

"I would just as soon shoot that little Black girl," one man said.

Beatrice disliked the way he said the word, because he spoke with hatred. Listening to him made her decide to like her own skin colour even more. She was a girl. She had brown skin. There was nothing wrong with her skin and nobody was going to make her feel bad about it. She had survived in the forest of Argilia. She could talk to every animal in the land. She made the best oatmeal in the world. Beatrice could read books and teach rabbits and crawl in and out of a crocodile's stomach and blast apart a pile of oatmeal with her slingshot. She wasn't anybody's *little Black girl*. She was Beatrice Lucinda Stackhouse. Period!

"Hang on," Croc Harry said.

"She's moving quickly," a man shouted. "It's a trick. Shoot her."

The men raised their rifles.

"Take your last breath now," Croc Harry said. Then he dove down. Her ears popped. Never had she felt his tail swing that fast. He felt as powerful in the deep as a galloping horse did on land. Once she had galloped on a horse. Who was she with? Her father? Had he taught her to ride? Metal bullets zinged through the water, steaming hot and smashing apart the rocks beneath them. She was almost out of air. They came up fast, suddenly motionless, by a log.

"Hang onto that log and just keep Horace in the bag barely out of water. Stay till I come back." He tossed her off. She held onto the log and kept Horace above the surface and looked over at the men, facing the wrong way, still shooting into the water.

"Careful," she whispered to Croc Harry, even though she knew he could not hear her.

Beatrice counted slowly. By the time she reached five, she saw a tail flash out of the water and flip the boat over. The two men fell into the river. They flailed and shouted, but could no longer shoot. She saw Croc Harry smash the boat apart with his tail. And then he disappeared. Seconds later, he scooped up Beatrice and Horace and swished them downstream.

They saw nothing else until the sun set and the river neared its end. The water fed into a deep pond and then shot out

over an edge. It tumbled way down into a set of massive tur-
bines. It would mean instant death to try to cross over, so
they climbed onto the shore. Beatrice led the way to a road
that seemed little travelled. There were no horses or carts, or
people. She found a small sign on a flat stretch of road. *The
Struggle: Ten kilometres.*

CHAPTER 30

One Last Grand Palaver

When they came to a river, they stopped and waited for darkness to fall. Croc Harry lay in the water, hiding among the reeds. Beatrice rested on his back, and Horace stayed on hers.

"Beatrice," Croc Harry said, "if I don't make it, please—"

"There will be none of that talk," Beatrice said.

"But Beatrice—"

"None!"

Croc Harry made a waving motion with his body, which was his way of saying "pay attention now." Just as Beatrice was about to ask him what he wanted to say, she felt the giant again, scratching at the door to her brain.

"I can feel bad vibrations," Croc Harry said.

Beatrice patted Croc Harry's head. "I've got this," she said.

"I feel his presence too," Horace said, "and I feel that he is not a wabbit-loving man."

Beatrice reached a hand over her shoulder to pat Horace's head. She got off the crocodile's back and walked through the water and up on to the riverbank, then turned her face to the sky and closed her eyes.

"Giant," she said, "you are wasting my time."

"I know you are on the move, Beatrice," he said.

She shuddered to hear him say her name. She did not like the idea that someone who wished to harm her also knew her name.

"This is my territory. I know you have to reach the castle with the three purple doors to enter the Queendom. But I shall intercept you, Beatrice. I shall destroy your companions while you watch. And then I will take you to my lands and steal your brain."

"I would sooner die," she said.

"Why don't we avoid more fighting?" he said. "Aren't you satisfied? You and your pals already hurt my little brother. If you open the door and let me in, I will forgive that transgression."

"That was your brother?" Beatrice said. "The one who shot me with the arrow?"

"The hunter. Not much of a conversationalist, but he shoots true."

"That is how you treat your own brother?" Beatrice said. "He was half-starved. His own family doesn't have enough to eat."

"Not your concern," he said.

"Some brother you are," Beatrice said. She could sense that she was provoking him, and as he got angrier, his face came more clearly into view in her mind. No hair, except the huge eyebrows, and a protruding forehead. She could see him purse his lips. Good. He was angry now. She was getting to him. If she could use his own energy against him, she could vault into his brain again.

"You let your own brother and his family starve," Beatrice continued, "and you call that leadership? You call that a way to run that world of yours?"

"Hey," he said, "no half-pint girl is going to . . ."

"Don't call me half-pint."

"Nobody defies me! I am the giant."

Beatrice knew that to upset the giant, all she had to do was talk back at him. It scared her to do it, but she knew it was necessary. She pretended to herself that she was acting in a play. She pretended that her role was to do the one thing that adults hated, which was to show them no respect. So she stepped into her acting role and looked for the best words to get under his skin.

"I'll show YOU who's boss," Beatrice shouted.

"Don't be sassy," the giant said.

"Don't call me sassy. I have a voice and I am going to use it. You're the one who is sassy. You're to blame for all of this. I'll slap you so hard, you'll wake up next Tuesday."

The giant's face turned red. He began to hyperventilate.

Beatrice's strategy was working. She could see the opening in his brain. She walked toward the door. One step. Two steps. Three. In she went.

She had glimpsed him in her dream, but now she hoped to get another look at how tall he was and the size of his legs and arms, and anything else that might show her how to confront him on The Struggle. But all she could see was what he saw with his own eyes. She could also see what he thought. She saw endless lineups of men, women and children. They were waiting for cold, stale food that ran out before everyone was served. Hungry people were then offered bread and jam to tattle on each other.

People were to keep to their own colour. They were not to be friends with or live with or love anyone of any different colour. People who were neither men nor women were kept in filthy camps. Many people had fled the Queendom to serve the giant because he had promised them jobs, food and homes. But in the Giant's Land, they were ranked and taught to hate each other. They were kept hungry. When they fought and bickered, the giant locked them in camps. Beatrice could not understand all that she saw, but she understood that everything about the Giant's Land was wrong. Even there, people needed help. But Beatrice would never be able to do anything about it unless she made it to the Queendom.

"I have seen you, Beatrice Stackhouse," the giant said. "And I will find you."

Beatrice ran to the exit and leapt from his brain.

* * *

Horace was jumping up and down on Beatrice's chest. "Get up, Beatwice, get up," he said, sobbing, hugging her, and sobbing again. "Wake up. Snap out of it."

Beatrice opened her eyes. She had fallen onto the rocks on the riverbank. Apart from Croc Harry and Horace, there was nothing on the massive bed of rocks but a lone purple flower. She wondered about the miracle of it taking root in a bed of rocks and growing strong against all odds.

"You were convulsing," Horace said. "Don't do that. We need you, okay? I pwomise never to upset you and always to listen to you, if you'll just snap out of it."

Horace used his paw to wipe her lips, gently. "You have white froth all over your mouth." He hopped nervously on the rocks as Croc Harry approached and opened his mouth, which was full of water. Horace reached inside for some water and splashed Beatrice's face.

"Was that crocodile spit?" she asked.

Horace raised his paws and frowned. "Don't look at me."

Beatrice gave Croc Harry a big hug and stood up. "Let's go," she said.

"Wight," Horace said.

"No more nightmares," Croc Harry said.

"It wasn't a nightmare. It was a vision. But let's go."

* * *

After they had walked without incident for an hour, Beatrice noticed a purple knapsack glowing in the dark. It sat on a long, flat cart on wheels. A harness ran from the back of the knapsack to the front of the cart. Inside the bag, Beatrice found a slingshot, five round purple stones that fit perfectly into her palm and a note written in purple ink.

The road ahead is dangerous. My powers are limited outside the walls of the Queendom, but this harness gives you one hundred times your usual strength. Pull the cart for as long as you can. As long as you are moving, Croc Harry, Horace and you will all be invisible. The slingshot and stones are for your protection. Get home safely.

Beatrice paused for a moment to study the note. Whose diction was that? Was it the Queen speaking to her? Ms. Rainbow? But she had no more time to consider it.

"Can you get up on the cart?" Beatrice asked Croc Harry.

The crocodile's voice was low and weak, and getting harder to understand. She had to hug him extra hard to make out his words.

"No need to pull me," he said.

"You must conserve your strength," she said. "Come on, get up."

Croc Harry was so exhausted after his long bout of road-walking that he could barely crawl onto the cart. Beatrice tossed her Beasack onto the wagon. She strapped on the special knapsack. She tightened the wide belt around her waist and the straps that ran up her chest and over each shoulder. With some effort, she began to pull Croc Harry on the road to The Struggle. Horace hopped along beside her. Once she got moving, it wasn't so hard to keep going. She pulled and pulled and pulled, and vowed to help him for as long as she could on this road. After all, he had carried her over lakes and rivers. She glanced back to say something to him but saw nothing. Then she looked down and could not see her own arms or legs or body. That came as a comfort. If she couldn't see herself, then she supposed nobody else could either.

She kept to the right side of the road and stiffened as she saw five mercenaries, in patrol, all carrying swords.

"The dirty Queen wants to bring the girl back, so she must be a leader in waiting. We are to kill the croc and the rabbit, and take her alive," the lead mercenary said. His eyes swept the road and kept glancing at the thick forest that grew up to the edge of the pavement. He and his fellow mercenaries walked right by Beatrice, Horace and Croc Harry, as she kept pulling.

Beatrice heard that word. *Dirty*. Whenever the giant or his brother or their people didn't like someone, they called that person dirty. Beatrice remembered nothing of the Queen, but she was quite positive that Her Highness bathed daily and had not a speck of dirt on her clothes.

A full moon slid out from behind the clouds. Beatrice

could see that the road had begun to rise. The forest hemmed them in on the left. On the right, she saw that they were on the edge of a hill. Up ahead, as the road steepened, the hill became a cliff.

The muscles in her legs were screaming. They felt full of lead. Her shoulders and back ached. Beatrice slowed down. Finally, the hill became too steep and she could pull no longer.

Just before the cart began to slide backward, Beatrice grabbed her Beasack, slipped off the special knapsack and said, "Quick, get off." She turned and saw Croc Harry again as he slid off the wagon instantly. She didn't want the wagon to fall into enemy hands, so she shoved it off the cliff and heard it clatter on the rocks below. She lay down quickly on Croc Harry. "Can you make it up that hill?"

"I must," he said. "So I will."

"Aren't you going to dignify me with the same question?" Horace said.

"Horace, can you hop up that hill?"

"I would hop up a mountain for you, Beatwice. I would hop up ten mountains. Ten thousand mountains. Ten million—"

"Save your breath. Just hop."

They climbed for an hour on a road that ran beside the edge of a cliff. At the top of the road, she could see a castle with three glowing, purple doors. Beatrice felt a sudden, aching awareness: she didn't even know her people, but for the first time since she had awoken in the forest of Argilia, she could imagine, and almost see, the faces and limbs of those she had loved. She could almost hear their voices. She wanted to be part of a family, part of a community, but she had been removed from them and didn't even know if they were alive. And she was not sure how long she could carry on alone.

Then she considered all the people who lived alone. What about those whose mothers and fathers and sisters and brothers had died? How did they keep going when there was no one left to love them? Even if your loved ones were all dead and gone, you still had to remember your people. You had to remember that they had loved you and you had loved them, and you had to believe that you had to keep going, if only to show others how to live and how to love. Beatrice suddenly imagined a village full of girls, each one having lost her parents and family, but each one moving forward, walking on and building a life for herself. Perhaps Beatrice still had a family. Perhaps she did not. She had Croc Harry and Horace, and she had the memory of Fuzzy, and she had herself, and that was enough for now. Beatrice would not give up.

Six mercenaries appeared out of the darkness, each with a sword at the ready. Their faces were smeared with mud. Five of them were tall and lean and looked like they had not been eating well. The sixth was a head taller than all the others and full of bulk and muscle and anger. That one had clearly been eating.

"They must be around here," one said. "Our intelligence reports said to intercept them on The Struggle."

Beatrice and Croc Harry lay flat on the road to make themselves as hard to see as possible.

Beatrice removed the slingshot silently from her bag, inserted a stone and pulled the sling back as far as she could.

Mist covered the road. Up ahead, Beatrice could see the purple doors.

The lead mercenary took a few steps forward and spotted them. "There! Attack."

They drew their swords and stormed forward. Beatrice let one stone fly and hit a soldier on the head. He fell over. She shot another stone and hit a second mercenary in the eye. He fell down screaming. She broke the kneecap of a third tall man, and he tumbled to the ground.

Two mercenaries advanced toward Beatrice. Croc Harry swept them both off the cliff with his tail. They fell screaming into the void. Croc Harry high-walked forward, beside Beatrice. The purple doors were only steps away.

Three steps away . . . Two steps away . . .

Beatrice reached toward the handle on the door and it began to open just before she touched it. The last soldier charged forward, blocking Beatrice's way to the door.

"Hello, Beatrice," he said. "I thought we might meet." She recognized that voice. She studied him in the darkness. Brian, the giant!

Croc Harry flew through the air, intent on catching an arm or a leg and taking the giant down. But the giant, huge as he was, was nimble. He stepped to the side and waited for Croc Harry to land. He dove on top of the crocodile's head, pinning him so he could not open his mouth. He kept his huge body out in front, well away from Croc Harry's thrashing legs. He wrapped his giant arm around Croc Harry's mouth and twisted and twisted until Croc Harry was forced to turn onto his side. His vulnerable belly was exposed. Croc Harry convulsed, but he could not get free.

"If you know what you're doing," the Giant said, "it's not so hard to wrestle a croc."

"Leave him be," Beatrice said. "I'm the one you want."

"You *are* the one I want," the giant said. "But first I have a crocodile to kill. He's not worth much anyway. If you had any idea who this croc used to be, you wouldn't travel with him so faithfully."

"I know everything," Beatrice said, "and he's my friend."

"Pick better friends. This one's about to die. Any last words, Croc Harry?" the giant asked.

"Wait," Beatrice said. "Stop, Brian! One question."

The giant looked at her, sword at the ready, with eyebrows raised.

"Why are you doing this? What did we ever do to hurt you?"

He lowered his voice and growled, "Your world hurt me, Beatrice, and there is nothing now that feels better than my hatred. It is pure. It is steady. I feed off it. It makes me strong. You see, Beatrice, I love to hate."

Out of the darkness just beside Beatrice, Horace Harrison Junior the Third launched the biggest, wildest, highest hop he had ever made since leaving Argilia. He flew through the air with the claws on his ten front toes and eight hind toes extended. He landed squarely on the giant's face.

"Ahhh," the giant shouted. Horace scratched and bit with all his might. The giant tried to swat Horace with his sword hand, but missed. He let go of Croc Harry's mouth to swat the rabbit with his other hand, and in that time, Croc Harry swivelled free.

The giant stood and held out his sword. Beatrice drew back her slingshot.

"You can't be serious," the giant said. "You can't hurt me with that useless toy."

Beatrice let the shot fly. It was the hardest, fastest, most vicious shot she had ever slung. It struck the giant cleanly on the temple. He dropped to one knee and roared.

"I was going to take you back, break your spirit and have you serve my land. But now," he said, "I just want to see you die and to see all of the Queendom mourn their so-called future leader."

The giant approached Beatrice. Beatrice felt movement in her Beasack. Something scurried down her arm. Down her leg. What could it be?

The giant took another big step. A third. A fourth. He was almost there. He cocked his arm and raised the sword high in the air. Then he stopped and cried out in pain. Fuzzy had raced onto his face and bitten his cheek.

"Fuzzy," Beatrice cried, "you're alive!"

The giant swatted the tarantula, who flew through the air, struck the purple door and fell to the ground, motionless.

The giant raised his sword again and brought it down fast, slashing toward Beatrice. Croc Harry shot through the air, bringing himself between the giant and the girl. The sword slid deep into his belly. The giant pulled out the sword. Blood poured from the crocodile's belly. Croc Harry let out a long, slow moan. Beatrice had never heard Croc Harry in physical pain before. The sound was agonizing. Beatrice would sooner welcome her own pain than see Croc Harry hurt. The purple doors were opening wider.

"Go in," Croc Harry told Beatrice and Horace. He opened his mouth, and even though they could not hear his words, they knew what he wanted them to do.

Horace flung himself, but the giant caught him and threw him to the ground. Horace lay there, unconscious and bleeding from the ear. Croc Harry kept staring at Beatrice. She knew exactly what he wanted. *Save yourself*, he was trying to say. *Save yourself. Get in that door.*

Croc Harry was limp on the ground, inches from the door. He was too weak to fight.

"I used to wrestle crocs," the giant said, "but never got to kill them." He raised his sword once more.

Beatrice was ready this time. She pulled back the sling, harder than she had ever pulled before, and let the shot fly. It barrelled straight into the giant's right eye.

The giant fell to the ground, writhing in pain. "Oh, nasty girl. Blind me in one eye." While he was on his knees, he drew back the sword once more. But he wobbled and fell. He moaned. He was still living, but just stunned. And blind in one eye.

Beatrice pulled the purple doors all the way open. She turned to the giant, who was getting up slowly.

"Don't call me pint-sized," Beatrice said, "don't call me nasty, and don't call me Black. Don't call me anything at all. Just leave me alone. Leave us all alone. If you show up here again, I'll shoot out your other eye."

Four huge soldiers stepped out of the castle. Each took Croc Harry by a leg and dragged him through the doors. Beatrice lifted Horace off the ground. He was bleeding and unconscious, but breathing. She found Fuzzy and picked her up gently.

"I got him," Fuzzy moaned. "Calisthenics!"

Beatrice leapt through the doors. She saw the giant stand up and wobble, and then step back. He turned and, as quickly as he had come, he disappeared into the Contested Lands.

"We made it, Croc," Beatrice shouted, and dove down to hug him. But he did not speak and he did not move. The four soldiers disappeared down a corridor. Six medics, all wearing plastic gloves, face masks and green operating gowns replaced them. One of them put a hand on her shoulder. It was a kind, warm hand. Beatrice didn't recall ever feeling a kind human hand before. But she knew kindness when she felt it.

"You'll be all right," the medic said. She was a woman. Her hand was as strong as it was kind.

"Look," the medic cried. "Someone kill that tarantula!"

"No, don't," Beatrice shouted. "That's Fuzzy. She's my friend. She saved my life three times."

Fuzzy slid out of sight and disappeared into the Beasack.

Beatrice hugged Croc Harry harder. She was covered in his blood, but she did not care. She remembered when, just like a mermaid, he had given her a ride, turning and playing in the deep waters. She thought about how he had come every morning to talk with her while she ate. She thought about pulling out his giant tooth and watching it fly up to meet the Big Dipper. She thought, most of all, about how lovingly he always said her name. Beatrice. Three syllables. Nice and slowly. Never two syllables. Bee-trice was not a sound that should be allowed. Not in a dictionary. Not on the planet. But he never said it that way. Croc Harry always was attentive to pronunciation: Beatrice. He said her name like they were friends and had been, for a thousand years. Beatrice could feel his heart slowing. She could hear his panting grow fainter. Then there was no more beating, and no more breath. She hugged him harder.

"Croc Harry, please talk to me." But her friend Croc Harry, the grand palaverer of Argilia, had no more to say.

A deep, commanding woman's voice came from the hall. "Take her to the saving room. She's covered in blood. Make sure she's okay. And sedate her now. The girl will be in shock. If the croc is still alive, effectuate transformation. Do it instantly, before he dies. The rabbit is still breathing. Transform him too. Find the spider. Let it live, for now."

Beatrice tried to say that Fuzzy was a *she*, not an *it*. But she had no more energy to speak.

"Hurry," the medic said. "Hurry. One medic for the croc. Two for the rabbit. Three for Beatrice, bless her heart. Treat that girl as if she rules the Queendom. Is that clear? Go!"

Beatrice shut her eyes and hugged Croc Harry more tightly. She could not imagine carrying on without his voice or spending a day without flying over his back through the water. She would not cry. She was home, but her only thoughts were with Croc Harry and Horace Harrison Junior the Third. She wondered, as she felt the prick of a needle in her arm, what could a 700-pound, 17-foot King Crocodile do to keep himself busy and happy in a walled Queendom? Probably not very much.

Beatrice imagined Croc Harry calling out to her as she sat in the morning eating oatmeal. Perhaps she would be in a kitchen. Seated in a chair by a table and waited on by servants. Perhaps he would be on a patch of grass. "There is ridiculously little for me to do on a patch of grass inside a castle," he would call out, "so please please please do palaver with me, Beatrice. Do me the kindness of engaging in a grand palaver."

Strong arms lifted Beatrice up, up, up, and away from Croc Harry. He was gone, but she was home. Wherever that was. Beatrice swam down, down, down. On the back of Croc Harry, she swam down into a bottomless pool of blackness.

CHAPTER 31

Have You Been Living Among Animals?

Beatrice awoke in a room with a window, a single bed with a thick purple comforter, three shelves of books and a breeze coming in from outside. For a minute, she thought she might have awakened in the forest of Argilia, and that she would soon be making oatmeal and palavering with Croc Harry as she sat with her legs dangling from the fig tree branch. But there was no woodpecker. No sound of wind in the leaves. Instead: children singing and playing outside.

Where was Croc Harry? What about his injuries? Who was taking care of him? Did people know that he could only make himself understood to a person who was touching him? And what about Horace Harrison Junior the Third? Was he free to hop? Was he hopping high again? And Fuzzy? Was she alive?

She slid her legs out of bed and discovered that she was wearing white pyjamas. It was a small, square room. She looked in the mirror. She was still short. Still freckled. Still had lovely brown skin. But her cornrows had disappeared. Instead, she had an afro the size of a volleyball. An afro so proud that it looked like a crown. There could be only one good word for it: a Beafro.

Apart from her bed, the bookshelves and a desk and chair, there was nothing but the open window at one end of the room and a portrait of a woman on the other end—a tall woman, with regal bearing, brown skin, full lips and eyes that seemed wise and educated and caring. She stood wearing a formal gown, with her arms hanging down and fingers interlocked. On an engraved plate under the painting, Beatrice read the words, *Her Majesty, Queen Arthuria.*

Beatrice walked to the window and saw children playing in a courtyard two floors below. They were skipping with ropes. Had Beatrice seen that before? She thought she had but was not sure. Out of the corner of her eye, she detected a blue splotch moving across the floor. She turned and saw Fuzzy scurry under her bed. Beatrice smiled. She would look for her later. On the window ledge, right where she placed her hands, was a small, circular, grey buzzer. Beside it, she found a note. Written in purple calligraphy. *Welcome, Beatrice. Please ring when you are ready.*

Beatrice felt a sudden sadness. Things would never be the same. She knew, without anyone ever telling her, that she would not return to Argilia. She had a terrible feeling about Croc Harry.

Beatrice rang the buzzer. The door to her bedroom swung open instantly. It opened to a large office with a couch and two chairs. Sunlight streamed in through large, magnificent windows, and at the far end of the office, a woman was sitting behind a desk. Queen Arthuria slid out from her chair, stood and gave a slight nod of her head. Tall, brown-skinned, with hair curled in a tight Afro around her head. Perfect posture. Flat, sensible shoes. She strode over to Beatrice and reached out to take her hand.

"I wondered when you might awaken," the Queen said.

"Are you my mother?" Beatrice asked.

The Queen broke into a huge smile. "Heavens, no. I have no time for mothering, or for marriage for that matter. I run the Queendom of Carolina, and it's a full-time job. I've got a giant leading a rebellion, trouble in the Contested Lands and news that the code to Argilia has been broken. We must have a serious debriefing about that, momentarily. Perhaps you know a thing or two about the situation. So, in short, I have no time for marriage. Husbands are high maintenance."

It occurred to Beatrice that she liked to run things too. She enjoyed telling people what to do. She sensed that she would have a busy life. Probably no time for a husband, either. She'd already looked after a high-maintenance rabbit. Loved him to pieces, but he was a lot of work.

"Is Croc Harry alive?" Beatrice asked.

"You do get right to the point."

"Well, is he?" Beatrice asked. "And what about Horace? He's a rabbit. You must have found him too!"

"How about if we have a spot of breakfast and get caught up on current events?" The Queen snapped her fingers. A person who looked about fourteen years old backed into the door, rolling a tray of food.

"Ma'am," the young person said to the Queen. "Miss Beatrice," they said to Beatrice.

The teen had long, brown hair. It was straight. Their skin was pale. Beige. They had blue eyes. Beatrice felt a huge wave of relief. In this world, people of different colours were allowed to live together.

"Are we related?" Beatrice asked.

The Queen let out a laugh. "My dear girl, you must cease asking every person you meet if they are family."

"No, Miss Beatrice," the person replied, "I am Wolf. I am in Grade 10, advanced educational stream, and this is my job."

Beatrice smiled. "You can just call me Beatrice."

"Yes, Miss Beatrice."

Beatrice walked over to the food tray, on which sat a bowl of steaming oatmeal topped with raisins, blueberries, brown sugar and cream, and put her hand on Wolf's arm. It was the first time she could remember touching a human being. She could tell, the instant her hand settled on the warm forearm, that this was a good way to convince a person of something: speak to them gently, and lay your hand on their arm.

"Beatrice is three syllables. There is no prefix, such as Miss. You do know what a prefix is?"

"I certainly do," Wolf said. "I'm in advanced. I learned that in Grade 2."

"Good. Three syllables. Beatrice."

Wolf smiled deeply and held Beatrice's eyes with their own. It felt awfully good to have a person smile at her.

"Beatrice," Wolf said.

"Nice to meet you, Wolf," Beatrice said. "I suppose we can still be friends?"

Wolf cast a quick glance at the Queen, who gave a nod of her head.

"Yes, Beatrice, friendship is a distinct possibility."

"Good," Beatrice said. "Could you tell me one little thing? It's something I've been wondering for a while."

"Yes, Beatrice," Wolf said.

"How old am I?"

Wolf glanced again at the Queen and received another nod.

"You are twelve years old, Beatrice," Wolf said. "Or, at least you were at the time of your teleportation, so you are returning at the same age. We have all been waiting for you. None of us could age, or grow, or get on with things until you came back."

"Thank you, Wolf," the Queen said. "That is quite enough information for now."

"Excellent," Beatrice said. "Thank you, Wolf. Am I too short for twelve years old?"

"For your age, you are in the fourteenth percentile," Wolf said.

"Pathetic," Beatrice said.

"You don't remember me yet, do you, Beatrice?" Wolf said.

Beatrice looked puzzled. There were so many things she could not remember.

Wolf smiled. "Don't worry. They say it will all come back. Do you remember our vocabulary lessons? Do you remember puzzling over the term *willing suspension of disbelief*?"

Beatrice smiled. She did remember that phrase. "Yes," she said. "It means temporarily agreeing to believe something unreal because it is pleasant to do so. But why do I remember that? How do you know about that?"

"When I was not at my own studies, I used to be your babysitter," Wolf said.

Beatrice paused for a moment to reflect. She had been living among crocodiles and tarantulas. She knew how to grease a fig tree with bear fat to keep out intruders. She had used a slingshot to fight off a giant. "I would like to be your friend, but I am in no further need of babysitting."

"If you say so, Miss Beatrice. I mean, Beatrice."

Beatrice turned to face the Queen. "Your Highness, it is going to be a very long day, indeed, and a very long rest of my life if I have to call you 'Your Majesty, Queen Arthuria' every time we speak."

"Ma'am will suffice," the Queen said.

"I have been sharing a forest with crocodiles, tarantulas, monkeys, bunnies and a rainbow, and none of them are big on formality. Could I call you Arthuria? Could we graduate to that? I have something important to say, and it would be easier if we were on a first name basis."

Beatrice walked toward the Queen. She put her arm out. Perhaps a hand on the forearm would work again.

The Queen shifted her arm, ever so subtly, out of reach of Beatrice.

"I am the Queen, so I am *always* the one to initiate personal contact," she said. "Is that understood?"

"Yes," Beatrice said.

"Yes, you may call me Arthuria."

"How about Artie?"

"Absolutely not. You may address me as Arthuria, but only in the privacy of my chambers. Out in the world, I still need respect. I demand respect. Out in the world, where I am still a woman, and where I am still Black, I am a Queen, and I must lead."

"Black? But Arthuria, you are brown."

"My skin is brown, but I am Black. So are you."

"A hunter in the Contested Lands called me Black. And the giant called me Black. I hated being reduced to a colour."

"You were right to be upset. They spoke with ugliness in their hearts. But Black is another thing when it is said in the right way. When it is said respectfully, it refers to people who have a common origin and whose ancestors came long ago from a place called Africa. Here in the Queendom, we have many peoples. We live equally, and we celebrate our differences. There are men, women, girls, boys and people of fluid gender. Wolf is of fluid gender—sometimes a little bit girl, or a little bit boy, or both, or neither. I am Black. You are Black. Your family—"

"Just what I wanted to ask about," Beatrice said.

The Queen paused. Wolf leaned over and whispered in Beatrice's ear. "One mustn't interrupt the Queen."

"Sorry, Arthuria," Beatrice said. "In the forest of Argilia, we—the animals and I—interrupted each other all the time."

"Quite all right," the Queen said. "Just a little habit to rectify."

Beatrice didn't agree that speaking freely among friends was something to be corrected, but she bit her tongue. She waited for the Queen to finish. She hoped the Queen wouldn't take long. Beatrice was bursting to get her thought out. So, she raised her hand, as she had been taught in school—that memory, too, was coming back to her—ever so slightly in the air.

"No need to raise your hand," the Queen said. "What's on your mind?"

"May I put my hand on your arm?"

"Why would that be necessary?"

"I'm used to touching someone when I speak. It's how I had to travel with my friends, when we left Argilia."

"Only in Argilia can humans speak with animals," the

Queen said. "And even in the forest, they can only do so if they are highly adept at communication. Your powers of empathy are, shall we say, unparalleled. All of which leaves me more than a wee bit nonplussed."

"Nonplussed?" Beatrice said.

"Heavens," the Queen said. "We do need to refresh your vocabulary. It means perplexed. Bewildered."

"So how about your arm?" Beatrice asked.

The Queen stepped forward and extended her forearm. Beatrice placed her hand on it. "Is Croc Harry alive?" she asked.

"In a manner of speaking."

"What does that mean?"

"Don't you wish to get dressed?"

They negotiated for a moment and came to an agreement. Beatrice would wash her face and brush her teeth and get dressed in the bathroom, and the Queen would stand outside the door and answer up to five questions. She would not answer a single additional question until Beatrice had eaten her oatmeal and returned to Her Majesty's office for a proper palaver because the Queen required an update from Beatrice before nightfall about the giant, and the Contested Lands and rumours that hostile forces were trying to crack the code to Argilia.

Beatrice turned one tap in the sink in the bathroom, and then the other. She had not remembered this. Not remembered it at all. Hot water poured from one tap and cold from the other. How convenient. How much easier than climbing down a rope ladder to bathe in the river.

"Where is Horace?"

"You shall see him soon."

"And where exactly is Croc Harry?"

"He is in two places, my dear. His body is in our animal hospital. We knew that you might not believe that Harry, as a crocodilian, was no longer. So Wolf, who happens to know you rather well, smartly suggested that you might want to see the body prior to cremation."

"Where else is he?"

"As a crocodile, after saving your life by taking a sword to the heart, he was moments from death. We got to him just in time. But, dear child, even if he had made it back to the Queendom without sustaining injuries, we would have transformed him promptly. He has been returned to his former state as a man. His name, as I believe you know, is Harold Crocton. He has been removed to our national penitentiary. He is serving a five-year sentence . . . I must reassure you that this is a far, far cry from the execution he would have faced for all the mayhem that he caused in the church on the day you nearly died."

"I wish to see him today."

"That is not a question."

"May I see him today?"

"No, that will not be possible."

"When may I see him?"

"We shall have to consider that matter. We don't, as a rule, allow Leader Designates—children who have shown sufficient talent, leadership and intelligence to be groomed for leadership of Carolina—to visit our national penitentiary."

"So what would you say to the following proposition, ma'am?"

She waved her hand and interrupted Beatrice.

"Your five questions are up, Beatrice," the Queen said.

"Then let me state my proposition, in one sentence. I will not eat or drink or consent to one single solitary bit of grooming or training until I have been given an opportunity to speak with Harry Crocton. I will not even speak to you. This is non-negotiable. You may punish me. You may starve me. You may lock me in a cage and feed me worms. I don't care. My mind is made up. I must see Harry Crocton, and that is not a question."

The Queen inhaled slowly. She wove her fingers together and placed her hands in front of her tummy.

"I am not in the habit of being dictated to," the Queen said.

Beatrice said nothing. Sometimes it was best to stay quiet. She decided that it would be impolite to mention that the Queen had ended a sentence with a preposition.

"This is not a democracy," the Queen continued. "However, I admit the situation is unique."

Beatrice kept her thoughts to herself. She was winning the argument, so why complicate things?

"Go ahead and finish getting dressed," the Queen said. "Give me a moment."

Beatrice heard a number of adults conferring in hushed tones in the Queen's room. In her bathroom were a dress and a pair of sandals. She was about to put them on. Wolf came in silently, but said not a word. They removed the dress and sandals and replaced them with a polo shirt, a vest, a pair of riding pants and riding boots. Beatrice got dressed. The clothes fit her perfectly. She stepped out of the bathroom and into the Queen's chambers. In addition to the Queen and Wolf, three women and two men were in the room. They all stood straight.

"Introductions later," the Queen said. "Follow us."

The Queen and Wolf led Beatrice through a series of hallways and tunnels. They took an elevator deep down into the ground. They opened the doors to the animal morgue. Croc Harry, or the powerful reptile who used to be Croc Harry, was lying motionless on a cold tile floor. He needed water for swimming. He needed sunlight to get warm. In this moment, she imagined he would especially appreciate his own thermoregulation. He would want to be as warm as pie in this moment. She supposed that Croc Harry needed bunnies, or antelope, in his ample belly. She imagined he needed all of these things. But she knew that he had said he would not want to live locked up in a zoo.

She could tell, by the manicured grasses and perfect bicycle

paths in her returning memory, that the very best thing awaiting him in the Queendom of Carolina would be a zoo, where
the highlight of his day would be eating a bunny tossed to him
while visitors snapped pictures. So Croc Harry got his wish.
It occurred to Beatrice that from the moment they left Argilia,
he had known that he would die once he had delivered her to
safety. He hadn't even seemed sad. He was a noble, devoted
crocodile. In her heart, they would be friends forever.

Beatrice lay down one last time on Croc Harry's back and
gave him a long, tender hug. "Goodbye, Croc Harry, and
happy hunting."

She stood, brushed off her pants and thought for a moment
that she would have much preferred bare feet and shorts to
pants and riding boots. Her Beafro looked perfect, but was
it too perfect? Hair twists and cornrows were better suited
for slingshotting and stone skipping. Beatrice hoped there
would be a place to climb ropes and build tree houses in the
Queendom. She would deal with that later. For now, there
was pressing business.

"Which one of you kind souls is escorting me to the penitentiary?"

The Queen waved away her assistants. She led Beatrice
through a courtyard and into a barn.

"Why are we going to see horses?" Beatrice asked.

"How else do you expect to get to the penitentiary?" the
Queen said. "I believe you have ridden before, correct? Today,
shall it be white, brown or black?"

Beatrice had ridden many horses. She knew all about horses. The colour did not matter. "I'll take the one that is quickest," she said.

"That will be the brown horse," the Queen said. "You will have one hour at the prison. Sixty minutes. Precisely. After-wards, you owe me a rather extensive palaver, entirely on my own terms."

"Sixty minutes is equivalent to three thousand, six hun-dred seconds, and I will savour every one of them," Beatrice said. "After which, if you wish, we may palaver until the cows come home."

The Queen smiled. "The forest of Argilia, I can see, did no damage to your precocious self. In case our rather rushed circumstances prevented me from saying so earlier, welcome home, Beatrice. We have been longing to see you again. We weren't sure you would make it back."

Beatrice did not smile back at the Queen. "You left me alone in the forest," she said. "You could have helped me."

"I did help you, as Ms. Rainbow."

"You are Ms. Rainbow?" Beatrice said.

"Not exactly. But I did communicate with you through the rainbow."

"You shouldn't have doubted me," Beatrice said.

"You really are an exceptional child," the Queen said.

Beatrice had no idea how exceptional she was, because for the longest time she was the only child she knew, but she decided in that moment that, yes, she most likely was highly exceptional. But every child was exceptional. Every child, she felt, deserved a chance to grow up suntanning on the banks of the Argilia River and learning how to mix oatmeal and peanut butter to glue shut the jaws of a crocodile.

Beatrice was about to speak, but the Queen raised her index finger to her lips.

A tall Black man came around the corner, leading a black horse. He gave Beatrice the warmest smile in the history of the Western hemisphere. And the Eastern hemisphere too. A white woman followed him, holding the reins of a white horse. Behind them was a small brown boy, about eight years old, black curls poking out from under his riding cap. He was leading two brown horses—one in each hand. He gave Beatrice a knowing smile. He wore riding boots. He hopped nervously from one foot to the other.

"Stop hopping," the woman said. "Stand up straight for the Queen. We must thoroughly revisit your manners. Have you been living among animals?"

"Yes, mother," the boy said. "I was with the animals, and with Beatwice."

Beatrice's mouth fell open. It stayed open. She knew that voice. She had heard it many, many times. Horace walked over and took his sister's hand. Just this one time, Beatrice decided, he could hold her hand for as long as he wished.

The mother smiled at Beatrice, nodded her head quickly in the direction of the Queen as she arranged the brown horse's harness, and raised a finger to her lips. Beatrice had been ready to dance on the spot and let out a scream, but with some great reluctance, she closed her mouth.

"Ma'am," the woman said to the Queen.

"Ma'am," the man said to the Queen.

"Ma'am," the boy said to the Queen.

"Ms. Stackhouse," the Queen said. "Mr. Harrison. Horace. I believe you can take it from here."

THE END

Penultimate Word From Author to Reader

Dear Reader:

This is an appendix. It's part of the novel, but not really. Sort of like a P.S., but considerably longer.

Anyway, stop reading right now. Seriously. Did you hear me? Stop.

You are not allowed to read this appendix unless you have already been reading this book, or somebody has been reading it to you.

Please note: This section that follows is NOT *The St. Lawrence Dictionary of Only the Best Words, Real and Concocted*. That dictionary has way over 5,000 pages. My publisher will not allow it. "Are you joking?" I was asked. "Do you think there is a single child in the Western hemisphere, or in any hemisphere, who would read a 5,000-page dictionary?"

So this is a compromise. What you see here is a tiny sampling. You might find it boring. In that case, don't bother. Really. Go curling or lawn bowling or try some other equally thrilling activity. But if you are the sort of person who likes to learn strange and silly words, you have permission to read on.

You may already know many of the words that Beatrice has been studying to improve her vocabulary. However, you can't know *all* of the words, because some of them are concocted. Oh. About that word. *Concocted* means "made up," or "nothing true about it."

Okay. You may now proceed.

With best wishes,

The Author

The St. Lawrence Dictionary of Only the Best Words, Real and Concocted

A

A fat lot: Not very much at all.

Abandon: To give up on someone. To stop looking for them. To stop caring for them. How would you like it if someone abandoned you in Argilia and said, "See if you can get along with that 700-pound crocodile"?

Abbreviate: Shorten.

Abhor: Hate.

Abscond: Steal. Make off with. Take without permission. As in "The thief absconded with the woman's purse" and "Don't abscond with other people's stuff." Not a good way to make friends.

Abundant: Many of them. Think of freckles. If there is one, there are usually many, which makes them abundant.

Accoutrements: Extra parts, or equipment. This word comes from the French and is spelled the same way in French. If you're planning to build a big vocabulary, try learning French. It will help your English.

Achilles tendon: The long, fleshy part of your body that attaches the calf muscle at the back of your lower leg to your heel. A sensitive body part. If it gets hurt, it becomes very hard to walk.

Advise: To tell people what to do without seeming bossy. Not easy to do. Try it sometime.

Align: Come together.

Alliteration: When two words or more appear together that each begin with the same letter or sound, as in "save celery" or "roaring rockets." This can get annoying very fast.

Antiscorbutics: Food or vitamins that prevent a serious disease called scurvy. Fresh fruit usually does the trick.

Antonyms: Words that have opposite meanings. *Antonym* is the opposite of *synonym*.

Apply to you: Affect you. Have an influence on you. For example, "The law of gravity applies to you." In other words, if you jump as high as you can, won't you fall back down to the earth just like regular folk? Or are you some sort of supernatural rabbit who can hop up and up and up before you start to come back down? Most living creatures—apart from flying insects, winged birds and a talkative rabbit named Horace—are ruled by the law of gravity. Mother Earth likes to keep them close. Just like a mother bear with her cubs.

Approbation: Approval.

Arachnid: A spider or scorpion. Great word, isn't it?

Assitudinous: Sassy and acting like a stubborn donkey.

Attitudinous: Mouthy. Argumentative.

Autobiography: Your life story, in your own words.

Avoidance: The act of staying away from someone or something. If a crocodile wishes to eat you, the avoidance of crocodiles might help you live longer!

B

Basest instinct: A desire that you would not be proud of and that you ought to ignore, such as to hurt someone. Be nice. Don't give in to your basest instincts.

Beautician: Someone who is paid to make you look good. Especially your hair, face, hands, nails or feet.

Bee's knees: An exceptional, highly admired, truly fantastic person or thing. If you're thinking about calling yourself the bee's knees—don't. Just don't.

Bicuspids: Your teeth with two points, located mid-mouth, between your canine teeth and your molars.

Bio-experiment: The creation of a magical forest containing most plants and animals and where all living creatures can communicate.

Black: When they use this word, the giant and his people are showing their hatred for Beatrice and for people who are Black. They are deliberately being rude and insulting to her. But as Beatrice discovers as she prepares to leave Argilia and as she re-enters the world of humans, Black is also a term of pride and belonging, referring to people who share a common identity and who come from, or whose ancestors come from, Africa.

Blended bowels: Horace means to say "blended vowels," which is what happens when you put two vowels side by side in a word such as *poem*.

Bloviate: Say too much. A person who is loquacious definitely tends to bloviate.

Bob's your uncle: This is one of the most ridiculous expressions in the English language. It just means "There you go." Or "It's that simple." Here are two explanations for the origin of this term. One is true and the other is concocted. Care to guess which is which? Here they are:

A singer-songwriter named Bob Schneider became well-known for a beautiful song called "Listen to the Water," which he wrote and performed for children. The children adored Bob and his song. While he strummed his guitar and belted out the song, they crowded around him and sang along. They all grew so attached to him that they came to think of Bob as their uncle.

A long time ago, the prime minister of Britain, whose first name was Robert, or "Bob" (his full name was Robert Gascoyne-Cecil), gave an important job to his nephew, whose name was Arthur James Balfour. After the nephew called the prime minister "Uncle Bob," the expression began to be used. It does not deserve to be in the English language. Shall we be done with it?

Bone to pick: Something to argue about.
Book people: People who like to read books. You could also call them *book nerds*, but that's a touch mean.
Boundless: So big that it seems to go on forever.
Branded: Had marks of ownership burned into their skin.
Broughtupcy: Having been taught good manners at home. Great word, isn't it? It comes from the Caribbean.
Bumfuzzled: Utterly confused. Believe it or not, this word is not concocted. Well, someone once concocted it. Now it is real.

C
Cacophony: A ton of noise, often made by a riotous bunch of birds or animals. People are animals, and we are the most cacophonous of all!
Calamoflation: The process of something becoming even worse than a disaster. The problem is becoming a calamity. Do you think this word is real?
Caliginosity: This is actually a real word. It means darkness.
Calisthenics: Strengthening exercises that use your own weight, such as pulling, pushing and running.
Calligraphy: Fancy, flowing handwriting. A lost art. These days, who has beautiful handwriting?
Capacious: Having lots of space.
Capitulate: Give in.

Carnivore: An animal that eats other animals. Many humans are carnivores, although Beatrice is not. Human carnivores usually get someone else to kill animals for them. Animals in the wild don't have that luxury.

Carnivorous: Behaving like a carnivore, which is an animal or person who eats meat. A carnivore is the opposite of a vegetarian, or herbivore. If you were living alone in a huge forest, you might wish that all crocodiles were vegetarians. Especially if the crocs were hungry and you were small and tasty.

Cavities: Holes in your teeth. If you have cavities, go see the dentist. But perhaps not Killjoy, as she is a dentist without a degree.

Cavort: Play around and have fun.

Cease and desist: An order to stop doing something.

Centre of gravity: Where most of your body weight is located. High up? Low down? A giraffe has a high centre of gravity. A crocodile has a low centre of gravity. Got it?

Chaotically: Wildly, without any pattern.

Civil war: A war inside a country.

CNA: This is like DNA, for crocodiles. It stands for *crocksyribonucleic acid*. It is a map for how crocodiles will grow. Decide for yourself if this word is concocted. *See also* DNA.

Cogitate: A fancy word for *think*. Three syllables, so it sounds fancier.

Comical: Funny.

Compensate: Make up for. Beatrice hates being short, so she compensates by throwing or slingshotting stones hard enough to hurt you—every single time.

Compensation: Sometimes the same word can mean two different things. Take *compensation*. It can mean *pay*, as in "He washed dishes for six days in a hot kitchen without compensation." Or it can mean a way of making up for something bad, as in "You treated me badly, so I want compensation."

Concocted: Made up. Fake. Invented. Like some words in this book. Often more interesting than real stuff. This goes for stories too.

Condone: Approve of, or support.

Consort: To hang out with. Spend time with.

Constitution: All this really means is *stomach*. As in your digestive system. Eating ten hamburgers would be bad for your constitution—because it would make your stomach sore. Constitution can also mean something entirely different. It can refer to a country's set of formal laws that almost never change.

Constitutional: Isn't this silly? We have just defined *constitution*, but *constitutional*—when used as a noun—refers to a regular walk taken for the good of one's health. As in "Grandfather goes for a constitutional every day after breakfast."

Controversial: Something people have strong opinions about. Some like it, and others don't.

Conversationalist: Someone who talks easily and a lot with others.

Converse: Talk back and forth with one or more people.

Crocodiliosis: What happens when a crocodile sprays his digestive juice on your skin. It is not going to be good. The croc is getting ready to eat . . . you!

Crocohypo-literosis: Fewer and fewer crocodiles are reading books these days. This problem is known as crocohypo-literosis. We need to address this problem.

Curds: Beatrice invented this pretend swear word. She could say something really nasty, but she knows that she should keep it clean.

Cuspid: A tooth with a point—a sharp enough point to cause you some harm if you were bitten. A word of advice: Do not walk or fall into any open mouth with cuspids at the ready.

Cwocowampoline: A trampoline located on the back of a crocodile, for the entertainment of gravity-defying, high-hopping rabbits.

D

Decrockestation: A complicated, life-saving technique that involves hurling a live animal from the stomach of a crocodile. You must move speedily, before stomach acid and gastroliths do their thing. Don't try this at home. If you must employ this technique, read the directions in the book *Survival Tips, Argilia Forest, 2090.*

De-escalate: To cool things down. Reduce the intensity of a disagreement or a fight. A parent might tell two fighting children to de-escalate the situation before they get sent to their rooms.

Defenestration: Nobody uses this word anymore. Try it out if you wish to make your friend or your school teacher open the dictionary. *Fenêtre* is French for "window." *Defenestration* means tossing someone out of a window. It also means the act of taking away someone's job.

Definition of a situation: What is really happening in a given moment, including the big picture. When Matilda tries to kill Fuzzy and then wants to hold back half of Beatrice's payment for teaching, the definition of the situation is that Matilda is a mean-spirited control freak who will act more and more badly if Beatrice lets her get away with it.

Detrimental: Hurtful.

Diction: This refers to the style of speaking. One might have careful diction, like a school principal, a nun or a queen. Or exaggerated diction, like a clown on a street corner. Or pretentious diction, like someone who had read this entire dictionary and was showing off their vocabulary. You can tell a lot about a person from their diction.

Diminutive: Sometimes folks like to use fancy words, instead of simple ones. Diminutive just means small. Very small. You could get to the point and just say *small*. Or you could pull out all the stops with four syllables and say *diminutive*. No real difference, except how it feels on your tongue. At times, a four-syllable word can be satisfying.

Dire circumstances: A bad way. A very bad way. If the circumstances are really dire, someone could die.

Disastroflated: Totally, entirely miserable.

Discriminate: Treat a certain group of people (or bunnies) badly, just because of the way they look.

Disintegrate: To break into tiny parts. A croc's stomach acid can disintegrate flesh and bones.

DNA: This is a real word. Honest. It stands for *deoxyribonucleic acid*. It is a chemical found in all living cells and is a map for how something (or someone) will grow.

Dollop: A healthy spoonful.

Dominate: To control, often in a mean or aggressive way. For example: "He dominated his little brother for five years until, one day, the little brother outgrew his older sibling."

Draw your attention: Get you to look at.

Dysfunctional: Not working properly. Hint: this is a great word for a spelling bee because many people guess that the first three letters are D-I-S.

E

Electrified: Killed by electricity.

Elevenses: A late-morning snack often eaten around 11:00 a.m. Sounds concocted, but it isn't. Read about it in *The Lord of the Rings*.

Embarking: Beginning. The word *barque* comes from the French for *sailboat* or *boat*. To embark is to get on a boat or to begin a journey.

Emotional neglect: Failure to take care of a person's feelings. Horace is convinced that he is suffering from emotional neglect at the hands of Beatrice.

Empathy: Caring for other people. Feeling their pain. Being interested in their situation.

Enterprising: Creative. Quick thinking. Able to create good situations. For example: "If you are not paying attention while crossing that river, an enterprising croc might have you for breakfast."

Enunciating: Means the same as *pronouncing*, but it's five syllables instead of three. So, it's just that much better.

Esquire: A polite title to add to a person's name. Generally, it means nothing at all except Mr. Fancy-Pants.

Estivation (or aestivation): A summertime hibernation that crocodiles and some other animals enjoy in hot weather. They dig into a burrow or cavern and wait for the dry weather to end and for the rains to return.

Eternity: A long, long time. Forever. Nobody likes people who talk for an eternity. If you tend to talk for an eternity, you may also find yourself alone for an eternity.

Exacerbate: Another enjoyable four-syllable word. All it means is to make something worse. The most fun thing about this word is putting the accent on the second syllable: Ex-ASS-er-bate. It's not your fault there's rudeness in that word, so go ahead and use it. Lean on it. Try it out on your teacher. It is seriously against the law to punish any child for leaning into the pronunciation of the second syllable of this word.

Executed: Killed.

Extensive palaver: Long conversation.

Extraordinarily: Very.

F

Fantabulous: Awfully good.

Figment: A piece, sometimes imaginary.

Fossil fuels: Energy such as oil and gas drawn from decomposed plants and animals buried deep underground. Once you use them, they're gone.

Fraternize: To hang out with someone and act like they are as close as family. When you fraternize with someone you don't like, that's called being fake.

Fulfilled: Satisfied. Feeling filled and full at the same time. Like a croc who has just eaten. Or a singer who gets an encore.

G

Gargantuan: Huge. Really huge. As big as big gets.

Gastificated: Having accumulated too much gas.

Gastrolith: A stone in the stomach of a crocodile. It helps grind up food. Can you believe that crocs eat stones?

Gavotte: Dance.

Gentlecroc: A nice, well-behaved crocodile.

Gentlecrockish: Behaving with good manners (for a crocodile).

Glandular: Relating to the glands, such as the part of the body that makes tears.

Gouzelum: You have to figure out this one all by yourself. It's kind of special. It's part of your body and your soul.

Grave consequences: Very serious problems.

Gravity: What goes up must come down.

Guilt complex: A tendency to feel guilt, even when you have done nothing wrong.

H

Half decent: Not bad. But not particularly good, either. If you say, "He's a half-decent writer," you are actually suggesting that he's not all that good.

Halitosis: Bad breath. It's even worse than it sounds.

Hallucinations: When your mind plays tricks on you and makes you see things that are not real, such as an elephant drinking chocolate milkshakes, a school bus dancing at a concert or a guitar running down the street.

Have every intention of: This is when you want something very badly and are planning for it too. For example: "Dad said I could not stay up late and watch the movie, but I have every intention of sneaking the laptop into my bedroom and watching the movie when everyone else in the house is sleeping."

Heavens to Betsy: A silly expression that means "oh my goodness," or "for Heaven's sake."

Held accountable: Held responsible.

High-walk: A crocodile moves over land in different ways. It can do a belly run, keeping its belly and tail on the ground and pushing forward with its tail. When it is chasing at high speed (while hunting, for example), it gallops or bounds, a bit like a rabbit, using first its two front feet to strike the ground at the same time and then its hind feet to land at the same time. It can only manage the gallop for a short sprint. Finally, for travelling overland at a slow, casual speed, it can do a high-walk, which looks a bit like a push-up. For the high-walk, it pushes up with its front legs—much shorter than the hind legs—to keep its head and body off the ground and does a diagonal strut: moving the front left leg and back right leg together, and then moving the right front leg and left back leg together.

Hippoflump: The body part that sits next to the gouzelum.

Hordes: Large numbers.

How do you like them apples?: This expression means "How do you like that?" And it suggests that you won't like it one bit.

Humanity: All people, together.

Hygienist: A person who cleans your teeth. This requires an element of trust: they don't hurt you, and you don't bite them. The birds who clean Croc Harry's teeth count on that element of trust.

Hyperactive: Can't stop moving.

Hypercrocksterfabulation: The process by which crocodiles make up lies.

Hyperventilate: Breathe quickly and deeply, much too fast.

Hyperverbal: Can't stop talking. Too many words, spoken too fast.

I

I have other fish to fry: I have other things to do. As in "Please don't make me wash the dishes. I have other fish to fry."

Immaculate: Perfectly clean. Don't you hate it when your bedroom is a pigsty but your best friend's is immaculate?

Imminent: About to happen at any moment.

Immobile: Not able to move.

Immortal: Not going to die. Ever.

Impervious: Resistant to, or not affected by.

Imporridgeable: This describes a person who is unable to live without porridge (which is another word for *oatmeal*). Scientists disagree about whether this is a medical condition or simply a food preference.

Imposition: A rule or something else that gets in your way and that you don't appreciate.

Imprison: To put in jail.

In all probability: Likely.

Inadequate: Not good enough. Have you ever got a lousy mark in school and thought that you were inadequate? Now you know exactly what it means.

Incessant: Something that will not stop. The more incessant it is, the more irritating too.

Incinerate: Burn up.

Insidious: Another way of referring to slow and steady harm—so slow that you don't notice, at first, that you are being harmed.

Insolent: Showing no respect.

Intact: All together and in one piece. Unbroken. Undamaged. Unscathed. Get the picture?

Intercept: Catch and get in the way of.

Interspecies: Between different kinds of animals.

Interval: The space in between things, or a pause in activity.

Intervention: An action to fix a problem.

Invoked: Called for.

Irredeemable: Hopeless.

J

No words here. Sorry.

K

Kicking the bucket: To *kick the bucket* is a sort of rude way of saying *to die*. Rude, but rather fun. Use it with your friends. Maybe not with the Queen.

Kindred spirits: People who think and feel the same way and have a special connection between them.

Kvetch: Some of the best English words come from other languages. In Yiddish, *kvetch* means to whine. In English, too, *kvetching* means complaining in a really whiny and irritating way. Kvetching will not win you a lot of friends. If someone tells you to "stop your kvetching," pause for a moment and listen to the sound of your own voice. Yuck!

L

Lacrimal glands: The part of your body, or the body of a crocodile, that makes tears.

Lambaste: This word feels truly great to pronounce. Say it. Accent on the second syllable: *lam-BASTE*. Feels good, doesn't it? Here is what it means: to criticize somebody severely. Give them a verbal thrashing. If someone lambastes you, it will not be a pleasant experience. However, if Beatrice has the opportunity, she would love to lambaste the men by the river who say mean things about her. Some cool synonyms also feel satisfying in the mouth: *berate*, *castigate* and *excoriate*.

The last thing from friendly: Not at all friendly.

Latitude: Room to make mistakes.

Law of gravity: When things go up in the air, such as baseballs or hopping rabbits, gravity pulls them back down to earth. Where they belong. What goes up must come down. Unless you have the fuel to make it stay up for a long time, like an airplane or a rocket ship, or unless you are talking about a bird with wings. But not all birds fly. Have you ever seen a chicken fly? Stop just one minute and imagine a twenty-pound Thanksgiving turkey. Imagine that thing trying to jump up. Gravity will pull it back down. If not for the law of gravity, any sensible turkey would take off and fly, and never end up bagged and frozen.

Litany: This word is sneaky because it has at least three meanings: (a) a bunch, as in, a litany of freckles, (b) a tedious list, as in a litany of complaints about badly scrambled eggs, (c) a long prayer—the kind that makes you want to sleep, even though you should be paying attention.

Longevity: How long you get to live. For example: "Eating fifteen bags of potato chips a day might be detrimental to your longevity."

Loquacious: Have you ever heard someone talk so much that you wanted to hit them? That person could be described as *loquacious*. Owner of a big mouth that simply will not shut.

Luminosity: Light. Consider this: when a word stretches into five syllables (*luminosity*) instead of one (*light*), you can be sure that Beatrice will hunt for it in the dictionary.

M

Malfunctioning: Not working right.

Manual dexterity: Ability to use your hands with skill.

Marginally more specific: Killjoy is showing off her big vocabulary. *Marginally* means "a bit." *More specific* means "more detailed."

Measly: Tiny, or unimportant.

Melancholy: A gloomy mood.

Mercenary: A paid soldier.

Mesmerized: So attracted to something (or someone) that the feeling is almost magical. Synonyms are *charmed*, *spellbound* and *bewitched*.

Met with hostility: Got a rude, unfriendly reaction.

Meticulous: Detailed. Careful. Focused on the little stuff.

Modicum: A small amount. As in "Could you show me a modicum of kindness and let me have another scoop of ice cream?"

Molars: The big teeth at the very back of your mouth. Good for crunching food.

Moral code: A set of beliefs about what is right.

Mounting irritation: Getting more and more ticked off.

Muckety-muck: A big shot, or important person. This term is not a compliment.

Mundane impediments like geography: When Fuzzy uses this phrase, it means "something basic, such as the distance between people." The individual words each have their own meaning. *Mundane* means "basic," or something that happens on a regular basis. An *impediment* is something that gets in your way. *Geography* is the study of place.

N

Naive: The quality of believing other people too easily, even when they are stretching the truth or lying. Or, not knowing much about how things work. A more polite way of saying "ignorant."

Niceties: Nice things.

Nictitating membrane: The third eyelid of a crocodile. A *membrane* is a layer. *Nictitating* is a fancy and rare word that means "blinking." The nictitating membrane is the crocodile eyelid that blinks and causes tears to fall.

No small potatoes: *Small potatoes* means "of little importance," so *no small potatoes* means "something that is actually important."

Nonchalant: Looking like you have not a care in the world. This is not easy when a crocodile opens its mouth and is so close that you can smell stinky breath.

Nonplussed: Confused.

North Star: The North Star shines the brightest in a collection, or constellation, of stars known as Ursa Minor. When Black people were escaping slavery in the United States, they often hid in the daytime and fled at night, making their way north by following the North Star.

Noxious: Poisonous. Enough to knock you out. As in "He hasn't brushed his teeth since Wednesday and now his breath is positively noxious."

O

Obliterate: Absolutely destroy. This can be very satisfying. For example: My friend had the school record for the 50-metre dash, but I ran so fast that I obliterated it. Now I hold the record.

Odoriferous: Stinky. Smelly enough to start an argument. As in a gym bag full of sweaty clothes left on a kitchen floor.

Olfactory skills: Ability to smell things.

Ominous: Threatening.

Once in a blue moon: Rarely, or almost never. If someone is said to do something once in a blue moon, you know it will be a special occasion and not to be missed. And by the way, if you are only visiting the dentist once in a blue moon, your teeth are in trouble.

Osities: Words ending with the letters *osity*, such as *luminosity*, *caliginosity* and *curiosity*.

P

An introductory note about the letter P: *The St. Lawrence Dictionary of Only the Best Words, Real and Concocted* makes the case that P is the most entertaining letter in the alphabet. Why? It is a bilabial explosive. To say it, you have to put your lips together and push. That's why it is more fun to say "potato" than "apple." What would you rather say: "polar bear," or "anthill"? Think of all the delightful words that begin with P. *Pumpernickel. Pappadam. Pop tart. Potable. Palaver.* The letter P is perfection indeed. Not to be disrespectful, but let's compare it to the letter A. *Alphabet. Align. Accede. Acid.* Come on! Those words are totally lacking in energy. Incidentally, the letter B is also a bilabial explosive, but not quite as satisfying as P.

Palatal valve: A valve, or tiny door that opens and shuts, at the back of a crocodile's mouth. Basically, a flap of skin that closes over a croc's throat. In case of emergency, such as if you are stuck in a croc's belly and need to get out lickety-split, it is possible to pull down the valve and climb through it. By the way, human beings also have a palatal valve, but there is no record of anybody climbing through one.

Palaver: To hold a long discussion. To talk and talk without necessarily reaching a goal. Also known as *chewing the fat*. This is only fun if the other person wants to palaver too.

Paraphernalia: A six-syllable word for *stuff*, or *various things*.

Penitentiary: Prison.

Penultimate: Next to last.

Perfection personified: Total perfection.

Perish: A fancy word for *die*.

Pernicious: Able to harm you slowly.

Perpetually: All the time. Constantly.

Perplexed: Confused, or bewildered.

Pincho: A little bit. Sometimes the very best words are stolen from other languages. *Pincho* comes straight from the Spanish: a *pincho de tortilla* is a piece of potato omelette. When it is warmed up and accompanied by a slice of baguette dipped in a bit of olive oil, it is truly superfactionous!

Pint-sized: A rude word for *little*.

Pique: French word for *anger* or *annoyance*.

Plover: Bird that lives on land, but close to the water.

Pompous: So formal that it is a bit silly.

Pop my socks: Believe it or not, to *pop socks* means "to die."

Poppycock: Nonsense.

Precocious: The quality—especially for children—of having advanced abilities. For example: Beatrice!

Predator: An animal that eats other animals and wants to do so. Now. If a predator is giving chase, you're in big trouble.

Proboscis: A long tube through which an insect sucks food.

Promenade: "A promenade" is a long walkway, and "to promenade" is to take a leisurely stroll. It comes from the French *se promener*. But here, "promenading to and from among the letters" is just a fancy way of saying "hunting for words in the dictionary."

Provenance: Where something comes from.

P.S. The P.S. is among the most stunning inventions in the world of writing. It stands for *postscriptum*. You studied Latin, right? The language is a total riot. You took it in Grade 8, right? If you didn't, why not? March down to your school principal's office today and hand over a letter demanding that the course be added to the curriculum. Anyway, we're getting off track. Let's return to *postscriptum*. In Latin, it means "written after." You know how sometimes you write a letter, finish it, sign it and then realize that you forgot to add a key detail? There's an easy solution. Write P.S. under your signature and say what you have to say. Keep it short. Shorter than this definition.

Pulsating: Vibrating.

Pureblood: No person's blood is more pure than any other person's blood. However, people who think they are better than others sometimes claim that their blood is pure.

Purity: Maple syrup can be called *pure* if you boil down the sap and don't add water to it. But blood can't be pure. Blood is blood. There are different types of blood, but no one type is better or more pure than another. People can't be pure either. People have ancestors going back thousands of years. They are a mix of everything. Calling some people "pure" is an excuse to treat other people badly.

Purposeful: Knowing what you want to do.

Put their finger on: Find, or locate.

Q

Quack: A nut. Someone who acts strangely.

R

Ragamuffin: The boys who pick on Beatrice when she is eating ice cream use this mean and insulting term to refer to a person wearing ragged, dirty clothes.

Reconnoiter: To look around and pay attention to what you see.

Refraction: The way light or sound gets bent as it passes from one medium (such as the air) through another (such as water). Sunlight gets refracted as it passes through water droplets. Because sunlight is made up of various colours, and because those colours get bent out of shape in different ways, sunlight passing through water droplets can form a rainbow. Violet bends a lot, but red bends very little, so they are never side by side in a rainbow. Think about that, next time you see the sun come out after a rainstorm.

Reign: Rule.

Repast: Meal.

Repel: Push back. Keep at a distance. If a crocodile is approaching, you should either run or repel the reptile. But repelling a crocodile is tricky business. Don't try it at home unless you have studied with Beatrice.

Retransformed: Changed back to.

Rigmarole: Bothersome, complicated nonsense. If somebody tries to put you through a whole rigmarole, run in the other direction. They are not your friend!

Robust: A robust person is vigorous and healthy. A robust cheese, on the other hand, is so strong and smelly that you might want to double-bag it before you put it in your fridge.

Roger that: Okay, got the message.

Ruse: A trick, an action that fools another person.

S

Scorch: Burn.

Scrumptious: So tasty that you'd like to take some off your grandma's plate and eat it yourself.

Scutes: The scales on a crocodile's back.

Segregation: The act of keeping people apart and treating some groups of people much worse than others. The hunter who shoots Beatrice with a poison arrow carries an identification card indicating that he believes in segregation. It is hateful to suggest that people of a certain colour or religion should be kept apart, or segregated. It's mean. It's foolish. And in the end, it will always fail. People will decide for themselves what they want to do, where they want to study and work and live, and whom they wish to love.

Self-extricate: Get oneself out of, remove oneself from.

Shenanigans: Activities that are not allowed.

Skedaddle: Take off. Get going.

Sleep apnea: A medical disorder that makes you stop and start breathing in your sleep. Sometimes it also involves coughing, snorting and snoring.

Smackifyingly: Very. Or, overwhelmingly.

Smidgeon: A small quantity. As in "I'll have just a smidgeon of cake, please, because I ate two other pieces when you weren't looking."

Socializing: Spending time with someone, or with other people, usually in a fun way.

Something of my origins: A formal way of saying, "A bit about who I am and where I come from."

Speech therapy: Training to help you learn to pronounce words.

Splendiferous: Have you noticed that the letter S is at the start of the best words for describing tasty foods? The person who invented *splendiferous* could have settled for *splendid*. The two words basically mean the same thing. But the final three syllables of *splendiferous* intensify the praise. Splendiferous sits right beside *savoury*, *sapid* and *superfactionous* as one of the most satisfying words to describe a superlative dish. Try it out on your grandparents the next time they serve you peach pie. They'll be so impressed, you'll get seconds.

Steel yourself: Get ready.

Stupendous: Fabulous.

Subject me to: Force me to undergo, or to live with. This is not a pleasant sensation. However, Horace is just a wee bit out of line when he accuses Beatrice of subjecting him to emotional neglect. As usual, the pint-sized rabbit is exaggerating. Obviously, Horace is just fine.

Submerged: Beneath the surface.

Substandard: Not very good. Far from the best. Not as good as reasonable people would expect. As in "It would be substandard dental procedure to use a shoestring to yank out a tooth."

Succulent: Very tasty.

Suffer fools gladly: The usual saying is expressed in the negative, as in "I don't suffer fools gladly." It means "I don't tolerate fools." But this begs the question: Who is the fool? What if the fool is the one who has no patience for other people? Just asking.

Sundog: If you imagine this is when a dog hangs out in the sun, think again! Here's the true definition: if you're watching closely and you have a bit of luck, when the sun looks like it is hanging close to the horizon, you might see sundogs, which are the images that look like other suns to the left and right of the real one. Sundogs result from the way sunlight passes through ice crystals high up in the air. You don't get to see them too often, so stop and enjoy them when you can. When the sky puts on a special show like that, it would be a crying shame to miss it.

Superfactionous: Best tasting in the whole world.

Superfluous: Unnecessary. More than enough. Too much. In Croc Harry's view, fingers and toes would be superfluous, given that he has a good tail and 69 teeth.

Supremacy: The soldier is carrying identification that suggests the false idea that one group of people is better than another group.

Survival Tips, Argilia Forest, 2090: No serious reader should be without this book. It could prove useful any time you find yourself alone and lost in a gargantuan forest. If you are looking it up, here are all the details: *Survival Tips, Argilia Forest, 2090.* Upside Down Publishing Ltd. Author: Anonymous.

It is a good idea to have this book on hand, in an accessible location and ready to use in case of emergency. Store it beside your fire extinguisher. If you cannot locate it easily, contact Dave, the friendly, bearded fellow who knows all about books, including those of the rare and ludicrous variety. Dave operates the bookseller King Croc Books. P.S. Dave does not have a last name, but not to worry. He knows everyone and is known by all. He keeps every manner of books about crocodiles on his shelves. P.P.S. Dave was responsible for curating the book selection in Beatrice's tree house. P.P.P.S. Isn't P.S. fun? You can just keep adding Ps and go on forever. But when you do, each new P should be sillier than the last.

Swift dismissal: Being fired very quickly from a job. Or being told to go away right now, as in when a military commander shouts at a soldier, "Dismissed!"

Sybberly: Ms. Rainbow taught this word to Beatrice. The sybberly is another mysterious body part, and entirely unique to humans. It is located just below the hippoflump.

Symbiosis: The way two people (or other living things) can help each other.

Synonyms: Words that mean the same thing or almost the same thing.

T

Teeming: Full of.

Teleport: Dear Reader, this term could have been defined earlier, but its meaning doesn't become completely clear until late in the novel. It's what you call a "slow reveal." But since you are now near the end of the novel, or should be if you are reading this, here we go. Teleporting is a high-tech way (if you know what you are doing) to zap a person, animal, food, or medicine lickety-split across great distances. No airplane, train or car needed. It is a way to move people around without using traditional means of transportation (you know: donkeys, horses, cars, buses, trucks, trains, airplanes, all that old-fashioned stuff). Teleporting was invented in the year 2050. After fossil fuels ran out in the year 2040, people had to invent a new, efficient way to move goods, animals and people around. It's very fast but also dangerous, and despite years of technological advancements, it doesn't always work. Also, you can only teleport something one way. No round trips. There's not a lot of energy to spare after the year 2090 in the Queendom of Carolina, and teleporting uses a great deal of energy. The rulers of the Queendom don't go teleporting every Tom, Dick or Harry. It's for special uses only and must be done by the proper authorities. Don't try this at home. It's against the law.

The cat's meow: Pretty well the same thing as the bee's knees: great, amazing, just peachy.

Thermoregulate: Control your own body temperature.

Thrice: Three times. One more than twice.

Tincture: A small amount.

Transgression: Crime.

Trespassers: People who walk or are simply inside someone else's property without being invited.

Trust: A deep belief that you can count on someone or something. You trust that your dad will not steal your lollipop. You trust that the sun will rise each day. You trust that the bank will not lose your money. Trust is knowing that you can rely on someone or something doing what they are supposed to do. Short words are sometimes tricky to define. Just one syllable. Short and snappy and packed with meaning.

Turquoise: Greenish-blue. The favourite colour of every reasonable person. Have you ever seen a pristine lake, high up in the mountains, fed by melting glaciers? Looks like that.

U

Unacceptable: There are many ways to say "not good enough," and here is another way. *Unacceptable* is something you can't accept. Like being offered a piece of chocolate, and then having it taken away.

Unappetizing: Can you think of something you really don't want to eat? It's unappetizing. Does not stir your appetite.

Uncertain age: Beatrice is so alone in the forest and has no memory of where she came from, so she doesn't even know how old she is. Her age is uncertain. How old do you think she is? Imagine a round number with two digits.

Uncouth: Rude. Uncivilized. Acting like you were raised by baboons.

Undignified: Lacking in dignity. Horace wishes to be taken seriously, so getting burned up by acid in Croc Harry's stomach is not his life's ambition.

Unflappable: Someone who doesn't get excited or worked up about things. Think of a flag that won't flap. *Unflappable.*

Unhinged: Loosened.

Unique: Special. Not like anyone or anything else. For example: "Mom ordered chocolate ice cream. Dad ordered vanilla. I chose something unique: strawberry licorice candy-floss ice cream. I wanted a unique flavour so Dad would not ask for a bite. Or a lick. It is so gross when he does that."

Unrelenting: Will not stop. This can be irritating. Heavy rains can be unrelenting. A toddler's screams can be unrelenting, especially if you won't give them the red lollipop in the store window.

Until the cows come home: Something that goes on and on and on. Think about it. When are the cows going to come home? If they're out there having fun grazing in the tall grasses, why would they bother coming home? If you are ordered to wash dishes until the cows come home, you know it's a severe punishment . . . because sometimes cows don't bother coming home.

Unwakeupable: Not able to be awakened. Usually because you'd rather avoid something, such as going to school.

Usher you: Lead you.

V

Vegetarian: You must know this word if you want to be friends with Beatrice. But just in case: a vegetarian is someone who does not eat meat. By the way, chicken and fish count as meat.

Verbal slap down: Telling somebody off. Using your words to back them off.

Violation: A breaking of the rules.

Visiting privileges: This can mean the right to work as a doctor or a dentist in a hospital, but it can also mean the right of a prisoner to be visited by friends or family in jail. When Killjoy uses the term, she means the right of patients to come back to see her again.

Vital signs: Signs of life, such as the beating of the heart, the movement of air in and out of the lungs, and brain activity.

Voltage: The power that moves electricity.

W

Wacky: Unusual. Odd. As in it's rather wacky to include a dictionary in a book for children.

Wecite: Horace can't quite pronounce the word *recite*, which means to read something aloud, usually in a formal, serious way.

Weighs on my conscience: Makes me feel guilty.

Without hiccups: A hiccup is a little spasm in the throat. But it is also a problem or a little setback. *Without hiccups* is a way of saying *without problems*.

Wolfed down: Ate quickly. Doing this looks rude. But sometimes animals or people wolf food down for a reason. If they don't, someone else may come along and steal it.

X

Not many words begin with X. One cool word is *xenon*, a colourless gas used in television and radio tubes. But since there are no televisions or radios in Argilia, and no laptops either, *xenon* doesn't appear in this story. If there's ever a sequel to *Beatrice and Croc Harry*, you'll find at least one completely ridiculous word beginning with X. Guaranteed.

Y

Yip-yapping: Talking too much. WAY too much.

Z

There are no words beginning with Z in this excerpt from the *St. Lawrence Dictionary of Only the Best Words, Real and Concocted*. You'll find no such words at all. Zero. Zip. Zilch. Sorry to disappoint you. The dictionary is incomplete. It is a work-in-progress. Because Z marks the last letter in the alphabet, this book is now officially over. If you are in any way dissatisfied or frustrated with this literary product, please write something of your own making. You've got this. Go for it.

Acknowledgements

Some people might say that writing is a ridiculous activity. Think about it. You spend years living in your own head, drifting away from dinner table conversations and walking right by friends in the park. During all those years of so-called work, you could have done something useful. You could have been flipping burgers, teaching children, filling cavities, building bridges or governing nations. But write a book? Years of work with no guarantee of readers? *Have you completely and utterly lost your marbles?* That is exactly what some clear-thinking people might say.

However.

Sometimes a writer just has to tell a story. Make up a good one. I write because I can. Because I must. It's one surefire method of feeling good about life. Before I began to write this novel, I had been stuck for a while. I was in a rut. I was grieving the deaths of my father, mother and sister. I didn't feel like writing. But I needed to fill the hole in my heart. I needed to comfort myself. So I returned to the one activity I have always loved: inventing stories straight out of the blue. This is the first time I have written a novel for children, but I hope it is not the last.

To write this book, I drew on two sources of inspiration: my late father Daniel Grafton Hill III (1923–2003), who concocted irresistible stories at bedtime and who used a litany of silly terms that made me laugh (*gouzelum* and *willy lump lump* would be two examples), and my fifth and youngest child, Beatrice Lucinda Freedman, for whom I used to make up bedtime stories about a clever girl who kept narrowly escaping the jaws of a giant crocodile. In our bedtime stories every night, Croc Harry would lure Beatrice close to his cavernous mouth. And every night, just when it appeared that Beatrice would become Croc Harry's dinner, she would outsmart him and escape to live another day. The laughter that Beatrice and I shared reminded me of some of the very best parts of being part of a family.

For Beatrice and my other children—Evangeline, Andrew, Caroline and Geneviève—and for my niece Malaika, I treasured building a household that played with language. For us, a ridiculous line (such as when Killjoy tells Croc Harry, "I decline to perform dental surgery in conditions of caliginosity") always gave us a moment to laugh and to admire inventive turns of phrase.

Although dreaming up a story is a solitary activity, I was never alone while imagining, researching, writing and revising this novel. I had the love of my children and my brother, Dan Hill, all of whom read and commented on early drafts. And I had the love, support, lively spirit and eagle eyes of my wife, the writer Miranda Hill, who has been with me every step of the way. Every family member asked, at least a dozen times, "Hey, when are you going to finish Croc Harry?" Now they can all stop asking.

* * *

In addition to my family, I relied on many other people for assistance.

Suzanne Sutherland, until recently the children's book editor at HarperCollins Canada, read and commented on many drafts of this book. Every time she stepped into the pages, Suzanne found ways to encourage me to make them better. When it came to proposing edits and asking for improvements, Suzanne's batting average was .917. In other words, if she made 1,000 suggestions, I accepted 917 of them. Can't beat that!

My long-time editor and friend Iris Tupholme (executive publisher at HarperCollins Canada) has been in my corner for twenty-five years and is always supportive, even though it takes me too long to finish my books. With this book and many others that came earlier, Noelle Zitzer, director of the managing editorial team at HarperCollins, always shows kindness, patience, practicality and support as she steers my work through the production phase. Thank you, Noelle, for being you!

I also wish to thank Catherine Dorton, who did a bang-up job copy-editing the manuscript. Catherine caught many slip-ups and shared a number of clever, creative suggestions as well. Hearty thanks as well to Debbie Innes for her incisive suggestions and proofreading.

My agent, Ellen Levine, expressed great enthusiasm when she stepped into this story and has done a fabulous job helping me place this and other books of mine with publishers. She and film agent Sean Daily have helped line up film deals and additional work as a screenwriter.

Some friends have been practically helpful as I worked on this book. Karen Grose cheered me on from the first draft through the last. Lois Concannon, Suzanne Crocker, Jaime Donofrio, Adrienne Kerr, Anne Lazurko, Tina Mirabella, Margaret Rosling, Daeja Sutherland and Agnès Van't Bosch all read and commented on early drafts.

Other friends encouraged me in numerous ways: David Chariandy, Daniel Coleman, Don Corbett, Alexa Dodge, Moira Dodge-Miller, Andrew Dodge-Miller, Becky Hill, Hartmut Lutz, Janet McNaughton, Mario Misasi, Jael Richardson, Bob Schneider, James Walker, Stephanie Kirkwood Walker and Janie Yoon.

I teach creative writing at the University of Guelph in Ontario. As it turns out, a number of my former students served as invaluable readers and advisors on this project: Laila El Mugammar, Dara Poizner, Maki Salmon and Laurie Sarkadi.

Cindy Henwood, Geneviève Hill, Laila El Mugammar, Ardo Omer, Celia Raymond and Karina Vernon advised me about issues of hair, identity and racism that my novel's protagonist, Beatrice Stackhouse, might have faced in and out of Argilia Forest.

Maki Salmon told me all about her pet rabbit Sawyer and introduced me to the quirks and sass of bunnies.

I relied on many sources of information about crocodiles. Most useful were the 649-page *Biology and Evolution of Crocodylians* by Gordon Grigg and David Kirshner (Cornell University Press, 2015) and *Crocodile: Evolution's Greatest Survivor* by Lynne Kelly (Allen & Unwin, 2006). Mary Anne White, professor emerita in the chemistry department at Dalhousie University, kindly advised me about acid in the belly of a crocodile. However, neither Mary Anne White, Gordon Grigg, David Kirshner nor Lynne Kelly are to blame for all the made-up stuff in this book. As for what is real and what is imaginary about crocodiles, tarantulas, rabbits and rainbows, I am pretty sure that readers will figure it out. If you are not sure about any particular detail, chances are it is a big fat lie.

I thank the late Eva Cassidy for the way she sang "Over the Rainbow." Of all the versions I have heard of that song, hers is the best. I listened to Eva Cassidy many times as I imagined Beatrice conversing with Ms. Rainbow. Usually, I tended to revise by pencil and type all the changes later. While typing late at night, to keep up my energy, I listened to singers I adored as a child and still love today: Aretha Franklin, Jackie Wilson, Gladys Knight, Mavis Staples, Sam Cooke and others. To my wife and children, I apologize for singing along.

My final thanks go out to all the children's book writers who offered such great entertainment when I was a child and whose stories beckoned me back to the Don Mills Public Library every Saturday. Their books were, and still are, great friends.